# THE DROWNING SPOOL

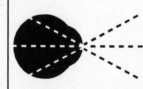

This Large Print Book carries the
Seal of Approval of N.A.V.H.

A NEEDLECRAFT MYSTERY

# THE DROWNING SPOOL

## MONICA FERRIS

**THORNDIKE PRESS**
*A part of Gale, Cengage Learning*

GALE
CENGAGE Learning·

Farmington Hills, Mich • San Francisco • New York • Waterville, Maine
Meriden, Conn • Mason, Ohio • Chicago

GALE
CENGAGE Learning®

**LIBRARY OF CONGRESS CATALOGING-IN-PUBLICATION DATA**

Ferris, Monica.
  The drowning spool / by Monica Ferris. — Large print edition.
    pages ; cm. — (Thorndike Press large print mystery) (A needlecraft mystery)
  ISBN-13: 978-1-4104-6752-2 (hardcover)
  ISBN-10: 1-4104-6752-X (hardcover)
  1. Devonshire, Betsy (Fictitious character)—Fiction. 2. Women detectives—Fiction. 3. Drowning—Fiction. 4. Needleworkers—Fiction. 5. Needlework—Fiction. 6. Large type books. I. Title.
  PS3566.U47D76 2014b
  813'.54—dc23                                      2013050944

Published in 2014 by arrangement with The Berkley Publishing Group, a member of Penguin Group (USA) LLC, a Penguin Random House Company

Printed in the United States of America
1 2 3 4 5 6 7 18 17 16 15 14

# THE DROWNING SPOOL

# ONE

For Betsy, it started in January, when the Courage Center's Olympic-size pool needed repairs. It was announced at her early-morning water aerobics class that the pool would be closed for twelve weeks, starting next week, and everyone was going to have to take a hiatus or find a new place to go during that period.

There was grumbling in the locker room after class. Twelve weeks! That was far too long to go without exercising. But where were they going to find another pool heated to ninety-three degrees? And one that offered a water aerobics class beginning at six thirty in the morning?

A woman changing for the Individual Therapy class that followed aerobics said, "I know a place that has a water aerobics class starting at seven."

"Well . . . Heated pool?" asked Betsy.

"Around ninety degrees or a little more.

The pool's nice, although not nearly as big as this one here."

But Betsy didn't need a big pool to stand and do jumping jacks in. "Where is this place?"

"It's a new addition to a senior-living complex in Hopkins. It cost them so much to add the pool that they're offering classes to the fifty-five-and-older members of the public to make some money. My mother lives at the complex — it's called Watered Silk — and she told me about it."

Hopkins was a suburb farther west of Minneapolis than Golden Valley, where the Courage Center was located — which put it closer to far-west Excelsior, where Betsy lived. So there would be a shorter drive to Hopkins for twelve weeks. Nice.

"Why is it called Watered Silk"? asked Betsy.

"The building that houses the complex was once a silk factory, back in the 1800s. One of the varieties they produced there is called watered silk. They actually found a piece of it inside a wall, or maybe it was under a floor, when they were remodeling. I guess they liked the term. It does have kind of a smooth, luxurious feel to it, which describes the complex itself. Everything is first-class over there, the residents really like it."

So when Betsy called the office, she should not have been surprised when she was quoted a price for three months' worth of thrice-a-week classes that was fully half again what the Courage Center charged. Not so nice.

Dismayed over the cost, she searched on her computer for alternatives. But all the other water aerobics classes in the area were held in pools far cooler than Watered Silk's, or were farther away, or didn't start as early; and none were less costly. So Betsy sighed and signed up.

Around twenty to seven on the first day, Betsy was guided by her GPS to a street on the west side of downtown Hopkins. The building was big, of dark red brick, old and plain. It had obviously once been a factory, perhaps built in the late nineteenth or early twentieth century. Four stories tall, it took up most of a city block, with a narrow alley separating it from a smaller, newer commercial building next door.

It was set far enough back from the street to accommodate a new stone and cement portico with a curved driveway leading underneath it to the main entrance.

There was a parking ramp across the

street, bi-level — the second "story" was the roof of the first — and there was no charge for parking. Betsy pulled in and found it almost empty at that hour of the morning. She parked and hurried across the street, under the cement portico, and into the broad entrance.

A pair of doors brought her out of the cold into a good-size entrance area, brightly lit and blowing hot air. She stopped in front of a pair of thick glass doors, tinted brown. But before she could press the button indicated for entry, the doors slid open.

The hall inside was tall. Really tall. Betsy's eyes were drawn up and up to an immense, very modern chandelier of crystal and chrome. The pale walls were bare except for one small painting in an elaborate frame. It was hung too far away for her to see any details other than it was red, and probably an abstract. The low-nap carpet had a pattern of dark gray curves and angles on a light gray ground. There was a long, plain buff couch near the framed art. A matching chair stood at right angles to it, with a chromed-metal-and-glass coffee table inside the angle. The lighting was gentle but adequate, and stronger on the right, where a beautiful wooden counter was guarded by a handsome, young African American man, who was smiling inquiringly at her. Betsy had a feeling she'd seen him before, but she couldn't place him.

"Betsy Devonshire," Betsy said, approaching him. "I'm here for the water aerobics class."

He checked for her name on a list, found it, and handed a clipboard to her to sign in. "Pool's down the stairs and to your right," he said, gesturing toward the back of the lobby.

It was then Betsy realized that the floor ended well short of the far wall. She walked over and saw a set of eight steps nearly the width of the lobby.

She went down to find a sitting area in front of four big windows and to one side a trio of doors — one was an elevator, one was marked PRIVATE, and the third had a glass insert in its top half through which she could see exercise equipment.

Through that door she found herself in a middle-size room reeking of cement and freshly laid carpeting and canvas, and full of new-looking treadmills, Exercycles, and even a set of lightweight barbells. A machine offered to test her blood pressure, and beside it was another glassed-in door leading into a well-lit room mostly taken up by a rippling pool.

She went in. The air was heavy with moisture and the smell of chlorine. The pool was rectangular, about twenty by fifty feet in size, and surrounded by a gray-tiled apron. The pale green walls featured a row of dark green tiles, which depicted a line of ancient-Greek-style dolphins leaping in perfect order.

A slender young woman with short black hair and dark eyes greeted her with a dazzling smile from the other side of the pool. She was wearing a navy blue Speedo swimsuit, and holding what Betsy recognized as the little kit used for testing water quality.

"Good morning!" she chirped. "Dressing room over there!" She gestured toward a pair of doors near a floor-to-ceiling window partly covered with condensation. The soft murmur from a fan showed why it was clearing from the bottom up.

The narrow dressing room extended past a set of six showers, then three sinks and two toilets, then into the locker area, which had a bench down its middle. The lockers were a mix of short and tall, painted sky blue.

Four women were already there. Betsy recognized two of them from Courage Center. "Hi, Rita, hi, Barbara," she said.

"Good morning," said one of the others,

an elderly thin woman whose swimsuit hung loosely on her. "I'm Eileen and this is Morgana." She gestured at the fourth woman, not so old but standing with the support of a walker. "We have to take a shower before we can go in the water."

"I'm Betsy," Betsy said, introducing herself. "Glad to be here."

The women took brief showers and went into the warm and humid pool room. Two men — one of them Dave from the Courage Center — were already in the pool. There were no steps into it, only a ramp. Betsy headed down it into the water, which, she noted with pleasure, was deliciously warm. Its sloping depth ranged from just under her waist to just over her shoulders.

The instructor stooped over a big, old-fashioned boom box and within moments the music started: a sixties rock song set to a disco beat. She jumped sideways into the pool at the deep end and announced, "My name is Pam and I'll be leading this class. Let's begin by rolling our shoulders." She led them through a series of stretches, and soon they were performing jumping jacks and cross-country skiing and hopping — first on one foot, then the other — while making the water boil with their hands.

They were nearly half an hour into their

13

routine when an old woman's shrill voice called, "Wait a minute, wait a minute, start over!"

They all stopped their movements — they were in the middle of downhill skiing — and looked around. Standing just outside the women's locker room door was a tiny woman in an old-fashioned, bright pink two-piece bathing suit. Her gray hair was uncombed, her white limbs and torso a collection of small folds and wrinkles with here and there a bump of bone, and her expression one of righteous determination.

"We can't start over," Pam replied cheerfully. "You're late."

"So I'm late, what does that matter? I want you to start over."

Pam said firmly, "Mrs. Carter, we are not going to start over. But come on in and join us." She went back to twisting vigorously at the waist, lifting her feet with each twist. The others followed suit.

Mrs. Carter came wading down the ramp, taking big, noisy strides, swinging her hands through the water when she got in deep enough. But then more quietly she found a place beside Betsy and, with a wink, started dancing a clumsy twist, feet firmly on the bottom.

When the class was over, Mrs. Carter announced loudly that Pam had to stay with her while she did more exercising to make up for being late. Pam cast her eyes upward but called for jumping jacks.

Getting dressed in the locker room, Betsy asked — bravely, because she did not know these people — "Is Mrs. Carter always like that?"

"No, sometimes she's worse," said Eileen with a grimace, then amended, "Sometimes better. She's got Alzheimer's, but it hasn't progressed far enough yet for her to get moved to the locked wing."

Morgana, the woman with the walker, said, "I think she's enjoying herself. Very energetic, you see her at all hours all over the complex. She really gets around." Her tone was pensive and she looked a little downcast — envious, perhaps, of Mrs. Carter's mobility.

As Betsy was walking through the big lobby to leave, a woman with curly red hair — more properly orange hair, a real "carrot top" — called after her. "Ms. Devonshire, can you spare a minute?"

Betsy stopped and turned. The woman was an Amazon, nearly six feet tall and strongly built, with gray eyes in a beautiful, lightly freckled face.

"May I help you?" Betsy asked.

15

"I sure hope so. I'm Thistle Livingstone, and I'm in charge of recreation and activities here at Watered Silk. You own a needlecraft store, right? In Excelsior?"

"Yes, that's right." Betsy braced herself to turn down a request for needlework materials; Crewel World, her shop, was not currently in a position to give product away.

"Do you teach classes, or know someone who does?"

Betsy nodded. "Yes, to both, for a fee. What kind of classes are you looking for?"

"Well, we have a stitchers' group that right now is knitting and crocheting caps to donate to Children's Hospital for preemies to wear. But they've been doing that for almost a year and are getting tired of it. They want something else, something new. Some of them can do counted cross-stitch, but those who don't have voted down learning how. They've asked if I can find someone to teach a class on something that's quick and easy, and a bit different, besides."

Hmm. Something fun and easy that wasn't counted cross-stitch. "How long a class are you thinking?" Betsy asked. "And for how many times per week? One night? Two? For how many weeks?"

"We'd prefer a daytime class, actually," Thistle said. "Say, one afternoon a week, from one to two o'clock, for five weeks. I can offer an instructor five hundred dollars plus the cost of materials."

A hundred dollars an hour was a lot of money. And none of it had to go to materials. Sweet! Betsy thought for a moment. "Have you heard of punch needle?" she asked.

"No. Is it difficult?"

"Not at all. Even done by beginners, the results are attractive. How many people do you think would come to the class?"

"We have over a dozen stitchers, but probably only seven or eight would take the class."

In Betsy's experience, an estimate of attendees at a class was generally too high, which meant this class would probably have a maximum of six students. That was a very comfortable number for a hands-on craft class. And apparently these people were experienced stitchers.

"Let me consult my calendar," said Betsy. "Then may I call you?"

"Certainly," Thistle said. "Thank you. Here's my card."

Later, over the phone, they agreed on Thursday afternoons for the class. Betsy frequently took Thursday as her day off —

she normally worked Saturday, and on Sunday the shop was closed — so she was free to teach the punch needle class herself. Five women signed up for it.

On Wednesday, between customers, Betsy gathered the material for seven kits: seven copies of a simple punch needle practice pattern of a heart inside a heart; seven Charlotte Dudney patterns of a baby chick among four eggs; seven each skeins of DMC floss in purple, orange, yellow-green, blue, lavender, and red; seven glass tubes, each holding a punch embroidery needle with threader; and seven Morgan Lap Stand embroidery hoops. The lap stands were a luxury, but they made the craft much easier. She put each set into a plastic drawstring bag with the Crewel World logo on it. She drew them all shut, and put the kits into a large attaché case along with an invoice for the materials.

The seventh kit was included because, almost as often as someone who signed up not appearing, someone who hadn't signed up would decide at the last minute to come.

On Thursday, Betsy had a quick lunch at Sol's Deli, next door to her shop, before driving over to Watered Silk. It was a sunny day, but cold. She signed in, and Thistle, who was waiting at the front desk for her, led her down a broad, well-lit corridor lined with support bars, clearly intended for use by seniors. They walked down the hall to an elevator, then up another corridor and into the building's library, a beautiful room with a beamed ceiling, a fireplace, and two large windows.

A long table built from what looked like real mahogany stood in the middle of the room and Betsy was dismayed to see a dozen women seated at it.

Thistle noticed the expression on her face and spoke quickly. "Not all the women here want to take your class. They just moved their usual meeting day and time so they could be here now to watch what you're doing." She leaned in and murmured in Betsy's ear: "They're nosy."

Betsy chuckled. "Which of you are here to learn punch needle?" she asked the members of the group.

"I am," said the one near the head of the table, a heavy-set woman with iron gray hair, raising her hand. "I'm Mildred."

"Me, too," said another, a sweet-faced, white-haired woman in a purple caftan with elaborate gold embroidery around the neck. "I'm Fran."

"And I," said an emaciated woman sitting in a wheelchair. She had an austere face and enormous, sad eyes. "I'm Estelle."

It turned out that Betsy's students —
there were five, as promised — all sat at one
end of the table. Betsy opened her attaché
case and handed out the kits. The women
immediately opened their bags and sorted
through the pieces. While they were occupied, Betsy got out her own kit and assembled the lap frame, made of a smaller
and a larger embroidery hoop connected by
three short legs, explaining as she went
along how to do it. The procedure was
simple enough that everyone assembled her
own without a problem.

"Punch needle is more properly called
Russian punch needle," Betsy said. She held
up a finished sample of the practice piece, a
red heart with a white heart in its center,
about four inches square. "See, on this side
it looks like a miniature hooked rug." She
handed the sample to the obese woman,
who fingered the pile admiringly, glanced at
the back side, and handed it along. The last
woman handed it back to Betsy. All were
smiling in anticipation.

"The reverse looks like parallel lines of
short stitches, which is what it is." Betsy
held up the back of the piece. "You work it
on this side, the reverse side, and the loops
form on the front.

"I want you to take up the smaller piece of fabric first, the one with two hearts on it."

Four of her students already knew how to loosen the embroidery hoop until it opened. Betsy showed them how to smooth the fabric across the bottom hoop, slide the top one over it, and tighten it again.

"Make sure your pattern is smooth and not pulled sideways or otherwise distorted." The very thin woman made an exclamation and a noise of frustration as she loosened the top hoop and adjusted her fabric.

"Let's start with the inner heart," said Betsy. "Pick a color and cut off a length about two feet long. This method of stitchery goes through floss really quickly, so you'll do it many times. This means you'll get lots of practice in threading the needle. When you get more skilled, you can cut your floss as long as one yard — even longer. You'll be working this with three strands of floss, and the skeins are six strands."

Betsy showed them how to tap the cut end of the floss to make the strands separate and pull three of them from the others. Most already knew the trick. Betsy smiled. How much easier it was to teach people who already had the basics down!

"Now, take out the punch needle from the glass tube," she instructed. The tubes had fat rubber stoppers on them. The punch needle was a little over three inches long, and consisted of a series of graduated cylinders, the last one a hollow needle with a hole in its tip.

"In the glass tube that holds the needle there's also a threader. It's a very fine wire, essential to punch needle but easy to lose, so keep careful track of it. If you drop it on the floor, it's next to impossible to find again. Best to put it back in the tube every time after you use it."

She showed them how to feed the threader loop-first through the hollow needle and up the shaft of the punch until it appeared at the other end. The floss was threaded through the loop and pulled back down and out the end of the needle. Then the blank end of the threader was poked through the hole near the tip of the needle and pulled through. Finally, the threader was removed and carefully stored in the glass tube.

Then the floss was pulled back until about a quarter inch was just visible through the hole in the end of the needle. One woman made an annoyed exclamation — she had pulled the floss completely through the hole and had to use the threader to pull it through again.

Betsy demonstrated the punching motion used to feed the floss into the fabric. Some of the women got up and came to stand behind her, watching. She kept her movements slow and deliberate, and the taut fabric made a little popping sound as the needle went through it.

"Punch through until it stops, lift the needle just barely back out of the fabric, move it a tiny way, less than an eighth of an inch, and punch down again," she instructed them. "Go slow until you get a feel for this."

The women began working on their practice piece. In about two minutes the room was filled with the sound of rhythmic thumping as the group's hollow needles pierced the pieces of tightly stretched fabric. The obese woman was fastest, the others more deliberate. Some of them turned their lap frames over and exclaimed in pleasure at the raised texture formed by their needles. Others saw with dismay that they were not punching the stitches together closely enough.

"To correct an error," Betsy said, "lift the needle up until the stitches you've made pull out. Then pull the floss back out through the needle until it's short above the fabric. If you want to retrace your steps, you have to turn the hoop around. Look on the shaft for a white line. That line shows the direction you should be stitching."

Betsy went to each woman, checking her work. She was leaning over one of her students when the door to the library slammed open.

"Wait a minute, wait a minute!" shouted the shrill voice of an old woman. "Start over!"

# TWO

The women at the table all looked at Betsy to see what she would do. "Come in, Mrs. Carter," she said. "I have a kit for you, sit down and take a look at it." She turned to the others. "Now, where were we?"

Mrs. Carter made a production out of coming to the table. She pulled out a chair, sat down with a thump, opened her kit, and spread the contents widely in front of her, poking at the lap stand parts, uncapping the glass tube that held the needle and threader and spilling them out. "What's all this stuff?" she demanded.

"I'll be with you in a minute," Betsy said, kindly but firmly. She turned to the others. "Remember to stay inside the lines, and to make little stitches in parallel lines without overlapping," she said. Then she went to Mrs. Carter and said, "Now, do you know anything about punch needle?"

"Of course not, otherwise why would I be

here?" Her tone was sharp, but then she winked, drew up her shoulders, and giggled.

She needed some help assembling the lap stand, but stretched the practice fabric on the smaller hoop with no trouble. She could in no way understand how to thread the punch needle with floss, but after Betsy did it for her, she began punching through the fabric with enthusiasm. "Yippee!"

"Slow down, slow down," counseled Betsy, then left her to it and went back to the others, praising their work, suggesting narrower lines to some and shorter stitches to others. Now and again one of them would turn the lap stand over and exclaim with pleasure at the look of the growing field of tight loops, sometimes stroking them with a gentle finger.

But when Betsy got back to Mrs. Carter, she found that she had begun to punch at random, twisting the punch needle so that it wasn't laying down the loops evenly, occasionally lifting the needle so far up that it was pulling loops out and leaving loose floss on the back of her fabric.

"This is fun!" exclaimed Mrs. Carter, holding up her work for examination.

"I can see you are enjoying yourself," Betsy said, noting that the random sprawl of loops had wandered from one heart to the other and even into the background. The woman smiled broadly and resumed attacking the fabric with rapid, irregular thrusts.

"Perhaps if you punched a little more slowly," Betsy began.

"Betsy, I'm about to run out of floss already," said Dot, surprised.

"Yes, that's the one big problem with punch needle," said Betsy, abandoning Mrs. Carter to her craft and going to the speaker. "It goes through floss at an amazing rate. You just let it come close to running out, pull up on the working side to empty your needle, and rethread to continue. If the needle empties on the front, go back to the last stitch and pry it up gently — very gently — with your needle so the loose end is on the back."

Betsy had to go around the class and reteach everyone how to thread the needle. It was a counterintuitive process; Betsy had had to resort to the instruction booklet repeatedly herself to learn it.

By this time Mrs. Carter had lost her threader, and three minutes' searching failed to turn it up. Fortunately, Betsy had brought along half a dozen extra ones, though she took care not to let her students see that, lest they get careless.

"I have an idea," said an observant knitter at the other end of the table, seeing Betsy about to slip a new threader to Mrs. Carter.

"What's that?" asked Betsy.

"I have a refrigerator magnet in my bag. I drop needles often — and it's very dangerous to step on one with bare feet — and the magnet is useful in locating them. Maybe if we ran it over the floor around Wilma's chair, you'd get that thing back."

"Wilma?"

"That's me!" declared Mrs. Carter, as if just remembering her own name.

"Brilliant!" exclaimed Betsy. "May I borrow your magnet?"

"No, you go ahead with the class, let me try to find the threader." She searched her stitching bag, found the magnet, and though a little stiff and uncertain in getting onto her knees, searched the floor beside Wilma. She swept the magnet — it was attached to a plastic poodle wearing a Santa hat — lightly around the carpet and, with a little happy exclamation, came up with the hairfine twist of wire. It took her less than a minute. Without rising, she held it up.

"Thank you, Melly!" said Mrs. Carter — Wilma — taking it and tossing it on the table.

"You're welcome, Wilma," said Melly,

beginning to struggle back to her feet.

"Are you all right?" asked Betsy. "Here, let me help you up." Melly only needed a little help but gave a half gasp, half groan as she straightened. Betsy walked her back to her chair and stroked her back as she sat down again. "Thank you so much, it was good of you to come to Wilma's aid."

Melly's "You're welcome" was accompanied by a smile so sweet that Betsy returned it with renewed gratitude.

As she went back to her end of the table, Betsy made a mental note to get a good strong magnet to include in her kit.

"Help me, Betsy," whined Wilma, holding up her lap stand. "I don't get it, this stupid thing was fine, but now it isn't working right again."

Betsy patiently showed her how to hold her needle so that it was facing forward, then watched over her for a few minutes, gently correcting her from time to time, until she seemed to understand that she needed to hold the needle with its white mark facing forward and that she should keep her stitches short and even.

"There it is, ha ha! There it is!" Wilma cried at last in a high, excited voice, having completed half a circuit of the heart. But as soon as Betsy moved on to another woman,

Wilma's needle twisted off center and her movements became random. "Wait a minute, wait a minute, it's all *screwjee* again!"

Craft maven Thistle, who had remained in the room to watch the class, raised her eyebrows at Betsy, signaling an offer to assist. When Betsy nodded assent, Thistle came to sit beside Wilma. "Here now, show me what the problem is," she said.

Betsy began explaining to the others that some punch needle stitchers clipped the loops formed by the needle, others didn't. It was a choice: fuzzy or smooth texture. She produced two identical patterns, one clipped, one not, and handed them around. While her pupils studied both samples, Betsy took notice of Thistle's conversation with Wilma. She was asking Wilma how to do the work, and listening to her repeat the instructions — a clever ploy, because it clarified them in Wilma's own mind.

Betsy came over to check on her and saw that Wilma's floss had run out without her noticing. Thistle raised her chin as a warning to say nothing, and Betsy decided to follow her instruction.

When the class was over, Thistle accompanied Betsy back down to the lobby. "What do you think?" she asked Betsy.

"They're picking it up so fast, I won't have anything left to teach after the next class," Betsy replied. "Except we're not being fair to Wilma."

"I'm sorry about her disrupting the class. She's a nice person, everyone likes her, and she wants to be a part of everything, but she's now at a stage where she simply isn't capable of learning anything new. I suspect by next week she'll have forgotten all about punch needle — I hope so, because I wasn't paying close attention to your teaching and couldn't put floss in that needle if my life depended on it. We'll pay for her materials, and I'll just put them in our craft supply cabinet."

"Someone told me she has Alzheimer's."

Thistle hesitated, then nodded. "Yes. For her, it's a slow-progressing disease, but eventually she'll have to move into the locked ward. I'll be sorry when that happens." Thistle touched her nose, then smiled. "Meanwhile, she's enjoying herself."

Betsy nodded. "I sensed that. I don't know a lot about Alzheimer's. Does she know that she has it? Is she scared?"

"I can't speak for her, I'm not one of her caretakers. I think most of the people with Alzheimer's understand what's happening to them, at least at first, and I'm sure they're frightened — I know I'd be. I think Wilma's being brave in the face of it. But I also think she's decided to enjoy the freedom to break some rules, to speak her mind, to behave selfishly. She's never done any harm to anyone, she's not cruel —" Thistle cut herself short. "I'm speaking out of school here, sorry."

"I understand that, but thank you for helping me understand her."

"Next time you come into the library, look at the big picture book on one of the side tables. Wilma used to be a well-known studio photographer, but she also did some nature photography and published a collection of her prints. At first they just look like scenes of lakes, rivers, fields, and forests. But if you look closely, you'll see there are animals in them, hidden by their natural coloring. Deer, rabbits, foxes — dozens of animals, and all of them almost invisible. Terrifically clever."

"I'd like to take a look."

"Come early next week — phone ahead so I can meet you at the door again . . . And here we are, back where you came in. Thank you for agreeing to do this, Betsy. I think everyone is enjoying the class. See you next week."

On the drive home, Betsy again reminded

herself to pack a magnet in her travel case — and to take a look next week at Wilma's book of photographs.

Back at the shop, Godwin, Betsy's store manager, was full of questions. "How was it? he asked. "Did they like punch needle? Did any men turn out?"

"Six students signed up, all women, and only one looks to be a problem. In fact, the other five are great!" Betsy's success with the class — and the handsome fee she was to collect — put her in an optimistic mood and she looked with favor around her shop.

It was looking very attractive. Indirect winter sunlight shone boldly through the big front window, making the rich colors of yarns and flosses glow. They and the carpeted floor absorbed sound, giving the shop a cozy, quiet feel. There were alternating double and triple rows of spinner racks marching across the floor, holding fancy silk and overdyed flosses. An old, well-polished library table stood in the center of the floor, a smaller version of the table in Watered Silk's library, its center marked with plastic bowls holding scissors, tape, knitting needles, samples of wool and floss, needles, threaders, and magnifying glasses for customers trying out techniques.

A triple row of eight-inch wooden pegs

stuck out along one wall, draped with thin skeins of needlepoint yarns ranging from white and pale yellow at one end, then shading across the rows into oranges, reds, browns, and blues, concluding in deep purples and black. A set of thin canvas doors hung on another wall, to which were pinned hand-painted needlepoint canvases.

Ceiling-high box shelves divided the shop. The front room was larger, and in the smaller room at the back, the emphasis was on counted cross-stitch. Every inch of available wall in both sections held finished needlework pieces, their beauty meant to intensify a customer's desire to stitch this one, then to stitch that one, then to stitch the next one, too.

Best of all, Betsy could see five customers perusing the merchandise.

Godwin saw the pleased way she was counting them and said, "I hate to bust your balloon, but . . ." He couldn't bring himself to finish his sentence, but Betsy knew what he was going to say anyway.

After the crush of post-Christmas sale-seekers, customer numbers had dwindled, which was not unexpected, just disappointing. But those who did come in weren't buying as usual. In fact, Betsy had been at wit's end trying to think of a way to boost business. She'd spent more of her outside-the-shop time working on the shop's web site. She tried posting tips and a list of frequently asked questions, and connecting them to items carried in her shop. She uploaded more photographs of projects finished by proud customers. She linked to Internet "how to" videos. She had increased the number of sales and classes Crewel World offered. All this effort helped, but not a lot.

Still, five customers on a weekday was pretty good.

But Godwin shrugged and shook his head. "They're just looking."

"Rats," muttered Betsy, then: "I don't know what we're going to do."

"Keep up what we're doing," Godwin said. "Sometimes it takes a while for things to sink in." He was sitting at the library table knitting a circular scarf in exquisite shades of lavender, pink, and purple wool. His fingers moved as if they had a mind of their own, and he barely even glanced at them as they worked the needles.

Betsy, noting the heap of fine wool on the table in front of him, said, "Why a circular scarf? I thought you loved fringe."

"I do. But this isn't just circular, it's a Möbius band." He lifted it up to show the half-twist in the circle.

Betsy came for a closer look. She said, "Gosh, that's clever, I should make one. Maybe in a shade of blue to match my new dress." She smiled thoughtfully and touched the scarf with its twist spilling from his needles. "When I was in my early teens, I learned about the Möbius strip in a math class. There's something magical about turning a two-sided object into a one-sided one. I used to wonder if it were possible to put a half twist in a three-dimensional object. Would it then be four-dimensional? Maybe if someone could get inside such a thing, he could stop time and live forever."

Godwin smiled. "There is a three-dimensional one, it's called a Klein bottle — and you can knit a scarf model of it." He shrugged. "I wouldn't make it of such beautiful yarn as this, but something sturdier. It's not exactly pretty, more of a novelty item, something for a kid to wear."

"What does it look like?" asked Betsy, trying to imagine its shape.

"Like a stocking hat whose skinny long end blends back into the side, like a handle. You knit it all in one piece, of course, no seams, and it's a double thickness, so it's really warm. You push the bottom of the bottle up inside to form the opening for the person's head. I could make one if you want." He looked inquiringly at her.

"Maybe I'll knit one myself." Betsy made a mental note to look it up on the Internet, as none of the shop's patterns for a Möbius scarf offered a Klein bottle hat pattern to go with it.

She walked to the gadgets-filled spinner rack to select a magnet for her class — and continued walking through her shop to see if anyone had a question. She saw one woman with an iPad typing information into it from a pattern on display. Placing an order on the Internet, no doubt. This was far from the first time Betsy had seen a customer doing this, and her lips thinned. Here was an explanation for why she had customers who weren't buying. How long could her shop survive if it served merely as a showroom for people shopping online?

Connor, Betsy's live-in boyfriend, was a handsome retired sea captain, born in Ireland but so long and far from his homeland that his accent was barely detectible. His courtship of Betsy had been long and arduous. Twice divorced, Betsy was wary of commitment. He fixed dinner that night, because Betsy was doing bookkeeping for the shop. While she waited for him to finish cooking, she logged on to Crewel World's

Facebook account and web site. She answered a customer's online question about Hardanger — which she illustrated with a photo of a particularly beautiful pattern of the embroidery. Not too infrequently, her Q&A column brought in a customer seeking the patterns and materials.

Then she went to her newest feature: reviews of products to be found in Crewel World. In one review, her friend and frequent customer Jill Cross had waxed enthusiastic over a new kind of scroll bar. Betsy was trying to think who she might ask to review the Morgan "no slip" lap stand when Connor called, "Dinner, *machree*!" The English spelling of an Irish word meaning "my heart," machree was his favorite term of endearment for her.

She went out to the dining nook to find a beautiful roast chicken posed on a small platter on the table. A coating of olive oil brushed on the bird before roasting had made the skin turn a delectable brown under a generous sprinkle of Nantucket Off-Shore Holiday Turkey Rub, left over from Thanksgiving. No wonder the apartment had smelled so delicious for the past hour.

"What's all this in aid of?" asked Betsy, noting the bowl of mixed vegetables and a little dish of homemade cranberry sauce also on the table. Connor had really outdone himself in the kitchen.

"Call it anticipation of Valentine's Day," said Connor in his pleasant baritone.

"You're too good to me."

"Nothing's too good for you." His smile lit up his face and Betsy's heart turned over. His competence in the kitchen was another reason she was glad to have him in residence — though not the main one, of course. They fell to eating. Betsy tried to go light on the cranberries, but Connor had found a recipe that called for triple sec flavoring, and the result was wonderful on the tongue. When he told her he had used Splenda instead of sugar, she took another helping.

About halfway through the meal, he said, "You know, the fourteenth of February is near. I'd like us to do something special to mark it. Would you like to go out to dinner? Or how about to the theater? We've neither of us been to the Guthrie for a long time."

Betsy smiled at him — he was such a romantic! But she said, "Valentine's Day is on a Thursday this year, and that's our open-till-eight night."

His face showed his disappointment. But her part-timers disliked working holidays, and Betsy felt their loyalty to her went both ways. Store manager Godwin, bless his heart, was normally willing to work weekends and holidays, but he liked Valentine's Day almost as much as Halloween, and she wasn't willing to ask him to work those days except in emergency. And Connor's romantic impulses, precious as they were, did not constitute an emergency.

"I'm really sorry," she said.

He thought briefly, then raised a forefinger. "I have an idea," he said. "Hire me."

"To do what?"

"Hire me as a part-timer at Crewel World, just for that day. Then at least we can be together."

Betsy would have laughed, but she saw he was serious. And now that she thought about it, it would be fun to have him working with her in the shop. On the other hand, mixing business with pleasure was risky. What if he had an idea for the shop that she didn't approve of? Could she be his boss and his mistress at the same time? "Do you have a green card?" she asked, beginning a jesting game while she tried to think of a reason to turn down his offer without offending him.

He instantly began to play along. "What do I need a green card for? I'm retired."

"But you want a job, and you're not a citizen, are you?"

He was, and she knew it. He looked mock-abashed. "I was going to go through the process, but I decided it would be less complicated to marry an American."

"To do that you have to be a legal resident — you *are* a legal resident, right?"

"I've been meaning to talk to you about that," he began, choking back a laugh. "That card I have will only pass casual inspection."

Her tone heavy with mock warning, she asked, "I take it you've found an American woman somewhere to marry so you can stay here legally?"

He was instantly serious. "Yes, I have. I have only to convince her it would be a good idea."

# THREE

On Tuesday morning, so early it was still dark out, Pam came through the main entrance of Watered Silk Senior Complex, nodded at the sleepy-eyed night guard, and went down the broad hall to the therapy complex at the far end of the building. Shucking off her long, down-filled coat, revealing a pink T-shirt and skinny jeans, she flipped on the lights in the small exercise room. She turned on the machine that measured pulse and blood pressure — it needed time to warm up. She hung up her coat, locked her purse in her office desk, and unlocked and went through the door that led into the therapy pool. She turned on the bright overhead lights. The air was warm and moist, and she could feel her winter-dry skin joyfully opening to it.

She turned on the underwater lights that illuminated the interior of the pool — and it was then she saw something large at the bottom of the deep end. She stared in disbelief. Oh my God, it was a person, arms out and legs apart, not moving. She took two steps closer. Yes, it was really there, a naked woman, with lots of long blond hair, facedown. Pam waited a few seconds for whoever it was to come up for air, but the person was motionless.

Her training clicked in, overriding her instinctive freeze. She pulled her winter boots off, dropped her keys and cell phone on the floor, and jumped into the water. She ducked under, grabbed the woman by one arm, and pulled her to the top. The arm was warm — the same temperature as the water — the skin rubbery, the joints stiff. Pam turned her over, noting with a sick feeling her half-closed eyes and foam-filled mouth. She did not recognize the woman, who had been young, petite, and really pretty. Pam could not imagine how she came to drown here.

Pam had taken a lot of lifesaving classes, but this was her first experience with an actual death by drowning. She grasped the woman under her chin and floundered with the body as she made her way to the shallow end.

The body's rigidity made it a clumsy thing to get out onto the apron. Pam pushed a thick wet length of pale hair out of the way to press two forefingers into the carotid artery, seeking a pulse. She was not surprised to find none.

She ran around to pick up her cell phone, picked it up, and dialed 911 with trembling fingers. When an operator answered, she said, too rapidly, "There's a drowned woman in our pool. A young woman, I don't know how she got in here, no one's allowed in here at night; in fact, I don't know who she is and she's naked and she's dead, no pulse —"

"Hold on, slow down," said the operator in a slow, soothing voice. "Where are you?"

"Oh, gosh, yes, this is Pam Fielding and we're at Watered Silk, the senior retirement community on Twenty-seventh in Hopkins, in the therapy pool, and I don't know who the victim is, I've never seen her before, she's way too young to be a resident —"

The operator, still in that calm voice, interrupted her with questions and made her repeat the information until Pam was nearly screaming into the phone. She finally tossed the phone down, ran back to the body, and began futile resuscitation efforts. After a minute, she was shocked to find herself sobbing.

■ ■ ■

The discovery of a drowned woman in an indoor pool was on the news that night. Betsy wasn't paying close attention until the reporter mentioned Watered Silk. Then she focused on the video accompanying the story. Yes, that was the front entrance of the senior complex — and there, that was a photo of the pool, Betsy recognized it from a brochure on amenities at the complex.

"Police are treating this as an accident, although they are investigating how the victim got into the pool, which is inside a secure building," the reporter said.

"And you're going to go swimming in that very water?" asked Connor with unusual fastidiousness.

"Not I." But that was because Betsy was going to be away from the next class in any case — she had a dental appointment. She called Watered Silk and was told that aerobics classes would resume on Friday.

At the class on Friday, clients who were not residents — Betsy, Dave, Barb, and Rita — hinted mildly that they wondered if their instructor, Pam, was the person who discovered the body. Pam admitted she was, but — with a nod toward the residents — she said she did not want to discuss it.

"Wait a minute, wait a minute, start over!" came a familiar cry, as Wilma charged into the pool. This time she was so late that the class was already winding down with stretches.

"Find any more dead bodies?" she asked Pam cheerfully.

"Mrs. Carter!" Pam responded. "That is a very rude question!"

Her tone surprised Wilma. "Pam," she replied, clearly abashed, "I apologize, I didn't know you were told not to talk about it in front of us." Then she continued, cheerful again, "I'd want to talk about it if it was me, lots and lots!" She began rolling her shoulders vigorously with the others. "I feel so good, I think we should swim a few laps today! What do you think, how about it, everybody?"

Pam sighed and dismissed the class — and this time she included Wilma.

The Monday Bunch was in session. An informal club of mostly senior women — and one senior man — its members gathered early on Monday afternoons around the library table in Crewel World to stitch, share stitching tips, and gossip.

"Did any of you see the hat Cherie Yonder

was wearing on Sunday?" asked Patricia in an amused voice. She had brought in a pattern she ordered from Crewel World after seeing it in a back issue of The Stitchery magazine. It featured one mostly red parrot and another mostly blue, a white and yellow macaw, and a black and gold toucan on a dense tropical foliage ground. "It looks like a box of crayons exploded," she'd declared. She was sorting through the Kreinik silks that she was going to substitute for the cotton floss the designer called for. Silk floss has more "loft" than cotton, so it would take fewer strands in the needle, which would decrease the extra cost for silk just a little.

"Who's Cherie Yonder?" asked Emily. She was working on a cross-stitched birth announcement for a friend whose baby was due in July. The family already knew it was a girl and were going to name her Riley. The theme of the announcement was sailboats — Riley's parents loved to sail.

Emily had found an old poem by George W. Cable and was carefully stitching an adapted version of it on the canvas:

There came to port last (blank) night
The queerest little craft,
Without an inch of rigging on;

I looked and looked — and laughed!
It seemed so curious that she
Should cross the unknown water,
And moor herself within my arms —
My daughter, O my daughter!

Emily, who had a son and two daughters, sighed at the deep emotion the poem evoked in her own breast. "Moor herself within my arms" — yes, that was the wonder.

"Cherie's new in town and she goes to our church," said Patricia. "And she always wears a hat." She tilted her elegant head sideways while she tried to decide which shades of orange she would use on the bird-of-paradise flowers among the foliage.

"I think that's really nice," said Alice, the widow of a pastor, who had seen parishioners whose only concession to the occasion of coming to church on Sunday was to wrap a towel around their swimsuits. A sturdy woman with broad shoulders, she was knitting a severely plain black cardigan with a rolled collar for herself.

"My mother wore a hat to church every Sunday of her life," contributed Phil, who was an old man, a retired railroad engineer. He was frequently found stitching locomotives and other rail cars, but lately he'd been working on a series of little shops, saying he

48

needed some buildings to go with the railroad station he'd stitched last fall. Today he was stitching the bakery.

"Oh, I love hats, though I hardly ever wear one," said Patricia. "Back when hats were in style, my mother wore them, too, for all occasions. But they were mostly —" She paused to think, then gestured at the crown of her head with her needle hand.

"Pillbox," supplied Betsy, remembering. She was seated at the checkout desk, going through registrations for a class on candlewicking.

"Yes, the kind Mrs. Kennedy made popular. These are" — she gestured again — "extravagant."

"The kind they're wearing in England," guessed Jill, whose two youngsters were now in first grade and preschool, respectively, so at last she had time to come to Monday Bunch meetings again. She was nearly finished with a famous cross-stitched alphabet monogram designed originally as the center of a quilt by a woman named Ida W. Beck. Very tall, slender letters overlapped in many colors in a shape something like the sound box of a violin. It made Betsy crosseyed just to look at it.

"Yes, that's it," agreed Patricia. "They're beautiful, really, but she's probably the only

49

woman in Minnesota who wears them."

"No, she isn't," said Bershada, who was an African American woman and saw extravagant hats in her own church on Sundays. She had two or three grand hats of her own. She was cross-stitching a line of animals — rabbit, duck, deer, cat (with a bird on its back), and squirrel — all listening intently to a bear reading a book to them. The pattern was done in black silhouettes and under it was the word "Storytime." It was going to be presented to the Excelsior Public Library, another in a series Bershada was making for them.

"Describe one of her hats," said Emily, whose three children, during the weekday, were either in school or with their grandmother. "I don't watch English TV."

"Well, this Sunday she wore a purple felt with a deep fold in the tall crown and a turned-down brim with a big bunch of feathers all curly on one side." Patricia was smiling at the memory.

"Sounds like something the Queen herself would wear," said Phil.

"No, the Queen has to wear something that doesn't hide any part of her face," said Doris in her deep, sandy voice. She was laboriously crocheting a scarf, homework for a class she was taking.

Emily said, "How do you know that?"

"I don't know where I read it, but I know it's true. Just pay attention to video and photos of her for a while, and you'll see. I don't know if it's a custom or a rule, but the royals never wear a hat that shades their eyes when they're in public." Her tongue appeared in a corner of her mouth as she chained two and turned a row.

Thoughtful frowns went around the table.

"You know, I think you're right," said Patricia. "That's interesting. I suppose so the people can go home from an event and say, 'I saw Her Majesty' instead of 'I saw Her Majesty's hat.' "

When the session broke up, Bershada remained behind. She waited while Betsy turned a fat skein of knitting yarn into a ball on a clever hand-cranked machine that attached to the library table, and sold it to a waiting customer who also bought a pair of size thirteen ebony knitting needles. Bershada's face was sad and it was easy to see the anxious look in her eyes, which she'd been careful to hide during the meeting.

Betsy had long since established a custom of paying close attention to the customer she was waiting on, making him or her the most important person in the room. It made her a popular proprietor, and often her care-

51

ful listening gave her an opportunity to add to her own or the customer's knowledge of the craft.

So she did not notice, until the customer left, that Bershada was carrying some kind of unhappy burden.

"Oh my goodness, Bershada, what's the matter?"

"Betsy, my sister and brother-in-law have a serious problem with their son, Ethan." Bershada, a retired librarian, was handsome and dark-skinned, with fine lips and a small, narrow nose. A little above medium height, she was slim, with an erect, almost regal bearing. Today she was dressed in a muted pinky-gold sweater (DMC 402, thought Betsy absently) and dark gray slacks. Her earrings were huge golden hoops.

"What kind of problem?"

"As you probably know, Ethan's a senior at the university, and doing well. He's working two part-time jobs to help with tuition and books — I don't know when that boy sleeps — and one of his jobs is night guard at Watered Silk."

"Uh-oh."

Bershada nodded. "Yes, he was still on duty the morning the body in their therapy pool was discovered, and he'd been there since midnight. So they're thinking he let her in. He's saying he didn't."

Betsy said, "Do they know what time she died? Could she have come in earlier, before midnight?"

Bershada shook her head. "There was some kind of gathering of eight or nine people on that lower level outside the door to the gym, which didn't break up until nearly one. The person who was on the desk before Ethan told him to keep an eye on them, so he did. He's sure none of them looked like the drowned woman."

And the police surely contacted them, thought Betsy, to see if they remember someone going into the gym/pool area.

Bershada continued, "Ethan says he didn't let her in the main entrance, or see her come in with someone else. He's a responsible young man, he pays attention to his job, he wasn't lost in a book, or sleeping. Tired? Yes, that describes his life right now. But missing the arrival of an adult, coming right through the door? Not likely, not likely at all."

"I'm sure the police know that."

"That's the problem: They don't. They've decided that since she couldn't have sneaked in, he must have let her in to swim. And that because she drowned, he's scared and lying about it. The fact that he's black and

53

she's white isn't helping, especially with this one cop, a detective, who seems to think that Ethan and the girl had something going on and he drowned her on purpose."

"Why would Ethan do that?" Betsy asked.

Bershada, without moving, seemed to back off a considerable distance. Her voice icy, she nevertheless answered, "This investigator seems to think that they had a quarrel. His theory is that, because Ethan is engaged to a young woman of his own race, perhaps this young white woman threatened to tell her they were having an affair and he thinks everyone knows that's the world's biggest no-no."

That shook Betsy into a proper frame of mind. "What wicked nonsense! I've only met Ethan twice, but he seems to me to be an intelligent fellow with his head screwed on right. He certainly doesn't strike me as the sort of person who would get himself in a mess like that. I can't believe that investigator is serious."

"I'm afraid he is, and he's in charge of this case."

"Ethan's mother and father must be sick about this."

"They're not sick. They're furious. And so am I. Betsy, can you help us? I know you're going to that place, Watered Silk, for exercise classes while the Courage Center pool is closed. Can you poke around and find out how that woman might have come into the pool without the man on the desk knowing about it?"

"Oh, Bershada —" Betsy began.

Bershada interrupted loudly. "You *have* to do it! The police think they know what happened! That it's Ethan's fault! They may even conclude that he's a *murderer*! If we can't find some other explanation, who knows what might happen to him? *Please,* Betsy!" Bershada's hands were clenching and unclenching around her stitching bag, and suddenly there were tears in her eyes. Bershada never begged, never wept.

Betsy came out from behind the checkout desk and took her friend into her arms. "Here now, here now, it's all right, everything is going to be all right. Of course I'll look into it, I'm sure there must be some simple explanation."

She could feel the tension in Bershada's shoulders relax. "Thank you," Bershada said, stepping back. She looked Betsy in the eye and smiled tremulously. "I was being silly, you were going to offer to help even before I asked."

"Yes, of course I was. You were just so

scared you didn't give me a chance to say so."

"You're a good friend." Bershada turned away to find and put on her long gray coat, then fumbled in a pocket for a tissue. "Thank you, Betsy," she said, "I just know you'll find out what really happened." Still wiping her eyes, she went out the door.

On Wednesday, Betsy went early to her water aerobics class. She lingered at the front desk after signing in. Now she looked more closely at the handsome black man manning it, and recognized him as Ethan. He frowned a little at her regard before realizing who she might be. "Hey, are you Ms. Devonshire? Did my aunt talk to you?"

"Yes." Betsy nodded. "I'm going to try to find out what really happened."

"You don't know how hard I'm wishing you luck." He spoke slowly, his forehead puckered with intensity.

"Thanks. I hope I don't disappoint you. So first, tell me about your job in this place."

"It's just part-time, four nights a week, midnight to eight. I found out about it from a listing on campus. I've been here almost eight months. It's a good job, no stress, no hassles, time to study. I man this desk and I do a regular little six-minute tour of the downstairs every hour." He held up his wrist. "They gave me this watch to wear on duty. It has an alarm that goes off at hourly intervals, reminding me to make my tour. So far, no complaints, from me or them. Until now, of course." He grimaced angrily, thumped his fist on the desk, then drew a calming breath. "Anything else I can tell you?" he asked.

"What do you know about the building?" Betsy asked. "How many entrances are there?"

"Five."

Betsy was surprised. "Five?"

He nodded. "Including the front door, five. They are all always locked but the residents have an electronic key that will open any of them, day or night. You've probably seen the key; it looks like an outsize credit card and you press it up against a white rectangle beside any one of the doors to unlock it."

Betsy nodded; every student in her needlework class here wore one around her neck. "What else by way of security?"

"There are nine cameras in the building, one at each of the doors, one at the entrance to the locked ward, two in the main downstairs hallways, and one in the kitchen."

He gestured at a big-screen TV at one end

of his long desk. It was divided into nine subscreens, and as Betsy watched, one of them grew a white spot just as someone entered the main entrance vestibule. The spot disappeared and Betsy recognized Rita and turned to wave at her. Ethan pressed a button and the door clacked sharply and slid open.

"Hi, Betsy," Rita said. She carried a zippered bag in one hand, and came to the desk to sign in.

"Hi, Rita. You go on down, I need to talk to this gentleman here for a minute."

"Okay."

Betsy waited until Rita was out of earshot, then asked, "Did that white dot mean a person was coming into camera view?"

"It means the motion detector went off. If someone hiding behind a corner rolls a ball down the hall, the white dot appears."

Betsy smiled. "Let me guess: Wilma Carter."

Ethan smiled back. "You got it. That lady has a wacky sense of humor. Plus, she turns up everywhere, and I think she sleeps less than I do."

"Do you ever miss that white dot alarm?"

"I did at first, but I rarely miss it now."

"But still, you do miss it sometimes. And

suppose it goes off when you're making a tour?"

"Well, okay, it could light up while I'm away. But like I said, those little rounds last six minutes, max. And if someone comes in, the only way to the pool is past this desk."

"There's an elevator at the bottom of the stairs," Betsy pointed out.

"Yes, from an upper floor *inside* the building. You'd have to get in, go to an upper floor, and come down on the elevator. Which has a nice loud *ping,* which I *didn't* hear that morning. Apart from everything else, the person doing that would have to be familiar with the building — and the drowned woman was a stranger. Nobody here can identify her."

Betsy nodded. "I see. So while it's not impossible, it's unlikely that some stranger could get in without your knowing it."

"Sure. And one other important thing: The door to the pool itself is locked, and with a for-real metal key. I think maybe four people have one. That door is only open when a staff member is in there."

"Is there a key here at the desk?"

"No. The two water therapists each have one, the head of maintenance has one, and the building manager has the fourth. None of them ever comes in at night."

"I see. Well, thanks, Ethan. Your Aunt Bershada has given me a hard puzzle to solve."

Ethan's face again twisted with anxiety. "It's a damned important puzzle. There *has* to be a solution that doesn't call for me to get arrested!"

# FOUR

The next day, Thursday, Betsy came in early
for the punch needle class. Even though she
had called ahead, she didn't see Thistle
waiting for her, so she went for a close look
at the framed piece of art.

It wasn't a painting but a piece of fabric,
a pure red, with vertical bands in paler red,
each marked as if many women with differently shaped lips had kissed the fabric. Betsy
had seen fabric with these markings before,
called moire, but she hadn't realized it was
the same as watered silk. The piece was
perhaps fifteen inches wide by twelve inches
high.

"Pretty, isn't it?" Thistle remarked from
behind her.

"How did they get that effect?" Betsy
asked, after an initial start — she hadn't
heard the tall redhead's approach.

"My understanding is that they ran the
silk between very heavy rollers, and that

pretty result is actually damage to the fabric. It was popular among the wealthy starting around two hundred years ago because watered silk was fragile and expensive." She smiled. "Sort of like the people who live in this complex today."

Betsy smiled. "Good simile. Or do I mean metaphor?" She shrugged off her own question. "And they used to make watered silk in this building?"

"Yes, though this wasn't the only kind of silk they wove here. The factory was in operation from 1887 until 1935. They did a couple of remodels, I don't remember which years they were, but somewhere in there, the piece you see here — which was about a yard long when it was found, split, stained, and dirty — got laid down under a floor. They saved the best part of it, and there it is."

Betsy took another look at the textile fragment. Even under glass, the fabric shimmered as if brushed by a delicate breeze. It was surrounded by a double mat in cream and ivory, and the broad and deeply carved wooden frame surrounding it looked like a real antique, its gold leaf flaked off here and there. Betsy could see how the people who built this place would appreciate the layers of meaning in the name Watered Silk. She turned around. "Let's go up to the library. I want to see the book of photographs Wilma Carter published."

"Right this way."

Betsy paid attention to the route they took, so she wouldn't always be dependent on Thistle to lead her to and from the lobby.

There were already three women in the library, punching away on their projects. Two of them looked up and nodded; the third was too deeply focused on her work to notice them.

Betsy walked over to the small table beside the fireplace. The book, which took up most of the surface of the small table, had a cover featuring a springtime meadow, fresh green grass poking up through the bent brown grass of the previous summer, with the edge of a forest in the background. *Minnesota's Secret Wildlife* was its title, with Wilma's name in smaller type in the bottom right-hand corner. Betsy sat down and put the book in her lap. Remembering what she'd been told, she spent about thirty seconds searching the dust jacket before she saw the pair of wild rabbits crouching in the mix of grass near the bottom center of the photo.

Thistle, standing beside her, gave her a few more seconds, then silently touched a place where the forest edge was marked with underbrush, and then Betsy saw the reason for the rabbits' flat-eared crouch: A wolf, head lifted as if he'd caught their scent, was studying the meadow with yellow eyes. His shaggy brown-gray coat made him almost invisible beside the bushes.

"This is wonderful!" murmured Betsy. She opened the book and quickly became absorbed in searching the photos for more examples of deer, beavers, turtles, and other animals cleverly hidden among underbrush, tall grass, evergreens, even in a tree-shaded pond.

"Ur-rmmm!" sounded a woman's voice softly. Betsy looked up to find all the members of her class present and waiting for her. She looked at her watch — she was five minutes late.

"Sorry!" she exclaimed, closing the book and putting it down on the table. "Welcome back. Have you all been working on the practice piece? Let's take a look." As Thistle had predicted, Wilma Carter wasn't present. The others had nearly completed their homework, and the results were all satisfactory. Even one that was barely half done was done very competently. The class was going splendidly. Life was good.

"Okay, you're clearly ready for a more complex piece," Betsy said. She handed out squares of thin, tightly-woven tailor's cloth printed with a simple outline drawing of a baby chick standing among four eggs. She placed on the table a great gleaming heap of DMC floss in lots of colors: three shades of pink, two of deep gold, three shades of green, two of yellow-green, two of blue-green, two maroons, a clear yellow, a light, medium, and dark blue, four shades of lavender, and so on, mostly pastels — these were Easter eggs, after all — many skeins of each color. There were exclamations of wonder and delight.

"You can take a pencil and draw patterns on the eggs, or you can make them solid colors," she said.

"Before we begin," said Estelle, the thin woman. She hesitated, then continued, a little shamefacedly, "I have to confess that I've lost my threader. I've been borrowing Nancy's, but can I buy just a threader from your shop?"

"As a matter of fact," said Betsy, "The shop carries a supply of them. They come four to a set. I'll donate this set to the class, so anyone who needs a replacement — up to four of you — can have one." She brought out a clear glass tube with four of the nearly invisible threaders in it. "Or, you can buy a tube of four for yourself."

"I need one, too," said Vivian, smiling in relief that she was not alone in having lost the implement.

"I'd better buy a tube," said Estelle.

"Fine, I'll bring you one next time."

The stitchers were busy drawing stars and curves on their fabric egg shapes when Betsy heard the familiar cry, "Wait a minute, wait a minute, start over!"

She looked up to see Wilma Carter hustling to a place at the table, a mischievous smile on her wrinkled face. Her lap stand was in one hand, and in the other she held a sewing bag made of a carpet remnant. She dropped the bag on the floor, then pulled a chair out and sat down heavily, scooting her lap stand out in front of her on the table. A glance at it showed her practice piece was nearly completed, albeit riddled with lots of cross-the-outline errors and gaps. "I ran out of floss," she announced. "Otherwise it would be done."

"I can see you understand the technique," said Betsy kindly.

"It takes a lot of patience," said Wilma, "and I'm not so patient as I used to be."

"You must have been extraordinarily patient to have captured those photographs of wild animals for your wonderful book."

"What book?"

Wordlessly, Betsy turned in her chair and pointed to the coffee-table-size book.

Wilma said, "They tell me that book over there has pictures in it I took, but I used to take pictures of people. They weren't wild animals." She chuckled. "Most of them weren't, anyway."

"That book is wonderful, sort of a *Where's Waldo?*, only with animals," said the plumpest of Betsy's students, Mildred.

"Where's Waldo?" asked Wilma, turning to stare at her. "Where *is* Waldo? Do you know?" Her face had gone blank and she seemed confused. "Who are you?" she asked Betsy, her voice frightened. "I don't know who you are!"

"I'm Betsy Devonshire, and I'm here to teach a class on punch needle."

"I don't know you, I don't know what you want! I don't want to be here! I need to go to my room!" Wilma's eyes were wide, her voice high-pitched.

"You're fine, I'm here with you, I can take you to your room," said Thistle, coming to put her hands on Wilma's shoulders. "You're all right, there's no need to be frightened. I'll take care of you. You know me, I'm Thistle."

Wilma looked up, then gave a nervous laugh. "That's a funny name. But wait, yes,

I remember you with the funny name. You teach us things."

Thistle laughed softly. "Yes, that's right." She helped Wilma to her feet and, leaving her needlework behind, led her from the room, one arm tucked companionably into Wilma's, talking quietly to her.

There fell a nervous silence.

Betsy said, "She'll be fine, I'm sure."

"Of course she will!" said Fran, with emphasis. "She just had a little lapse, it could happen to anyone."

"No, it couldn't, not like what just happened," said Estelle. "She's ill, she's got a deadly sickness. Let's not pretend she's going to be all right. Please; God, don't let it happen to me."

"Amen," said two other women quietly.

"Now, where were we?" said Betsy, reclaiming their attention to the task at hand. "When you're coming close to the border on your pattern, don't put a stitch directly on the border if you're going to outline it in another color. Now, look at your punch needle. You'll see that the narrow red sleeve on the silver needle is actually in three segments. If you pull one off, that will raise the nap on the front of your pattern. Pull two off, and it's even higher. You might want to make your chick stand out from the eggs by making the nap higher on him. But be sure to put the little segments back into the glass tube you store your punch needle and threader in, so you don't lose them. And be careful pulling them off and even more so putting them back on, as the point of your needle is really sharp."

Thistle hadn't returned by the end of the class, so Betsy was glad she'd paid attention when she'd been escorted to the library. She was able to find her way to the main entrance with no problem.

Wilma was crying like a child who's been spanked. She was sitting on her bed, hands on her cheeks, her thin body racked with sobs. "I — I — I — can-can-can't do *anything* an-any mooooooorrre!" she cried. "It's — it's *wrong*, w-w-wicked, stu-stupid. I'm *stupid*!"

"No, you're not," said Thistle, with a glance at the resident RN, Nurse Peggy Humphrey. Wilma had taken hold of Thistle's hand and would not let go. Thistle was wishing the RN would say something helpful, but she was just standing there, nodding encouragement. "You're just a little confused right now," said Thistle.

Sullenly, Wilma said, "I don't want to have Alzheimer's anymore."

"I don't blame you, I wouldn't want it, either." Thistle glanced imploringly at Nurse Humphrey, who added a shrug to her nod. Wilma had told her that she didn't know the nurse and wished she would go away. But the nurse was clearly not going to leave. She was staying out of Wilma's line of sight and seemed to Thistle to be of the opinion that Thistle was doing quite well and should continue.

"Is there something you *do* want?" asked Thistle, who was beginning to imagine Betsy wandering the halls in a futile search for a way out.

Wilma thought for a few moments. "I want a pattern, a stitching pattern." She thought again. "A cross-stitch pattern. Punch needle is too hard, but I already know how to do cross-stitch."

"Do you want me to go ask Ms. Devonshire to bring you a cross-stitch pattern?"

Wilma considered that. "I don't know any Ms. Devonshire. How would she know what to bring?"

"Betsy Devonshire owns a needlecraft store, she could probably get you any pattern you want."

Wilma brightened. "Even Psyche Goes into Cupid's Garden?"

"*Who* goes into a garden?"

"Psyche. That's the pattern I want." Wilma smiled as if letting Thistle in on a big mystery. "Maybe it's Psyche *Enters* Cupid's Garden. It's *so* beautiful, a woman opening a door into a garden full of flowers." Wilma gave a theatrical sigh, and touched her breast with her free hand. "Beautiful," she murmured.

"All right. Let me try to find her and ask her to bring you that pattern."

After a moment, Wilma reluctantly released her tight grip on Thistle's hand. "Okay," she said. "Will you come right back?"

"Of course, if you like, as soon as I ask Ms. Devonshire about a psychic going into a garden with Cupid."

"Yes." Wilma wrapped her arms around herself and began to rock to and fro. "Don't be long," she whispered. "I keep forgetting."

"I'll be back as soon as I can." Thistle hurried back to the library, but Betsy had already left. She checked at the front desk and discovered that Betsy had signed herself out. Thistle went back to Wilma's room, but by then the woman had lain down and gone to sleep, her arms still wrapped tightly around her thin shoulders.

When Betsy got back to Excelsior, she

dropped in at the shop to see how things were going.

Godwin was waiting for her, fairly dancing with anxiety and distress. "I'm *so* relieved to see you! I left a *message* for you upstairs, but now I can tell you in *person*. You'll also find a message from *Bershada*."

"What's happened? What's the matter?"

"Bershada said to tell you that Ethan's been fired. There was no notice or anything, they just phoned him and said he shouldn't come in anymore, they'll mail his pay to him."

"Did they say why?"

"Bershada says no, he was an at-will employee, which means they can fire him for any reason at all. They don't even have to give a reason, in fact."

Betsy felt her heart sink. Was the next thing an arrest? How was she going to face Bershada? Was this fine young man's life to be destroyed before it could begin?

# FIVE

The Northwest Coin Club met one evening a month at a community center near the shore of Lake of the Isles, in an upper-class neighborhood in western Minneapolis. Long tables were arranged in an open rectangle and the members, all men, sat around its outside border. The room was decidedly minimalist in design, color, and style of furnishings.

The club's members were mostly middle-aged and well-to-do — they included a judge and at least two attorneys — but they were friendly and just a little boisterous. There were lots of handsome sweaters on display, a couple of blazers, and one bow tie, worn by the judge.

Godwin had decided that if his partner, Rafael, was going to continue collecting coins, he'd better take an interest in it himself and so he'd come with Rafael to this meeting. After all, Rafael had taken up

73

needlepoint, right? But Rafael hadn't taken more than a passing interest in knitting, so Godwin hadn't bought any coins except for a pair of shiny dimes minted the year he was born.

Before the meeting got started, a few of the members showed off their newest acquisitions. One started a discussion about whether or not to keep the size and value, even the fact, of their collections secret so as not to attract thieves. This set off a sidebar in which several members shared indignant anecdotes of burglars who stole collections and spent valuable coins in vending machines.

Godwin could have told a tale or two about priceless handmade lace or heirloom needlework selling for a dollar apiece at garage and estate sales, but he decided that wasn't the point, especially with this crowd.

The meeting was called to order right on time.

Acronyms like ANA and PCGS were thrown around carelessly during the meeting. Godwin guessed the *n* in ANA stood for "numismatist," a twelve-dollar word that meant "coin collector." PCGS had something to do with coin grading, a subject of intense interest among collectors. Any sign of wear diminished the value of a coin dramatically, Rafael had told Godwin, and there were at least sixty-five grade levels.

A big topic was the coming March Regional Coin Show. Club members who were coin dealers were offered a low rate for space in the coin show catalog. Buying an ad also entitled them to be mentioned on one of the billboards that would be strategically placed along freeways I-35W and E and I-94, crossing Minneapolis and St. Paul — one of the members owned a billboard company.

Godwin had once attended a coin show with Rafael at which Rafael had purchased two coins that turned out to be phony — that was the main reason Rafael had decided to be more loyal in attending meetings like this, and Godwin had decided to support this decision.

The speaker at this meeting was one of the members of Northwest Coin Club, an IT expert with a strong Mexican accent. He talked about the five-hundred-year post-Aztec history of Mexico as seen through its coinage. The mint in Mexico City was established in 1635, the speaker noted, and had operated continuously since then, despite numerous revolutions. It was in fact the oldest mint in the Americas. He handed around examples of Mexican coins. Godwin was amused at how many members casually hauled out pocket-size lighted magnifiers to examine them. He'd thought only Rafael habitually carried one. As he watched Rafael closely examine a big silver coin minted during Mexico's First Empire period, Godwin wondered if Rafael was going to expand his collection into this new arena.

When the meeting ended, they came out to find the predicted snow had instead fallen as freezing rain. The first two members of the club to exit the building whooped as their feet slid dangerously on the sidewalk leading to the parking lot, and their cries alerted those who followed to tread carefully.

*"Madre de Dio!"* muttered Rafael as he nearly fell.

Godwin clutched Rafael's arm to steady himself, and slid around until they were facing each other. They embraced, and Godwin started to giggle.

"Don't, don't," warned Rafael, teetering on the very edge of his balance, but he began to laugh as well, and the two stood awhile, holding each other at the elbows, snorting and choking with badly repressed laughter.

"Get a room!" advised someone from behind them, his voice loud and cheerful.

Rafael, prepared to take offense, turned to glare, and his feet went in two or three directions. The man — it was the club's president — was grinning even as he was whirling his arms like a double windmill and sliding toward them on the ice.

"Whoa!" he shouted and involuntarily joined their embrace. They all three laughed and, still joined, began edging down the sidewalk toward their cars.

But the slippery drive home wasn't funny.

On Friday, Betsy woke to a world transformed. Everything was clad in a coat of crystal, from entire buildings to the smallest twig, and all of it glittering under a frozen sun.

Trucks strewing sand and salt had been busy, so the main roads were safe to drive on. But the side streets Betsy took to get to her water aerobics class had not yet been serviced with de-icers and she drove at an uncertain crawl to the parking ramp across the street from the building.

It was close to the start time of her exercise class when she entered the building. She grabbed the sign-in clipboard to scribble her name and the ID number she'd been assigned and only when she put it down again did she notice that Ethan had already been replaced.

"Already?" she asked the thin young woman sitting there.

"Already what?" The woman's voice was high-pitched, a child's voice. She looked very young, too, dressed too casually in a maroon sweatshirt with a zombie's face printed on it. Her ears were lined with silver knobs and another knob pierced the side of her nose. Her eyelids were thickly blackened with mascara.

"They've already hired you to take the place of Ethan Smart. He's the person usually on at night."

The woman shrugged. "I don't know anyone's name, I'm new. This is only my second night on duty."

Betsy's dismay over Ethan's absence was obvious. She thrashed her way angrily through her exercises, drawing sideways looks from the instructor and fellow exercisers.

"Kind of energetic this morning, weren't we?" asked Rita in the locker room after the class as Betsy yanked on her underwear.

"I'm not energetic, I'm angry. They fired Ethan."

After a blank pause, Rita said in a slow drawl, "Ohhhh-kay?"

"He's the young man who's usually on

78

the desk when we come in."

"Oh, the one you were talking to the other morning? The African American fellow? What did he do to get fired?"

"Nothing!"

Rita was scandalized. "You mean they fired him because he's black?"

"No, of course not," Betsy said, slamming a foot into a sock. "They fired him because they think he let that woman who drowned into the building."

"Ah." Rita pulled her corduroy trousers out of her locker and began to step into them.

"And I'm going to prove they're wrong."

Rita smiled at Betsy. "Another mystery for you to solve. Good luck."

Betsy stopped at the front desk on her way out. "I'd like to speak to whoever is in charge of security in this complex," she said to the woman on duty — a different woman from the one she'd seen when she arrived. This woman was tall and stout, a black woman in dark green silk, with an elaborate hairdo and wickedly long painted finger-nails. So, here was the person who manned the desk during the working day.

"If you're interested in applying for a position, I have an application right here for you to fill out." The woman was already reaching into her multitiered filing tray.

"No, that's not what I want to do."

The woman paused without taking her fingers away from the tray. "Do you want to leave a message, then? Admin personnel aren't here until nine."

Betsy looked at the big clock on the wall behind the desk: eight fifty. "I'll wait," she decided.

She went to sit down. The plain buff chair was hard and uncomfortable. On the low metal-and-glass table were two stacks of brochures, each touting Watered Silk as a wonderful place to live: One was titled "Living in Comfort" and the other, "When It's Time to Decide." The first encouraged seniors to come live at Watered Silk, the other was directed toward adult children or grandchildren who might choose Watered Silk for their aging relatives. The color photos in each were identical, however.

Very shortly after 9 a.m., an administrative assistant in the person of a young-looking Hispanic woman came to take Betsy down a long hall and up one floor in an elevator to a small office. There was no name on the door, just the word *Security* in white letters on a small sign. The office was painted a soothing blue and there was a piece of art on one wall depicting an autumn creek meandering among brilliantly colored trees. Betsy started to look for a hidden squirrel, then caught herself and looked instead at the stern-faced woman in a wine-colored suit who sat behind a wooden desk. On the desk were an antique pen set and a small wooden block engraved with the name Woodward.

"How may I help you?" asked the woman in a beautiful low voice that contrasted startlingly with her expression.

"I'm Betsy Devonshire. I'm enrolled in your water aerobics class and I am also teaching a needlecraft class to a group of residents. I'm a friend of Bershada Reynolds, who is the aunt of Ethan Smart, your night guard who was recently fired."

The woman looked a bit bewildered at this complex of connections to Watered Silk. "Yes?" she said encouragingly.

"Ms. Woodward, I want to know if he was fired because you suspect he let a nonresident, nonemployee into the building, who was later found drowned in your therapy pool."

Woodward sat back, nonplussed for a few moments. "I'm afraid we don't discuss personnel matters with people who have no official need to know," she said. Then, with a hint of worry in her beautiful voice, she added, "Are you an attorney representing Mr. Smart or the family?"

"No, but —" Betsy began, then stopped. The woman was right, of course. "I'm sorry, I should have thought of that before I came to see you. Bershada is a good friend. She and Ethan's parents are upset about this, and my reaction to their distress overrode my common sense."

Woodward sat forward again, her expression sympathetic but also relieved. "I can understand that," she said. "I am also sorry that I can't help you in this matter."

"Yes, well, in turn, I understand your position. I hope the problem can be resolved." Betsy stood. "Ethan will deserve a big-time apology when it is, and perhaps an offer to give him his job back."

Woodward's mouth thinned. "I hope so, too," she said, but not, Betsy thought, with complete sincerity.

That evening Betsy and Connor were watching the local TV news. "The woman found drowned in a therapy pool at a senior residence complex in Hopkins has been identified," the reader intoned. "She was Teddi Wahlberger, aged twenty-five, who lived in Excelsior." A photo of a very pretty blue-eyed blonde was displayed on the screen, her long hair in a disorderly but attractive tumble past her shoulders, a big smile on her face. The name under it was the more formal Theodora Wahlberger.

"Oh, how sad," said Connor. "What a waste."

"Autopsy results are pending," the announcer continued. "How Ms. Wahlberger came to be in the therapy pool of Watered Silk, a secure building, late at night is not yet known."

There was no mention of Ethan Smart, and moments later the reporter went on to a story about a big nonfatal pileup on I-94 caused by slippery road surfaces, as an introduction to the station's ever-jocular weatherman.

One result of Betsy's changes to Crewel World's web site came in the form of a morning visit by a poorly dressed woman carrying a big, dirty, off-white bundle of fabric. She was short and a little plump, with a wistful look in her dark eyes, as if she'd had to make too many sad decisions in her life. Her old quilted parka was almost the same silver-gray color as her short, wind-ruffled hair.

"I found this in my garbage can a few days ago," she said. "I put the can out by the

83

curb for pickup the night before and then the next morning I found that one of my wastebaskets hadn't been emptied. So I brought it out to add to the can, and this was stuffed in on top."

She unfolded the bundle, which proved to be slightly malodorous as well as dirty and torn. Betsy took a step back. It was a bedsheet, a very old one to judge by its thinness and by several long tears, which were parallel splits. But the top edge showed a broad line of Hardanger stitching, complex and beautiful. Betsy stepped forward again, her eyes sparkling with interest.

"I hoped you'd be interested," the woman said, reading accurately the expression on Betsy's face. "This is that same kind of thing you wrote about on your web site, right? Hard anger. Or is it har danger?"

"Hardanger," said Betsy, pronouncing it HAR-dahng-er. "It's Norwegian embroidery. This is beautiful work."

"That's what I thought, too," said the woman. "What I want to know is, can it be cut off this raggedy old sheet, cleaned up, and put on something else?"

"Certainly," said Betsy. "In fact, I hope you will do that exact thing. You say you found it in your garbage bin?"

"Yes," said the woman, nodding. "I don't

know how it came to be in there, it wasn't one of my neighbors mistaking my can for their own, I asked them." She stroked the embroidery with a work-thickened forefinger. "I never seen anything like this Hardahng-er before." She pronounced it carefully. "My grandmother used to do all kinds of embroidery, but nothing like this. This's got little bitty holes cut in it." She hesitated, then asked a little too casually, "Is it valuable?"

"Yes, but not many people collect it. It's generally of more value to the family that inherits it. I'm surprised it ended up in the trash. This is certainly heirloom quality, and has probably been in someone's family for a long time."

"How long? Is it really old? Like an antique?"

Betsy leaned in for a closer look. She didn't do Hardanger — she found its serious demand that every stitch be done perfectly intimidating. She thought it hard to believe the assessment by advanced stitchers that the craft was relaxing. But she'd seen a lot of it, and had sold a lot of copies of Janice Love's book on advanced Hardanger, *Fundamentals Made Fancy,* so she knew complex work like this when she saw it. She recognized the pattern of one repeating segment as Spider in a Lacy Web, and another as the wonderfully complex and delicate Edelweiss. Geometric shapes made of satin stitch were set among the open work and were strong contrasts to the nubbly Dove's Eyes. There were a lot of variants of Dove's Eyes, and the edging was an incredibly complex broad strip of open work called Spider Web Flowers, in which the tiny cut-out squares were linked in rows and filled with tightly wrapped threads and Greek crosses. The whole thing made an intelligent repeating pattern that was simply ravishing.

"It's impossible to tell just from the embroidery itself," Betsy said. "On the other hand, the sheet is badly worn, so it's likely old. Perhaps more than fifty years. I don't see a single bit of damage to the Hardanger, but work of this sort is often amazingly sturdy. It's sad that the last owner of this didn't realize that it could be moved to trim a new bedsheet."

"I was going to put it on a table runner."

"That would also be a good use for it. Then visitors to your home could admire it."

Betsy and the customer discussed how best to clean the Hardanger and safely cut away the ruined bedsheet. Then Betsy took one of her biggest plastic bags and began folding the sheet into it.

Meanwhile, the customer looked around at the displays in the shop. She said, "I used to knit my sister a sweater every Christmas, but I haven't knit anything for such a long time." She paused. Then, "So long as I'm here," she murmured, and the wistful look in her eyes turned to yearning. She walked over to touch the skeins of spring pastel yarns heaped in baskets. She hesitated a long while over the ones on sale, then picked out three skeins of wool so pale a yellow it was almost cream, another skein in earthy brown, a simple sweater pattern, and two pairs of steel knitting needles. She paid by check, and with an abstracted, smiling good-bye, as if already knitting and purling in her mind, she left the shop.

# Six

The next morning, Jill was standing at the door of Crewel World, waiting for Betsy to unlock it. The coffee was just starting to perk, filling the space with its warm, dark fragrance. Betsy had turned on the Bose, tuned at a low volume to a light jazz station. She unlocked the door to let her friend in. Jill paused for a few moments just inside the door, listening with pleasure. She was of Scandinavian descent, not the least intimidated by below-zero temperatures — which it was outside. But still, she was clearly enjoying the comforting warmth of the shop.

"Sometimes," she murmured, "on cold, starry nights in Minnesota, if you stand really still and listen really hard . . . you'll freeze solid."

Betsy was surprised into laughter. "Is it that bad out?" she asked.

"Of course not. It's nearly the middle of February, the worst is over. Every morning the sun comes up earlier, and it goes down later in the evening. The sparrows are already squabbling and I expect snowdrops under our front window any second."

Betsy laughed again, because the sparrows were still silent and snow still rose nearly up to Jill's windowsills. "So, wassup, girl?" she said, mimicking the slangy vernacular of youth.

"I have some news for you. Well, more for Bershada and Ethan and his parents. Lars, among others, talked with Mike yesterday and Mike said something very interesting about the autopsy performed on that body in the pool." Mike was Detective Sergeant Mike Malloy of the Excelsior Police Department.

As had happened before, Betsy felt as if her ears had grown large, hairy points, which she swiveled in Jill's direction. "What did Lars tell you?"

"Two things. The first and most interesting is that when the medical examiner opened the victim's body, she smelled lavender."

Betsy blinked. "What?"

"Lavender. As in bath salts. As in, the victim was drowned in a bathtub, not a therapy pool. There were bath salts in her lungs."

89

After a startled moment, Betsy smiled. The smile began at the tips of her toes and broadened as it flowed upward to her face. "Well then! What great news! So she wasn't drowned in the therapy pool! And that means Ethan isn't to blame!"

Jill nodded. "She must have been brought there after she was dead. Probably to make it look as if she drowned there, not at home in her tub."

"Or in someone else's tub," amended Betsy. "But never mind, Ethan would hardly bring a dead body along with him to work. So he's cleared."

"Well, he's cleared of killing her and of bringing her to Watered Silk. But not of letting someone else bring her in."

That dashed icy water on Betsy's glee. "Ah, I see. Yes. Well, that's a puzzle yet to be solved. But we progress. What's the other thing Mike said?"

Jill said soberly, "She was ten weeks pregnant."

They looked at each other in shared heaviness of heart. Here was a double human tragedy. Betsy said softly, "Oh, how awful! Two lives lost — did she know, do you think?"

"I would think so. Ten weeks, that's two and a half months. Unless she was totally oblivious, she would know."

"Husband?" asked Betsy.

"She had never been married."

"Was she seeing someone?"

"That hasn't been established yet, or at least Mike didn't say anything to Lars about it." Lars was Sergeant Lars Larson, Jill's husband and an officer on Excelsior's small police department. Since Teddi, the drowned woman, was from Excelsior, Mike Malloy was now involved in the investigation.

"How was she identified? By her parents?"

"Her roommates had reported her missing and gave Mike a link to her Facebook account, and the photo on her Facebook page was a match. Her parents have been notified — they live out of state."

"That pregnancy could be a motive, couldn't it?"

"Sure. That's probably where Mike is focused."

"But now we know Ethan didn't kill her, right? This will be such a relief to Bershada and his parents! Or do they know? Has anyone from the police spoken to him?"

"I don't know. This changes the way this case has been handled up till now, but I don't know who is telling who what."

An hour later the phone rang, and Godwin

picked up. "Crewel World, Godwin speaking, how may I help you?" He cocked his head, listening. "Certainly. Hold on."

Godwin called Betsy to the phone. "It's Thistle Livingstone."

Betsy took the phone. "Hello, Thistle. What can I do for you?"

"Wilma Carter has asked me to ask you if you can get her a counted cross-stitch pattern called A Psychic Enters a Flower Garden."

"Does Wilma do counted cross-stitch?"

"She told me she does. Or did."

"Hmm," said Betsy. Perhaps that was a skill she had retained. "I don't think I know of that pattern. I don't suppose she knows the designer or manufacturer?"

"She didn't mention one."

"Let me do a search. I'll call you back, okay?"

"Thanks."

Betsy was pretty sure the pattern wasn't called A Psychic Enters a Flower Garden, but she did an online search anyway. She wasn't surprised when it didn't come up.

"Goddy," she called at last, "did you ever hear of a cross-stitch pattern called something like A Psychic Enters a Flower Garden?"

Godwin came out from the back of the

shop, where he'd been putting a new shipment of patterns into a display. His expression was thoughtful. " 'A Psychic' — are you sure?"

"I'm sure that's not the name of the pattern, but it's tickling my memory somehow."

"Try Psyche," said Godwin. "Isn't there a pattern about Psyche and Cupid's garden?"

"Ah, you've got it! And so, I think, do we." She called up the shop's inventory, and sure enough there was the pattern, already in the shop. Psyche Entering Cupid's Garden was a big, elaborate pattern, 188 stitches wide by 300 stitches tall, done in 92 shades of DMC floss, designed by Abracraftdabra. It was a close copy of a painting by Pre-Raphaelite painter John William Waterhouse, and depicted a woman in a pink, sort-of-ancient-Greek gown, pushing open a wooden door in a cut-stone wall into a garden with a temple in the background. The detail was exquisite. It was not something Betsy would even attempt to do herself.

"Want me to kit it up?" Godwin asked.

"I don't think so." Surely Wilma couldn't stitch this. Maybe it was something she had done before she became ill, and she was just remembering it.

"Who's it for?"

"Wilma Carter. She apparently used to do fine needlework. I know people with Alzheimer's sometimes retain old skills, but whether she is one of them, I don't know. I feel bad about her botching the class on punch needle, so I'd like to do this favor for her. But let's not pull the floss for it until I make sure it's something she can do." The chart was only twelve dollars — twenty in large-print format — but ninety-two skeins of DMC floss would bring the price up to something like a hundred and fifty dollars.

Betsy put the large-print version into the attaché case she took to the stitching class. She wanted to talk with Wilma.

Then she called Bershada and invited her to meet for lunch at Sol's Deli, right next door.

They sat together over thick sandwiches of three kinds of lunch meat and two kinds of cheese. Betsy asked, "Have you heard the autopsy results?"

"Have they got results? What do they say?"

"The woman, whose name is Teddi Wahlberger, didn't drown in the therapy pool, but in a bathtub full of lavender-scented bubbles."

Bershada put down her sandwich hastily, as if fearful of dropping it in her surprise and confusion. "What?" she said.

"She drowned in a tub of scented bath salts. The medical examiner smelled lavender during the autopsy and found traces of bath salts in her lungs. Teddi wasn't drowned in the Watered Silk pool but somewhere else, and then brought to the pool."

"But . . . why?"

"That's not known yet. My theory is that she drowned — or was drowned — in a bathtub, and someone wanted it to look like she drowned somewhere else."

Bershada shook her head as if to clear it, the frown still in place. "Why would someone want it to look like she drowned at Watered Silk?"

"I don't think Watered Silk was chosen on purpose. A lake or river would have been fine. But there isn't any open water this time of year, so she was brought to the therapy pool."

Bershada's brain kicked into gear. "That means it had to be someone who knew about that pool. I mean, it's not like they advertise on television and radio that they have a pool."

Betsy nodded. "And it must have been someone who knew Ethan would let them in."

"No! Girl, Ethan did not know anything

95

about a drowned woman in that pool! He was as surprised as he could be over it! He never saw that woman before, he never let her or a friend of his or a stranger into the complex that night, he swears to it!"

Betsy studied her friend's adamant face. "Okay, I believe that's exactly what he told you."

"Betsy, what he told me is the *truth*!"

"Did he let *anyone* through the front door that night?"

Bershada started to say no, but thought better of it. "I don't think so. Maybe. Why?"

"Maybe the person responsible works at Watered Silk. Or lives there. No, wait a minute, employees and residents have their own keys." Betsy rubbed the underside of her nose vigorously. "I wonder if they've reviewed the camera tapes that record activity by the doors. Probably, probably. But why didn't they find something to help them with this? After all, that woman didn't come up out of a drain or down a chimney; she came through a door in somebody's arms."

"Or in a laundry cart," said Bershada.

"Laundry cart?"

"You've seen them, they're big things, made of white canvas, with little bitty wheels at their four corners. Of course

Watered Silk has them, right? A body would fit into one of them, if it was folded up good. And you could cover it up with laundry."

An image swam up before Betsy's eyes. She'd seen those very carts in hospitals and hotels.

"Sure!" she said. "Of course! Someone could wheel that thing in one of the back doors and no one would think a thing of it! Bershada, you're a genius!"

# SEVEN

Sergeant Malloy was brought into the august presence of Ms. Felicia Colt, administrator of Watered Silk. The office, on the first floor and overlooking an attractive walled garden with a tall fountain in its middle, was large enough to accommodate a mahogany conference table with six chairs and a big antique wooden desk.

Ms. Colt, on the other hand, was almost a little person. Probably not quite five feet tall, she had dark hair in a Dutch bob, a white silk blouse with a big collar, and a black suit that fit her tiny frame exquisitely. She came out from behind her desk to put a tiny hand into Malloy's big one. Her grip was warm and surprisingly firm. Her voice, when she spoke, was equally firm, with a hint of warmth — a good voice for a person in charge.

"I hope I can be of use to you in your investigation," she said, taking him in approvingly with her fine dark eyes. "Please, take a seat." She went back behind her desk and managed to climb up into her executive chair in a single graceful movement. Its seat was high enough that she did not appear dwarfed by the size of her desk.

Mike chose one of the comfortable leather chairs facing her desk. "Thank you for agreeing to see me with such little notice," he began.

"This is a terrible thing that has happened to us," she replied. "We need to get to a solution quickly so we can move on."

"We would like to solve this quickly," he said. "But I personally am not in favor of making an arrest just so we can declare it solved."

"You don't think, then, that Ethan Smart had anything to do with Ms. Wahlberger's death?" she asked him.

"No, ma'm, I don't. It is not possible that he let someone into the pool. For one thing, he didn't have a key to the pool room door. For another, a quick review of the tapes from the camera that night do not show anyone coming in the main entrance carrying a body or pushing a laundry cart or dragging a trunk big enough to contain a body."

"So whoever brought that woman's body

into the building must have come through one of the other entrances," said Ms. Colt.

"Well, we are reviewing the other tapes from cameras trained on the other doors, but so far we haven't seen anyone coming in with a body-size bundle or container. Is there an entrance not guarded by a camera?"

She shook her dark head. "No."

"Something on the roof, perhaps?"

"No. There used to be a big entrance down in the machine room, back when this place was a silk factory, but it's been boarded up for decades — since long before we came here."

Malloy nodded. He had seen that pair of heavy double doors blocking the entrance from the alley, high and broad enough for a truck to drive through. The beams holding them closed were huge, fastened with iron bands, dirt and dust ground into their grain. They had obviously not been used in many years. It would take a week of work to get them to open or — if someone was in a hurry, with a body to get rid of — a dozen sticks of dynamite.

"So how do you think they got the body of Ms. Wahlberger into the pool?" Ms. Colt asked.

"I think if we could find that out, we'd

know who to arrest."

"Is there anything I can do to help?"

"Whoever brought the body here must have known about the pool. In fact they were so familiar with the place, they knew a way in that even you don't know about. That means somebody here is connected to the murder. Somebody here, an employee or a resident, is either the murderer or knows who the murderer is. What I'd like you to do is get out your list of employees and your list of residents and run your eyes slowly down them. See if a name doesn't jump out at you, even a little bit."

"All right, I will do that, and I'll contact you if a name does leap to my attention."

"Thank you." Malloy stood. "Meanwhile," he said, daringly, because it was really none of his business, "you might reconsider the firing of Ethan Smart."

"I will take your recommendation under advisement," she said, in a chilly voice. Clearly she was offended at his putting his oar in where it did not belong. But maybe it would have an effect.

On Wednesday Betsy came a few minutes early to her water aerobics class, this time to have a quick talk with the instructor, Pam, standing short and slim in her Speedo swimsuit at the deep end of the pool.

"What are you doing right after class?" Betsy asked.

"Working out some routines for special-needs clients. Why?"

"Could I talk with you for just a little while? Maybe fifteen minutes or so?"

"What about?"

"Finding the body of Teddi Wahlberger."

Pam literally took a step back, and her eyebrows lifted. "What makes you think I'd answer any questions about that?"

"I've been asked by a member of Ethan Smart's family to look into the circumstances of her being brought to the pool."

Pam looked slantwise at Betsy and said accusingly, "You're not a police officer."

"No, I do this as a private citizen."

"A PI? I thought you owned a shop that sells embroidery stuff."

"That's right, I do. This is a sideline. It's something I've been doing for several years. I have a list of satisfied clients."

Pam hesitated so long that Betsy was sure she'd refuse. But finally she threw up her hands and said, "Oh, what the heck. Sure. See me in my office, off the exercise room, as soon as you get dressed."

"Thank you."

Wilma was on time for the class, appearing bright, interested, and energetic. But she looked at Betsy without any sign of recognition, so Betsy didn't tell her she'd found the cross-stitch pattern she'd asked for. There'd be time for that later.

Pam was in an imaginative mood today. She called for different sets of exercises, such as touching the right foot with the left hand, and then touching the left foot with the right hand, repeating that movement four times before changing it to lifting alternating feet behind and reaching for them with opposite fingers four times. Repeat. Repeat. She had them do jumping jack arms while making cross-country ski movements with their legs. She even had them skipping across the pool, a movement Betsy hadn't done since childhood and found surprisingly difficult to do in the water.

Wilma, whooping with glee, did the exercises with no apparent trouble and a lot of splashing. Since it was easier to splash in the shallower end of the pool, she stayed there — which was just as well, since the others mostly stayed in the deeper water.

At the end of class, as they climbed up the ramp to the apron, Wilma winked at Betsy and said, "See you on Thursday!" So she *had* recognized her. Or maybe she just had a lucid moment. Whatever the case, she stayed in the pool to splash some more.

Betsy showered and dressed hastily, then went through the exercise room and between the two treadmills to Pam's little office. It was brand new — like the rest of this end of the facility — and ferociously neat. It was also stiflingly hot.

"They're working on the heat problem," Pam said. She was dressed in a sleeveless knit top with white and blue stripes and white shorts. She stood to shake Betsy's hand across her small desk.

"Too bad you don't have an outdoor window you could crack," said Betsy. The temperature outside was seventeen degrees, which would have cooled things down in a hurry. Three of the office walls were solid, painted cream, bordered by a couple of file cabinets and a credenza topped by a computer. The computer screen displayed the logo of Watered Silk (a red streaming banner with a single watered silk mark like a stylized kiss in the center, which Betsy thought amazingly risqué for a retirement center). The logo drifted across the screen, bumping diagonally off its borders.

The wall with the door into Pam's office also featured a large window overlooking the exercise room, the kind of double-paned window that does not open.

"What can I do for you?" asked Pam, sitting down again, and resting her clasped fingers on a single file folder in the center of her small gray desk.

Betsy sat in the wooden-armed upholstered chair. "Tell me how people can get into the pool area without going through the door."

Pam looked past Betsy at the door to the pool she could see through her window. "They can't," she said.

"I did," Betsy pointed out. "I came to it from the locker room."

Pam shrugged that off. "But you came into the pool area first through that door." She nodded at it. "Then into the locker room, and then out again. There's no back entrance."

"What about the men's locker room?" asked Betsy. "Is there another way into the men's locker room than from the pool area?"

Pam hesitated, then shook her head. "No, I'm sure there isn't."

"Ethan told me that the door to the pool has a key lock, not an electronic one."

"That's right."

"Who has a key?"

"I do, as does my fellow physical therapist,

the administrator, and the head of maintenance." Pam's fellow physical therapist had come into the pool room near the end of that morning's class, and remained there with Wilma.

"That's all?"

"Yes."

"So even if someone managed to get into the building without being seen, she couldn't get into the pool area."

"Not without a key," Pam said, a trifle smugly.

"But someone did, obviously."

That wiped the smug look away. "Yes." Pam put a slender hand sideways over her mouth for a few moments, her eyes wide and blank. "It was the most awful thing that's ever happened to me."

Betsy did not reply, and after another pause, Pam continued, "I can't think how she got in there, if the night guard didn't let her in. I mean, there's just no way."

"But Ethan didn't have a key, so he couldn't have let her in, or the person bringing her into the pool," said Betsy. "I'd like to know why he was fired."

"Maybe he wasn't fired, maybe he quit. I mean, it doesn't seem fair to fire him, does it? So maybe they didn't. They haven't told me anything about it."

"Have you ever loaned your key to some-one?"

"No . . ." Pam frowned and bit her top lip. "Well, actually that's not true. The last time I went on vacation, I gave my key to my substitute. She left it in the desk drawer, I found it when I got back." Pam gestured at her desk.

"When was this?" asked Betsy.

Pam thought, then turned to her computer and brought up a calendar. "Five months ago. I was gone for twelve days."

"Was your office locked? The desk drawer?"

Pam drew up her shoulders a little. "No."

"So how long was the key to the pool in the drawer?"

"Just overnight. I called my substitute about it, and she said it never left her key ring until she left it in the desk drawer on her last day."

"May I have her name?" Betsy had been rummaging in her purse for the reporter's notebook she carried when sleuthing. She brought it out, along with the beautiful wood-cased ballpoint pen Connor had given her.

"Heidi Langstrom. She's now at Courage Center."

Betsy nodded. Heidi was one of her water

aerobics instructors over there, and a licensed physical therapist. She would call her later today.

"Now, Teddi Wahlberger was found naked in the pool, right?"

Pam frowned and her lips thinned as if in pain. Clearly she was distressed that Betsy knew this. But then she nodded. "Yes, that's right."

Betsy continued, "We know she was brought to the pool already dead, possibly in an attempt to make people think she came here to swim and drowned in the pool. But to make that ruse work, her clothing should have been here, too. Was there clothing belonging to her in the locker room?"

"No, it was piled up near the ramp. I didn't look through it, of course, but I remember there was a beautiful fur jacket on top. It might've been fake fur, but it looked real. And a pair of high-heeled leather boots. Both black."

"Was there a purse?"

"I didn't see one, but it could have been under the coat."

"Anything else?"

"I think I remember seeing one end of a bra sticking out at the bottom. It was black or dark brown." She was frowning in an earnest attempt to be thorough. "That's all I remember. But it was a pile of clothing, obviously more things were under the coat."

"You're sure you've never seen the woman before?"

"I'm sure." She shuddered and rubbed her fingers together as if to wipe off the remembered feel of dead flesh.

"Any idea how long she'd been in the water?"

"No. She was stiff — that's rigor mortis — but I don't know how long it takes for that to set in. I understand that the warmer the body is, the faster it takes hold, though, and our pool is right around ninety-three degrees. I locked up at four in the afternoon the day before. Residents can get into the exercise room at any time; their pass keys will open that door. I haven't heard that any resident reported someone in the pool."

"Have you ever left the key to the pool in your office?"

"No, I keep it on my key ring."

Betsy could see that Pam was getting impatient, and she couldn't think of anything else to ask, so she thanked Pam and left the building.

She was sitting at a stoplight when it struck her: That coat should not have been on top of the pile. When a person undresses,

109

the outer garments come off first, then the inner. Underwear last. But Teddi's bra was on the bottom, her coat on top. Did that mean anything? It would have if it were not already known that Teddi didn't stand there, undressing herself. Right?

The car behind Betsy's honked; she was in danger of sitting through a green light. Betsy hated when she sat behind an oblivious driver. Connor had once remarked that she was a little quick to blow her horn at drivers slow to realize the light had turned. Betsy had determined to reform, and once sat while a woman in the car ahead of her carried out some interaction with an unseen person in the passenger seat — changing a diaper, judging by the movement of her arms — through two green lights. She had turned to Connor then and said smugly, "See?" And Connor had not said anything about it again.

The car behind her honked again. So here she was, caught in the same error. Blushing and angry, waving an apology, she hurried through the intersection and focused on her driving the rest of the way back to Excelsior.

Once in the shop, she took care of a customer, then phoned the Courage Center and left a message for Heidi Langstrom to call her at her convenience.

A little before noon, Heidi called. "Just a few quick questions," Betsy said.

"The repairs on the pool are moving right along," Heidi said promptly. "We'll reopen on schedule."

"That's great," said Betsy, "but that's not what I'm calling about."

"Oh?"

"You took over at Watered Silk while Pam Fielding was on vacation, right?"

"Yes, that's right. Is that where you're going in the interim?"

"Yes. Pam says she gave you the key to the pool, and that you left it in her desk drawer the last day you worked there."

"That's right. Was there a problem about that?"

"Was her office locked when no one was in there, do you remember?"

Heidi hesitated. "I . . . don't remember — I don't think so. Why, was her key missing?"

"No, it was there. It's just that the key is the only way into the pool area, and they're supposed to keep a tight hold on it."

Heidi chuckled. "Skinny-dippers a problem over there?"

Betsy dutifully chuckled back. "Not that I know of. Well, thanks, Heidi."

"You're welcome. Say, wait a second! You don't think that's how that drowned woman got into the pool over there, do you?"

"I don't know how she got in. Nobody does."

"Oh my God, I hope not. But wait a minute, I don't see how I could be responsible, that was nearly six months ago, and this woman drowned just last week. But now I'm gonna worry till somebody finds out how. Jeez. Well, see you in a few weeks."

# EIGHT

The following Monday, Betsy asked Bershada to stay after the Monday Bunch meeting broke up.

"I'm so sorry I couldn't solve Ethan's problem with Watered Silk," she said. "The police no longer think Ethan drowned that poor woman, but they reached that conclusion on their own, not because I brought them some information."

Bershada nodded. "But they still believe he let into the building whoever brought her body to Watered Silk. Maybe they don't believe it with the same conviction as before — but still." She thought for a moment. "It turns out there are some holes in their security. It could have been someone else who works there, or even someone who lives there. I think it was a resident; after all, some of them are no longer thinking very clearly."

"That's true. But the problem remains:

There are only four keys to the pool itself, and Ethan had access to none of them."

"So that would seem to mean the people they should look at are those four. Who are they?"

"Pam and Jaydie, the physical therapists, and Felicia Colt — she's the administrator of the complex — and whoever is the head of maintenance. I don't know his name." Betsy frowned at this lapse. "I should find that out, shouldn't I?"

Bershada nodded. "Maybe Ethan knows, I'll ask him."

She called Betsy later that day. "Ethan says his name is Paul Juggins, with two *g*'s. He lost his job, too."

Betsy, surprised, laughed. "Juggins? Are you serious?"

"That's his name, according to Ethan. Why?"

"It doesn't matter. Does Ethan know how to contact him?"

"No. Sorry."

But Juggins was not a common surname, and Betsy quickly found a phone number for a Paul Juggins living in Hopkins.

Mr. Juggins was an angry man. He kept saying, "Who is this? *Who* is this?" And "Well, what do you expect me to say?" And, "I don't work there anymore, I don't know what they're doing now." His voice was deep and resonant, and might have been pleasant if he weren't so angry.

Finally, Betsy said, "Can I buy you lunch? Or dinner?"

"What?"

"If you will agree to sit down and talk to me, let me explain what I want from you, I'll buy you lunch at the restaurant of your choice."

He asked suspiciously, "Talk about what?"

"The woman who was found drowned in the therapy pool."

That brought on an explosion of remarkably creative profanity, mostly regarding the improbable recreational habits of Watered Silk staff. Betsy held the receiver a little away from her ear until the image-laden noises faded to mere grumbling. Then she said, "I want you to tell me how you think someone brought that already dead woman into the building."

"Already dead? Who told you that? How do you know she was already dead? Hold on; do you think *I* had something to do with it?"

"I'm not asking if you did it, I'm asking you — an expert on the layout of that building — how it was done."

"Who told you I'm an expert?"

"You worked there how long?"

There was a brief pause, then, "Six years, since it first opened."

"So you must know every nook and cranny of the place. You know all the entrances and exits. You went into places nobody else gets into. I bet, if you thought about it, you could tell me probably three ways to get into that building that nobody else knows about."

Juggins fell silent, except for some noisy breathing. "Well . . ." he finally said.

"Will you meet me so we can talk?" she pressed.

"Who are you again?"

"My name is Devonshire, Betsy Devonshire, and I'm doing a private investigation into the firing of Ethan Smart."

"Yeah, they tossed him out, too, the poor bastard. Private investigation, huh? How much will you pay me?"

"Not one red cent. The motive here is justice — maybe we can get you your job back, too."

"Huh." Another noisy interval. Then a long, deep sigh. "All right, okay, and I'll let you choose the place to buy me lunch."

"Can you come to Excelsior? We've got a couple of nice places. When can you come?"

"Gimme your number, I'll call you back."

Betsy half expected him not to call, but he

did, thirty minutes later. "How about Wednesday at noon?" he said, nice and calm.

Betsy was surprised to see that Juggins was an African American man, then a little ashamed of her surprise. But his grin on seeing her expression made it clear that he enjoyed her reaction.

"Yo, y'all want me to talk lak this?" he drawled. "Or, p'raps you would prefer this?" he continued in a very convincing British accent.

They were standing beside a table in Sol's Deli. Juggins was short, broad, and balding, with intense brown eyes in a brown face. He looked to be in his middle thirties, maybe a little older. He was dressed all in brown, jacket, denims, boots. A tiny gold earring gleamed in one ear. He had a close-cropped black beard only a little longer than his hair, and he smelled strongly of cigarette smoke.

"Who are you, really?" asked Betsy, amused and confused in equal parts.

"I'm an actor," he said.

"Ah, of course," said Betsy, enlightened.

"And I want to apologize for my behavior when you first called me. I'm going through a complicated breakup with my wife and I keep getting phone calls from people trying to get in the way."

Betsy said, "I understand. Shall we sit down?"

She suited the action to her words, taking off her coat, pulling out the little chair with wire legs and back, and sitting down at the tiny, marble-topped table, one of two in the room. Juggins pulled off his jacket to reveal a brown sweater and sat down across from her.

Sol's Deli was probably original to the building. It had a white stone floor set with random black squares. The front window was large, uncurtained, streaked in the corners with condensation. Across from the window were two big, white, slant-fronted cases, one filled with meats, cheeses, olives, peppers, lettuces, and other sandwich fixings, the other with salads: potato, egg, macaroni, two kinds of coleslaw. Behind the cases lurked the owner, whose name was Jack, not Sol. He was a tired-looking man with dark, sad eyes, and a stomach that slopped into his stained white apron. He wore loose-fitting clear plastic gloves on his hands. The smells of preserved meats and vegetable soup filled the air.

Juggins sat down across from Betsy. "Surprised I'm an actor?" he asked.

"Yes, and I'll bet you at least started out with a specialty in comedy."

He grinned. "Why do you think that?"

She grinned back. "Because Juggins is an obscure British nickname for a simpleton."

His grin disappeared. "Funny how many people don't say that out loud, at least to my face."

"Yet . . ." Betsy began, and stopped herself from going on. Because what if she was wrong?

He laughed at her discomfort. "All right, it's a stage name, picked because I know what it means. And I still specialize in comic roles, so I've never changed it. But I'm also a janitor. A very good janitor, a certified pool operator, with a boiler license. I'm also a competent pipe fitter, a good electrician, and an adequate carpenter. When I told my dad I wanted to be an actor, he said I should acquire some backup skills that couldn't be outsourced to India or China. I apprenticed myself to my mother's uncle, who is a contractor, *and* got a college degree in fine arts, and so I can support myself while I wait for my big break. Meanwhile, I do commercials and get various roles in theaters in the area. I've been to LA twice but had to come back both times."

"Both you and Ethan are black. Do you

think that had anything to do with the fact that you two are the ones who got fired from Watered Silk?"

He shook his head. "No," he scoffed. "Somebody brought a dead body into a secure building and somehow got access to a key that hardly any people have, though one of them is me. It was done late at night. Ethan was on duty from midnight till eight, I was there until ten the night it happened, trying to fix an exhaust fan in the exercise room. Hell, *I'd've* fired the both of us."

"Can you tell me anything about the woman whose body they found?"

He shook his head. "Nope. I couldn't believe someone would do such a crazy thing as bring someone to the pool just to drown her. And now you say she was already dead? I don't get it."

Juggins told Betsy that people came and left the building only rarely at night. "It's mostly emergency-response people who come late at night. You know, because someone has a heart attack or a stroke or something. But there's no curfew, so if a resident takes a notion to go for a midnight stroll or drive to Chicago for a concert, there's nothing to stop her from doing so. And I have a pretty good idea that those electronic keys get handed around. A resident will mislay one and get a replacement, then find the first one and give it to a friend or relation. I've seen it with my own eyes, people who I know for a fact don't work there or live there coming in using those keys." He raised both hands. "But it's not my duty to say anything, so I don't. Or didn't."

But the pool was a different matter. "When I was just a kid," he continued, "I lost a good friend who drowned in a swimming pool, so I have a healthy respect for any body of water deeper than four inches. If someone on my staff needed to get into the pool area to clean the apron or test the water or change a lightbulb, I went with him or her myself to unlock the door. And I stayed to lock it again, unless Pam or Jaydie was there. There are people living in Watered Silk who no longer have a strong survival instinct, if they had one to begin with. There are some exceptions, but the seniors who live there are, by and large, morons." He smiled to show he was exaggerating — but it wasn't much of a smile.

Still, Betsy thought, that was rather strong criticism. But he was probably still angry at being fired and taking revenge any way he could.

"Did you get another job yet?" she asked.

"Oh, hell, yes; people who can do as many things as I can do in maintenance will always find work. But I thought I'd found a home at Watered Silk."

Betsy could think of no other avenue to explore after her conversation with Juggins. She felt guilty that she couldn't help Ethan. Bershada said it was all right, that he'd found another night job that paid the same, but Betsy read disappointment in her eyes.

# NINE

Thursday was Valentine's Day. For breakfast, Connor fixed heart-shaped pancakes, using a spatula to shape them. The batter didn't always cooperate, so he kept the most lopsided ones for himself. Dressing for his day of working in the shop, he had put on his most elaborate Aran sweater, the kind worn for centuries by Irish fishermen. It had large knots down the outside of the sleeves and Celtic braids in a triple row down the front. The sweater was old, and countless washings had turned it from its natural pale brown to pale ivory. With it he wore new jeans and comfortable loafers. With his close-cropped graying brown hair and sea-blue eyes, he looked both handsome and approachable. Betsy felt her heart warm to him when he sat down across from her and, smiling, said, "Syrup, machree?"

"You are so good to me, sweetheart," she said.

After breakfast they went downstairs together, down the narrow back hall that led to the rear door into Crewel World. Even though Betsy had made this trip countless times over the years, it felt unusual this morning. Betsy's cat, Sophie, knew why. She came behind them, mewing anxiously. Incorrigibly fat, with her long white fur splattered generously with tan and gray on top of her head, along her back, and up her plumed tail, she was gracious and graceful, as much a part of the shop's gentle atmosphere as the spinner racks of floss or the baskets of yarn. She was anxious because, like all cats, she was comfortable with routine. The routine was that Betsy came down with Sophie, opened the back door to allow her to scoot in first, let her explore briefly to see if there was anyone already present who might offer her a tidbit, and then Sophie would jump into a wooden chair with a blue cushion to await said anyone.

Today, however, Sophie was at the back of a procession, and Connor's presence in the parade confused her. Betsy tried to help by unlocking the door and pausing long enough for the cat to weave her way through the maze of legs and trot through the back room and into the shop. Not unexpectedly,

124

there was nobody waiting with a fragment of sandwich or cookie to slip to a greedy cat, so she jumped onto her cushion, turned around twice, and lay down. Things were back to normal.

Connor stayed in the back room to start the coffeemaker brewing and the electric tea kettle heating — paying customers were offered a free beverage. Betsy turned on the lights, then tuned the Bose radio to a soft jazz station and put the start-up cash in the drawer. She ran a carpet sweeper around the front and back of the shop, and did a little dusting.

Their first customer was a handsome middle-aged woman, tall and slender, with keen blue eyes, a long nose, and a wide mouth. She wore a black wool coat trimmed at collar and cuffs with Persian lamb and a hat also of Persian lamb. The hat wasn't the usual Minnesota winter helmet, but sat at an angle on her bright chestnut hair. It had a high crown and a little brim that curved up on one side and down on the other. Betsy hadn't seen a hat like that in person for a long time — and had never before seen the woman wearing it.

"Good morning," said Betsy. "How may I help you?"

"A friend loaned me this magazine," said

the woman, with just a trace of a southern accent, holding out a back copy of *Just Cross Stitch*. "I told her I was looking for a cross-stitch pattern of daffodils that wasn't too difficult, and she found this in her stack — she keeps all her back copies of stitching magazines." A slip of paper had been tucked in to mark the page.

Betsy took the magazine and opened it at the bookmark to find a stylized pattern of three yellow daffodils with green stems and leaves on a blue ground. It was designed by Angela Pullen Atherton, to be stitched on white Jobelan or Aida with ten colors of DMC floss, the finished result to be about ten inches square.

Connor came up to the checkout desk for a look. "Say, that's really pretty," he said.

The woman turned to regard him, a little surprised. "Don't mind me," Connor said, smiling, "I just work here."

The three of them, in consultation, decided on Aida, to be stitched using gold-plated size twenty-four tapestry needles. They agreed that Connor should pull the skeins of Anchor floss from the set of very small drawers that held them in numerical order.

As Betsy was processing the woman's credit card payment, Connor said, from his place at the drawers, "May I say that I love your hat? I had an aunt who wore hats; my sister has several pages of a photo album full of pictures of her in her hats."

"Why, thank you. It's harder to wear a hat outdoors in a Minnesota winter. I'm afraid I'll reach up one winter day to make sure I still have both earrings and one of my ears will crack right off in my hand."

Connor laughed — he had a great laugh. He said, "And earmuffs would spoil the look, right?"

Her wide mouth twitched with amusement. "Very true."

Betsy said, "I don't think I've seen you in here before. Are you a visitor to Excelsior?"

"No, I'm a new resident. My husband and I moved here from Nashville, though we both grew up in Pittsburgh. A woman I met at church, Patricia Fairland, is a stitcher, and she told me about your shop. I used to stitch all the time, and now that our third child is in college, I have time to get back to it."

"Oh, yes, Patricia mentioned you this past Monday. You're Cherie — oh, I can't remember your last name —"

"Yonder, as in from far away."

"Yonder. All right. I hope we see you often. And if you have time, there's a group

127

of stitchers who meet here Monday afternoons starting around one thirty. Patricia's
a member."

"All right, thank you. I'll try to come. I'm
sure I can use some support as I try to bring
back some old skills."

Later, as the time approached for Betsy to
leave for her punch needle class, Connor
appeared more obviously anxious.

"Do you think I should call a part-timer
to come in and help?" asked Betsy.

"No, of course not. We're not that busy,
I'm sure I can handle things." But he kept
looking out the big front window as if afraid
a difficult customer might come in.

Then, suddenly, he relaxed. A man had
entered, wearing a familiar brown uniform,
carrying a white cardboard cube around
nine inches square. Connor signed for the
UPS package and brought it to the library
table. "Happy Valentine's Day," he said,
smiling as he handed her the cube.

"What's in it?" asked Betsy. The brown
lettering on the side of the box said Norman
Love Confections. It looked big enough to
hold an awful lot of chocolate, but when
Betsy took it, it wasn't heavy.

"Open it," suggested Connor.

Inside the top was a flat, silver foil surface
— the box was lined with insulation. Under

the insulation, on the bottom, was a plastic bag of something frozen solid. Beside it was a light green box with a mitered top, about eight inches long and maybe three inches wide, too small to be a container of ice cream. It was tied shut with a white ribbon printed with hearts.

She looked at Connor, who was smiling proudly. "Go on," he said, gesturing at it.

She took the box out — cold in her hand — and opened it. On top was a strip of cardboard showing beautiful heart shapes in softly blended colors: purple, pink, gold, mottled, and swirled. Under the tissue were ten candy hearts, each just over an inch across and not quite half an inch thick. A rich smell of cocoa wafted to her nostrils.

"Try one," said Connor, still smiling.

Betsy picked the dark brown heart with a swoop of white on it. She bit into it and her senses were assaulted with an incredibly smooth-textured rush of chocolate, not milk, not dark, so intense she had to sit down.

"Shut the front door!" she said, and Connor, recognizing the expression of surprise and pleasure from a cookie commercial, began to laugh.

He sat down beside her to watch her finish the heart in two slow bites. With the last bite in her mouth, she slowly leaned sideways until her shoulder was against his, and he put his arm around her. She was unable to say anything for a minute after the last swallow, but just sat there, leaning against him and enjoying the lingering taste of the chocolate, replaying those delectable moments in her mind.

"That is the best chocolate I have ever eaten," she said at last. "And this day with you is the best Valentine's Day I have ever spent. Ever. Thank you."

"You are welcome, machree," he replied solemnly.

"Where did you find this place?" she asked.

"Peg wrote to me about it." Peg was Connor's daughter, who was currently on an archeological dig outside of Mexico City sponsored by the University of Florida. "Her current boyfriend grew up in Fort Myers, where this confections place is located. She raved about the chocolates he sent her, so I decided to let you try some, too."

Connor was as severely chocoholic as Betsy. He was already casting an envious eye at the little green box in front of her, so she pushed it toward him. "Try one," she invited him.

"Thought you'd never ask," he said, and chose one covered in subtly blended colors of red, orange, and yellow, with silvery gray on the sides. The card said it was called Sunset Kiss.

He bit into it, inhaled lightly to capture all the flavor, and closed his eyes. "Very, very nice," he said, nodding over and over as he savored it. "This one's mango."

Betsy loved mango, alone or in any kind of mixture. Knowing this, he leaned toward her. "Have a taste," he said, and kissed her.

"Yum," she murmured, and kissed him back, warmly.

Then she determinedly closed the box over the remaining chocolates. "These are too good to eat all in one sitting," she said. "Let's put the rest upstairs in the refrigerator. Each of us can get one piece a day until they're gone." She was half hoping he'd object, but he only sighed and went upstairs.

Oddly enough, it was in that moment that she realized how much she loved him.

Betsy hustled over to Sol's for a couple of sandwiches — beef with horseradish spread — and potato chips. She made the same deal with Connor she usually made with Godwin: He could eat half her potato chips in exchange for his kosher dill pickle. Then she reapplied lipstick and drove to Hopkins for her punch needle class.

Most of her students had finished or nearly finished the chick-and-eggs pattern. Thistle had phoned Betsy on Monday, saying they wanted some more patterns, so now, up in the library, she opened her attaché case and brought out a selection.

While they were choosing, she looked at the chick patterns they'd been working on. Joy had not only made the chick a higher nap than the eggs, she had chosen to clip the loops — and she'd clipped them just a little shorter at the edges than at the center, giving a rounded effect that was, in Betsy's word, "Brilliant!"

Joy blushed at the compliment. "If I'd had more colors, I would have made the edges just a little darker than the centers, too," she said.

"I'll get you all the colors you want when you punch the next one," offered another student. "I'm making a floss run to Michael's next week. "But I want cash in advance, no checks."

Vivian had nearly finished her pattern. She said, "I couldn't think of a design for the last egg, so I just punched it in yellow green. But I remember as a child an aunt and uncle who had a farm, and their chickens laid speckled eggs. How would I make a speckled egg? Do I pull out what I've stitched and then do the speckles and then punch the color around them?"

"No," said Betsy, "it's easier than that. You can leave the egg as is, if you're satisfied with the color, but now you look at the needle on your punch." Vivian held up her punch.

"Now, slide off one segment, to make what you're going to punch stand up higher than what's already there."

"Yes, yes," said Joy. "You told us about that at the first class; it's how I worked my pattern."

"Okay," said Betsy to Vivian, "take off one segment, and thread your needle with a short length that is the color of the speckles."

"Maroon, I think," said Vivian. She pulled off a segment and put it carefully into the glass tube the needle was kept in, then cut about fourteen inches of the floss, divided it in half, and put three threads into her needle.

"Now," said Betsy, "punch here and there randomly over the green egg. The speckle color will stand up just a little higher than the ground color so it doesn't get lost. Here's a tip: Do fewer than you think you should. You can always add more."

Vivian punched three times, then turned her lap stand over to look at the result. "How sweet!" she exclaimed. "Just like I remember!" She punched a few more times, then lifted the needle to pull the end free. "Thank you, Betsy!"

She handed her work around to show the others the result she'd achieved, and two other women decided they wanted speckled eggs, too. "I'd like to make my blue egg speckled," said one. "But I've already got a pink stripe on it."

"Find the end of the floss on the stripe and pull gently," said Betsy. "It will come out and you can repunch it."

"Wait a minute, wait a minute, start over!" came a familiar cry. Wilma rushed in. She was wearing an ill-fitting orange dress and a green cardigan.

"Hi, Wilma, come sit down," said Betsy. "I have something to show you."

"Really?" said Wilma eagerly, hurrying to sit at the table. "What is it?"

Betsy reopened her attaché case and got out the Psyche pattern she'd found in her shop, which was printed on sheets of copy paper and came in a Ziploc bag. On top was a color photograph of a finished model. She handed it to Wilma, who looked at the picture of the beautiful woman with her pink gown falling off one shoulder, her auburn hair pulled into a careless fat knot at the nape of her neck.

"I stitched this pattern a long time ago," Wilma said with a shrug. She looked at it again, more thoughtfully. "It's making me think of something. My husband had auburn hair, maybe that's what it is. But it turned all gray and then he died." She looked around at Thistle, standing behind her. "His hair wasn't as bright as yours, but he went through the door and died." She turned back to face Betsy. "Did your husband go through a door and die?"

"No," said Betsy. "He's still alive. But I did divorce him."

Wilma winked at Betsy. "Tossed him out the door, eh? Good for you!" She looked down at the pattern. "Out the door, out the door," she chanted, and tossed the pattern back at Betsy, who took it and opened her case to put it in. But Wilma shouted, "Did I say you should put it away? Give it back, it's mine!"

Betsy complied, and Wilma ripped open the plastic bag and strewed the multiple sheets of the pattern across the table. "Unlock the door!" she said loudly. Some of the sheets slid across the table to fall on the floor. Wilma stared at the result. "Oops, sorry! I'm sorry! So sorry!" She began to cry, softly at first, then louder and louder, until she seemed almost hysterical.

Thistle stepped forward to put her hands on Wilma's shoulders, but Wilma shrugged them off angrily and choked back her tears to growl, "Don't touch me! This is between Betsy and me!" She looked at Betsy and said in a small, pleading voice, "Will you take me out of here?"

Thistle said at once, "Her room's 412, fourth floor, go left off the elevator."

Wilma said in a dignified voice, "Come with me, Betsy."

Betsy looked at the other women. "I think you all did a splendid job. I'll be glad to bring a catalog of more punch needle patterns, if you like."

Thistle said to Betsy, "I'll write down the patterns they choose from what you brought, and we can settle up later."

"Come on, come on!" said Wilma, starting for the door, one hand reaching out behind her. Her tone had turned cheerful and there was a mischievous smile on her face, though her cheeks were still wet with tears.

Outside the library, Betsy asked, "Which way to the elevator?"

"Did I say I wanted to go to my room? Ha!" She started walking swiftly down the corridor, the skirt of her orange dress fluttering around her thin legs. She wore old-fashioned red sneakers.

Betsy hurried after her. "Where are we going?"

"I want to show you something!" said Wilma.

"But my coat and purse are back in the library," said Betsy.

Wilma laughed loudly. "Follow me, follow me!" She hurried ahead and ducked through a door.

Betsy slowed down. Had she gone into someone's room? What if she frightened someone, raising a fuss and refusing to come out? But as Betsy got closer to the door, she saw the glowing red EXIT sign over it. She pushed it open and found herself in a stairwell, all concrete. She could hear the soft pattering of rubber-shod feet going down and followed as quickly as she could. She should not have agreed to bring Wilma to her room, but now that she'd done so, she was even more anxious not to lose her.

Wilma exited the stairwell on the first floor and fled across the lobby to the broad stairs down to the therapy-pool level. When

Betsy followed, she could just see the top of Wilma's white hair as she made her way down the steps. "Ha ha ha!" Wilma crowed, the sound floating up the stairs.

Betsy glanced at the woman behind the desk near the entrance, who rolled her eyes and shrugged elaborately. Apparently this sort of behavior was familiar to her.

At the bottom of the stairs, Betsy saw the elevator doors just closing and threw up her hands in aggravation. But then she saw someone with white hair just inside the exercise room, and quickly went to peer through the glass. There were three women and two men in there, using the treadmills and bicycles. And Wilma was already halfway across the floor, heading toward the pool room.

Betsy followed quickly. Through the glass insert she saw a man and a woman floating on their backs in the pool while Pam and Jaydie were pulling and lifting their arms.

As Betsy opened the door, she was met with a wet blanket of hot, moist air. Down the pool's apron Wilma hustled, her old woman's voice wafting behind her. "Ha ha ha!" She turned into the entrance to the men's locker room.

"Hey, Wilma, wrong door!" Betsy called.

"Whoa, Mrs. Carter, watch where you're

going!" shouted Pam from the pool, and the two floating seniors tried to lift their heads to watch.

"I'll get her," Betsy said, and hustled across the tiled floor, hesitating only a moment before opening the door.

The men's locker room, a mirror image of the women's, was empty except for Wilma at the far end, where the lockers were. She turned to look at Betsy. "Well, come on, come on!" she said cheerfully.

"I'd prefer it if *you'd* come on," retorted Betsy. "I'm supposed to accompany you to your room, not play 'catch me if you can.'"

"Catch me if you can, catch me if you can!" Wilma laughed and went through another door, this one very plain with a small sign on it that read AUTHORIZED PERSONNEL ONLY.

Betsy waited, but Wilma did not come out again. After a few moments, Betsy went to the door and knocked on it. "Wilma, come out of there!"

No reply.

This was getting ridiculous. Betsy sighed and opened the door.

But no one was in there.

It was a closet, full of mops and buckets and brooms and other paraphernalia of the maintenance trade. Shelves held cleaning fluids and powders, rags and towels. A thin chain hung down from the ceiling, and when Betsy pulled it, a low-watt ceiling light came on.

By its light Betsy could see yet another door near the far end, closed. On it was a sign reading HAZARDOUS MATERIALS — CHLORINE, and under it, again, AUTHORIZED PERSONNEL ONLY.

Well, she reasoned, since Wilma had not come out and was not here, obviously she had gone through that door despite the warnings.

Betsy reluctantly opened it. She found herself on the verge of a big, deep space, a machine room, brightly lit. There was a soft sound of machinery — a smooth-running electric pump, perhaps — and a faint gurgle-rush of water through pipes. Betsy was at the top of a set of metal steps overlooking the room below. It had a concrete-block wall on one side, but the other walls were built of ancient brick and stone. Two big white tanks stood near the far wall, shorter than the propane tanks often seen outside farmhouses, but fatter. Pipes of different diameters led into and out of the tanks, into and out of the concrete blocks, and into and out of a blue cylinder about nine inches in diameter attached to the far wall. Several gauges on the wall wiggled their needles. Clearly all this machinery had to do with filtering, treating, and circulating water in the pool, which must be on the other side of the concrete-block wall.

Near the tanks, an old wooden desk looked as if it were a relic from the old mill era. File folders were stacked on it, and next to it stood a set of metal shelves crowded with big three-ring binders and fat instruction manuals.

In the right-hand wall was an immense pair of ancient wooden doors that filled an opening big enough to drive a team of horses through. But thick wooden beams bound with heavy metal bands fastened them permanently closed.

Wilma was standing beside the pair of doors. "I told you there was a door," she said proudly.

Before Betsy could point out that the doors were blocked, Wilma put her hand on a smaller door set into the nearer of the big ones. It had a high sill, and a thick timber ran across the upper portion of it. An ancient padlock on a heavy metal latch was further proof against its opening.

There was a doorknob of some dark metal below the padlock, and Wilma grasped it with both hands, pressing and moving it in a small circular motion, as if it were a crank. After a few tries, the door opened. Betsy, astonished, saw that it led outside.

"Ha ha ha!" said Wilma as she stepped over the high sill, ducked under the timber, and went out into the cold.

# TEN

Betsy stumbled down the steps, which seemed steeper than normal, or perhaps she was just alarmed, even panicky. She had to get Wilma back inside!

Wilma had slammed the door shut and Betsy twisted the knob frantically without getting it to turn. She took a quick, calming breath and pressed inward, then up, around, and down, trying to imitate what Wilma had done, but with no result. She tried again, pressing harder, and the knob turned in her hands and the door opened. She had to duck her head and lift her feet high to get through the opening. It was shockingly cold out there, and goose bumps were raised on her bare arms.

She found herself in the narrow alley between Watered Silk and the gray brick commercial building next door. She looked in both directions without seeing anyone. Deep, frozen ruts scattered with dead cigarette butts made it clear the alley was in use, but there were no vehicles present, either.

Hoping there was still a crumb of sense in Wilma's head, Betsy turned right, toward the front of Watered Silk. In as much of a hurry as she could manage, she slithered and slipped up the alley to the street, where she saw Wilma standing bewildered near the curb. Betsy hurried to her.

"Oh, hello," said Wilma, taking her by the arms, but showing no sign of recognition. "I'm so, so very cold! Can you take me to my r-room?"

"Yes, of course. Come on, let's get back inside. How ever did you find out about that door?"

"Psyche enters Cupid's garden through a door," said Wilma. She appeared to be guessing what Betsy's question meant. Her teeth were chattering.

"Who is Psyche?" asked Betsy, forgetting her own chill and putting her arms around the trembling woman as she walked her toward the portico over the entrance. A stiff breeze plucked at their clothing.

"She was a beautiful Greek woman. The goddess Aphrodite was jealous and then angry that her son Eros fell in love with her. Aphrodite gave her impossible tasks, but

144

she succeeded in performing every one of them." Wilma's bright tone reminded Betsy of a teacher trying to engage the interest of a dull pupil. "Psyche is often depicted with butterfly wings, which is a lovely image, isn't it?" Wilma began to cry. "So beautiful, so beautiful."

"There, there, it's going to be all right, you're going to be fine," soothed Betsy, tightening her embrace. Wilma's frame was thin and her face was pale. Betsy ran her hand up and down Wilma's arm. "Come on, keep walking. We need to get indoors, it's cold out here."

"I'm afraid something serious is wrong with me," said Wilma. "How did I get outside?"

"You came out through a door no one knew would open."

"Psyche knew it would open. The talking tower sent her to Taenarus after Aphrodite tortured her."

"Oh, Wilma!" sighed Betsy, exasperated.

Wilma stopped and pulled away from Betsy to explain, patiently, "It's an old Greek legend, my dear, about the tasks Aphrodite set for Psyche because she was angry that her son Eros fell in love with a mortal. In the end Eros married her and they had a daughter, Hedone. Anyway, lots of people know about that door. I told people about it myself."

"I see. Come on, we're almost home." They stepped under the portico, where the wind was funneled and strengthened. Wilma staggered and Betsy braced herself in support. She opened the door to the vestibule and rapped impatiently on the inner door.

It opened with a clack, and the black woman behind the desk stood, alarmed. "Wow, where did you two come from? Mrs. Carter, how did you get out of the building? And why is neither one of you wearing a coat?"

Betsy said, "Wilma surprised me by showing me a different way out. I'm going to take her up to her room. Please call someone, she may need medical attention; she's confused and she's terribly cold."

"I'm fine, I'm okay, I'm fine, I'm okay!" chanted Wilma, still trembling. As Betsy led her toward the elevators, Wilma broke into song: "My object all sublime, I shall achieve in time, to let the punishment fit the crime, the punishment fit the crime!" She began to giggle and kept giggling, between verses from *The Mikado,* all the way up to her room.

It was five thirty before Betsy got home.

146

She staggered as she came up the stairs, exhausted both physically and emotionally. She had been questioned, not always kindly, by the administrative staff at Watered Silk and two policemen. She had gone down with them twice to the pool-mechanics room to demonstrate how to open the door, once with the policemen, then again with Ms. Woodward from Watered Silk Security. Detective Sergeant Burgoyne was angry with Wilma for not telling someone on the staff about the door, but this did him no good at all because she had lost all memory of it and thought he wanted to talk about seeing Betsy at water aerobics class. And the Watered Silk administrator seemed to be angry with Betsy for following Wilma down into the machine room.

When she came into the apartment she saw Connor, slouched deeply on the loveseat, reading a paperback novel. He tossed his book aside and rose, concerned, when he saw her. "Are you all right? Where have you been? I've been calling and calling but you had your cell phone turned off." As he got nearer, he saw the look on her face, of depression and exhaustion. "What on earth has happened?" He took her attaché case from her, set it down, and helped her off with her coat. "I was really worried about you!"

"I found out how Teddi Wahlberger's body was brought to the Watered Silk pool. Wilma showed me."

"Really? That's wonderful! But why so unhappy about it?"

"The police and the Watered Silk staff have been hammering at me. I thought they'd never let me go. I think they're angry that they didn't discover it themselves." She walked down the short hallway into the living room.

"How was it done?" he asked, hanging her coat up in the little hall closet.

"There's a huge old door on the alley side of the building that is supposed to be blocked, but isn't. It's located down in the machine room, where the water for the pool is pumped and filtered."

"How did Wilma find out about it?"

"I have no idea. She's gone off the deep end again and can't explain anything."

"But she told you." He came into the living room and took Betsy gently into his arms.

She leaned against him and spoke to his shoulder. "No, she showed me. She was so disruptive in class that I tried to take her to her room, but she got away from me and I chased her into the men's locker room —"

Connor snorted in surprise and Betsy smiled. "I know, she is always going into places she doesn't belong. Anyway, she disappeared into a maintenance closet, which turned out to have the entrance to the pool's filtration system at the back of it. And down there is a big set of doors dating back to when the place was a factory. A couple of big beams are fastened across them. And there's a little door in one of the big doors. It looks like it's blocked with a board nailed across it, and it has a big padlock, too.

"Anyway, someone, sometime, somehow cut the little door behind the board so the board hides the cut. And rigged the hasp so it only appears to padlock the door. And there's a doorknob that seems to be unusable, too, only it isn't. You kind of wriggle it and it turns."

Connor stepped back and made a whistling shape with his lips. "Who knew about this?"

"That, my dear, is the question. Wilma has apparently known about it for a while, she went right to the door and opened it on the second wiggle."

"What do you think?" asked Connor.

"I think she saw someone using that door, someone who didn't see her watching. She wanders around the building at all hours of

149

the day and night, and she loves secrets — I told you about that wonderful book of photographs of hidden animals. She probably thought it was fun not to tell the staff of Watered Silk. Though she told me she *had* told people. I wonder who?"

Betsy went to her easy chair and fell backwards into it. "Whew," she said, "I'm glad to be home." She leaned her head back, closing her eyes. "I keep asking myself, who might have rigged that door so it would open?"

"How about that Juggins fellow? After all, it's his bailiwick. Did he know Teddi?"

Betsy's eyes stayed closed. "He says no, and in a way that makes me inclined to believe him." She frowned without opening her eyes. "Although he *is* an actor." She sighed. "You know, cops can be doggone rude. They talked to me like I must know who messed with that door and just didn't want to tell them who it was."

"Didn't they play 'good cop–bad cop' with you?"

Betsy smiled and her eyes opened. "Just 'bad cop.' There was just one officer to talk to, the others were Watered Silk staff. But he was really mean. I wonder if he's the one who was angry because he thought Ethan was fooling around with a white woman. I

150

should ask Ethan if that detective's name is Burgoyne." She sighed. "I think they're floundering, they don't know who did this. They're as lost and confused as I am, and it's making them angry. Me, it's making depressed."

"Would you like a nice cup of tea?" Connor asked. People of the British Isles think a nice cup of tea is the answer to any woman's distress.

Sometimes it is, Betsy thought. "You're wonderful. Yes."

He went into the little galley kitchen to heat some water. Betsy closed her eyes again and fell into a near doze. In a few minutes he was beside her with a cup of tea on a saucer accompanied by two peanut-butter cookies.

She took a sip. It was sweet and had been lightened with a dollop of milk. "Lovely," she said, comforted.

Connor sat on the loveseat with his own cuppa. "What do you want to do now? Or are you resigning from the case?"

"I'm thinking about it. But before I do, I'd like to talk to someone who knew Teddi. Still, can I at least wait until tomorrow to start back in? I'm bushed."

Jill came into Crewel World the next day

very close to closing time, with her two children, Emma Beth and Erik, in tow. She wanted to buy a counted cross-stitch pattern of hydrangea blooms to hang in the entryway of her house, to match the bushes in her front yard. "Do you have something by Thea Gouverneur?" she asked Betsy. "I like her designs."

"That's good, because I have at least four of hers, and three of them are hydrangeas," said Betsy.

Jill picked one that was just the head of a single giant flower, mostly blue but with some pink petals in it. The bushes in her yard were blue and pink, blue for Erik and pink for Emma Beth. "I wish there was one that had all three colors," she said, "blue, pink, and white." She turned to Betsy with her lovely Gibson-girl smile, her gray eyes shining with unexpressed news.

"Oh, Jill!" exclaimed Betsy, and she hurried to give her a hug.

"Hug me, too!" demanded Emma Beth, who was six.

"Me, me, me, me!" chanted Erik, who was four and a half.

The two children attached themselves to the adults, all four of them laughing.

"When?" asked Betsy.

"End of August."

"Which, another boy?"

"I don't know. I may not want to know."

"So what does this do to your plan to get that private-eye license?"

Jill stepped back and shrugged. "That can wait. I can be a PI after menopause, but the window for having children is narrowing. And I wanted at least three."

"Are you all right?"

"All is very, very well — touch wood." Jill bent over and touched the wooden toggle that fastened her daughter's knit hat under her chin. Like Betsy, Jill only thought she was not superstitious.

Emma Beth looked up at Betsy. She was radiantly fair, her hair almost white, her complexion palest ivory, her large eyes a clear light blue. She was wearing royal-blue leggings and coat, and her hat was bright yellow. "Do you have any bubbles you need for me to snap, Aunt Betsy?"

Erik smiled his most winning smile. "Can I have popping bubbles, too, please?" he said. His hair was a golden red, his eyes dark gray. He was tall for his age, just a few inches shorter than his sister. He was wearing forest green snow pants and ski jacket, and his knit hat was white.

Betsy agreed she had some bubbles that needed popping and went to the checkout desk to pull out two sheets of bubble wrap. In short order, the two children were seated at the library table in the middle of the room, their expressions serious, their little fingers busy.

Jill and Betsy stood just out of earshot near the box shelves that divided the needle-point part of the shop in front from the counted cross-stitch section in back.

"Any other news?" asked Betsy.

"How could I have other news newer than yours?" Jill replied. "You've blown that case wide open by letting Wilma Carter show you that secret way into and out of the complex. But these young people: What was the attraction of a secret entrance, anyway?"

Betsy smiled at her. "Sometimes I think I'm younger than you instead of older. Ever hear of skinny-dipping?"

"Who was — oh. Teddi. But how did she know about it?"

"I don't know. But people rarely go skinny-dipping alone. So someone else must have known, and showed that entrance to Teddi — or Teddi knew and showed someone else. And there were probably others. This was too delicious a secret to be kept, don't you think?"

"That sounds very logical. But who is the person who first discovered it?"

"That is the question of the hour. Neither the Hopkins police nor the Watered Silk staff can find a connection between Teddi and Wilma. But we'll find out more, I hope, when Wilma is able to remember the secret door again."

The next morning, as Betsy and Connor were relaxing over a second cup of strong black Irish tea — Betsy couldn't tell it from black English tea, but Connor insisted there was a difference — the phone rang. Betsy was closer, so she got up to answer it.

"Betsy, it's Jill." Her voice was hushed.

Betsy was alarmed by her tone. Had something happened to the baby Jill was carrying? "What's the matter?" Betsy asked.

"Wilma Carter is dead. She was found dead in her bed this morning. No sign of foul play, but this was certainly unexpected. An autopsy will be ordered."

Betsy was struck dumb. Her first foolish thought was, *No more "wait a minute, wait a minute."*

Then she found her voice. "God have mercy on her soul, poor thing! Oh, this is *terrible!*"

Betsy hung up and Connor was beside her an instant later. "What is it, machree?"

Betsy leaned in and Connor took her in

155

his arms. "Someone has murdered Wilma!" she said, and burst into tears.

"Murdered? Are they sure? How was it done?"

"They don't know — they aren't even sure it's murder. But I am, I most assuredly am!"

# ELEVEN

When Betsy came down to open the shop the next morning, Godwin was already there. The lights were on, the coffee was brewed, the Bose was broadcasting something light and sparkling from NPR. Godwin turned sad eyes on her and said, "Oh, my dear, Jill called to tell me to be extra nice to you today — and why. Do you want to go back upstairs?"

"Thank you, Goddy, but no. I'm upset, of course, but I think I'll do better if I'm at work."

"Do you really think it's murder? After all, she was old and had a terminal disease."

"Alzheimer's doesn't kill suddenly. The path downward is a long one, and she was far from the bottom. It could have been a heart attack or stroke. All the same . . ."

"All right," Godwin said, nodding. "Maybe the autopsy will tell us something."

"I hope the autopsy is clear."

■ ■ ■ ■

Wilma Carter's funeral was a church service in the Hennepin Avenue Methodist Church in Minneapolis. A big, roughly circular building of gray stone, it had a tall, elaborate, delicate spire rising from its center, supported on slim flying buttresses.

Preston Munro; his wife, Sonja; and Tony Halloway, Sony's father, crossed the street together, preparing to enter the church. Tony, a tall man with a respectable paunch, was wearing a black suit, white shirt, and black silk tie under a dark gray wool overcoat. Preston, tall and thin, with dramatic cheekbones and piercing dark eyes, was wearing navy blue slacks, light blue shirt and tie, and dark brown blazer under a lined raincoat. Sony, also tall, and strongly built with thick golden hair swept back from her face, was in a deep green dress, black low-heeled shoes, and a light gray long coat with a black fox collar.

Preston was there under protest, though he was trying to conceal it. He had met Wilma only three times in his life: once at his wedding, again at his son's christening, and once at Watered Silk. His father-in-law, Tony, was Wilma's nephew, which made her his great-aunt-in-law, too distant a relation to be important. And although Tony remembered Wilma fondly from her younger days, he had finished grieving for her long before she died, when she stopped knowing who he was. Sony was sad and a little bitter — she had loved Wilma and resented the attitude of the two men with her.

The interior of the church was a descending semicircle, with the altar at the bottom and the pews in the nave rising upward, and a choir loft surrounding it. Wilma's coffin, closed and covered with a magnificent purple and gold pall, stood near the altar. An enormous wreath of white lilies rested on it. Sony wondered where the wreath had come from.

She was surprised at the large turnout. She knew Wilma had been the widow of a Minnesota Supreme Court judge — but he had died twenty years ago. *I guess the political class have long memories,* she thought. Looking around, Sony recognized several important Minnesota political figures among the sixty or more mourners. While the organ played, she read the service bulletin. There was a brief biography. She was glad to see the mention of Wilma's amazing book of wildlife photographs. It had won the Minnesota Book Award the year it was published. Sony had her own cherished copy and her son, Little Tony, loved to look at it.

The minister came out in a black cassock, white surplice, and purple stole. He was a short, rotund man with a great shock of white hair and an air of dignity. His voice, amplified by the microphone, was very deep. "We have gathered here this morning in God's presence," he began, startling Sony into thinking for a moment he had mistakenly opened his prayer book to the marriage service. But he continued, ". . . to remember the life of Wilma Carter, and to commend her soul into the gracious care of our Lord and Savior, Jesus Christ."

The service was moving, the music familiar, including a beautiful restatement of Psalm 23.

"O God," concluded the minister, "give us now your grace, that as we shrink before the mystery of death, we may see the light of eternity."

The eulogies were touching and heartfelt, though one politician seemed to think they were here to honor Wilma's late husband rather than Wilma herself. Tony had been asked to say something, but he'd asked Sony to speak for the family.

Sony had wrung her heart out on two

160

pages. She clutched them tightly as she made her way to the lectern. But standing there, behind the covered coffin with its lilies, she lost her ability to speak. She cleared her throat twice, then wiped her eyes with a handkerchief and finally managed to begin, "Great-Aunt Wilma was funny and creative, brilliant and fearless — and a second mother to me. She loved Valley Fair, and would take me on the roller coaster as many times as I wanted to ride. I never thought of her as old, and was shocked when she was diagnosed with Alzheimer's.

"She loved the outdoors, especially the Boundary Waters, where she would take me camping and fishing. She taught me to admire nature on its own terms. She loved politics a little less, but worked hard on her husband's behalf when he was campaigning. And she . . . she loved me.

"She taught me to live life to the fullest. I will never forget the way she'd come hurrying in to my birthday parties, late as usual, calling 'Wait a minute, wait a minute, start over!' " She had to pause while a rush of reminiscent laughter filled the church. "Or how she'd rush ahead at the State Fair, calling, 'Come on, come on, follow me!' Oh, Aunt Wilma, I know where you are now, and I hope someday to follow you to that happy place. I know we're supposed to say 'God rest your soul,' but somehow I think you're too busy to rest, trotting around heaven with your camera, catching angels unaware and Saint Peter in his bath."

Sony didn't hear the congregation's appreciative laughter this time. She stumbled back to her seat, where Preston put a good, strong arm around her, and her father blew his nose like a proud trumpet.

The final hymn was one not found in the hymnal, but entirely appropriate for Wilma: "How Can I Keep from Singing?"

After the service, while they waited for Wilma's coffin to be loaded into the hearse for its trip to the cemetery, Sony noticed a group of four or five men and one woman standing a little to one side. They looked alert and professional. Who were they? Sony wondered. Why were they here? She slowed as she passed and heard the woman say, "What did the autopsy show?"

One of the men, shorter than his companions, with a freckled face and thin lips, said quietly, "Atropine."

As she listened, Sony felt Preston come up behind her. As he took her by the arm, she pulled him not toward the door but off to the side, where she heard the freckle-faced man say, "Someone got into the box

162

of Exelon kept in a locked cabinet in her room, and injected a fatal dose of atropine into the back of one of the foil packets. The used packet was found in a wastebasket and it had a tiny puncture in it."

"Oh my God," murmured Sony.

One of the other men turned to look out the open door and saw her. She immediately took Preston's arm and went out to stand on the porch. She looked at Preston, whose expression was grim. He had heard it, too. Murder! Great-Aunt Wilma had been murdered — and the police knew it!

After the next Monday Bunch meeting, Phil and Doris stayed to talk with Betsy. Phil, in his rather loud, hoarse voice — he was a little deaf and didn't always wear his hearing aids — said, "I know you tried to help Bershada's nephew after he lost his job at Watered Silk, and that didn't go too good, so maybe we shouldn't try to get you to help us with an even bigger problem that has to do with it all over again."

Normally, Phil was direct, so this circumlocution made Betsy wary of what was coming. Still, she said encouragingly, "What's the new problem?"

"You know that drowned girl was pregnant."

163

"Yes."

Phil hesitated, so Doris spoke up. "Phil's grandnephew Tommy — Thomas Shore is his name — was the father of Teddi Wahlberger's baby."

"Oh my," said Betsy. "So now he's a suspect?"

"Oh, yes, definitely," said Phil.

"Is he under arrest?" Betsy asked.

"Not yet," said Phil. His old-man's face, rumpled as an unmade bed, was further disordered by eyebrows that twisted upward unevenly, and by the severe downward turn of his wide, thin-lipped mouth. "He's a nice, sweet boy," insisted Phil. "He didn't — he couldn't — not ever — wouldn't — kill anyone!" He wrung his broad, strong fingers hard. His eyes were shiny with tears, but he didn't break down.

"How did the police identify Tommy as a person of interest?" asked Betsy.

"They talked to Teddi's roommates," said Phil, "and they said Tommy was one of the men Teddi was dating. There are at least two others, but they could only find one of them. I hear they took DNA samples from the two they had, and lightning struck Tommy."

"The problem is . . ." said Doris, halting as she glanced at Phil.

"Yeah, all right, the problem is, Tommy lied to them. First, he said he never heard of Teddi Wahlberger. When the roommates said Teddi invited a guy named Tommy over to a barbecue a couple of times, and described him, he finally admitted it, but said he'd never, er, well, you know." Phil was old-fashioned; intimate details were not to be shared in mixed company.

"But then," said Doris, "it turns out he was the father of that poor unborn child. So now he says that he never heard of Watered Silk and never knew anything about an indoor heated pool over there."

"And they don't believe him," said Phil.

"I can see why," Betsy said.

"Yeah. So, is there anything you can do to help him?"

"I don't know," she admitted. "I suppose I can try. How about I start by talking to him? Do you want to arrange a meeting, or will you give me his contact information and I'll get in touch with him directly?"

"We've already told him we're going to ask you for help," said Doris. "He's agreed to talk to you. He's really scared — and so are we."

Phil handed Betsy a slip of paper. "Here's his cell number. He's waiting to hear from you."

■ ■ ■ ■

The next day, Betsy was sitting in a booth at the Barleywine, Excelsior's microbrewery, waiting to meet Thomas Shore for lunch. A couple of minutes late, he came in shyly, looking for her. She waved, and he came over to her.

He was handsome — almost pretty — short and trim with a young face and a vulnerable cast to his features. Betsy was surprised; she'd been told he was twenty-four, and here he looked about nineteen. He had a fresh, unlined complexion and rosy cheeks, though his hands, while clean, bore the thickening that comes from physical labor, and he had walked in with an adult tiredness. He wore work boots, stained jeans with a split at one knee revealing long underwear, and a dark-brown turtleneck sweater under an old mock-sheepskin coat with a torn pocket. Heavy, fur-lined gloves were stuffed in the intact pocket. There was a farm-animal smell about him.

"Hello, Mr. Shore," said Betsy.

"Hello, Ms. Devonshire." His voice was light but not thin. He slid in opposite her. "Can we get our food right away? I have to get back to chores before I go to my job."

"All right."

Betsy ordered one of those salads that feature six kinds of lettuce, cherry tomatoes, purple onion, black olives, sweet yellow peppers, celery, carrots, and feta cheese, with a balsamic vinegar and oil dressing. She asked for a diet ginger ale.

Tommy had a bacon cheeseburger and skin-on fries, and a big mug of pale ale. He ate quickly, as if he hadn't been fed for a week — another reason to think he was surely younger than twenty-four.

Betsy said, "I'm pleased you agreed to talk with me face-to-face."

Tommy chewed and swallowed before responding. "Uncle Phil and Aunt Doris said you are like magic when it comes to detecting crime." His smile was hopeful.

Betsy waved her fork dismissively. "Oh, sometimes I can see through a problem, find a missing link, or make a connection. I do it in my shop all the time. And when it comes to crime, it usually happens when I try to prove the innocence of someone who's been falsely accused."

"Wow, that's me!" He put his burger down, his light-blue eyes shining. "Can you really do that? Will you do it for me? I have this feeling that any second a big hand is gonna grab me from behind, slap the cuffs on me, and start telling me I have the right to remain silent."

"Has that ever happened to you before?"

His eyes shifted briefly. "No, never."

He was lying. Betsy gritted her teeth and pretended she didn't know. "If it happens, invoke it."

"Invoke it?" Tommy looked as if he wasn't sure what "invoke" meant.

"Say you don't want to answer any questions without your lawyer present." Betsy had a strong feeling he was going to need this advice.

Tommy looked alarmed. "I don't have a lawyer. Are you saying I should hire one? How much do they cost? I don't have any money."

"A good one is expensive. But the state has to provide one for you if you can't afford one."

Tommy nodded. "That's right, that's part of that rights thing they recite when they arrest you."

"Pay attention to it, and tell them you won't answer their questions without a lawyer. Then stick to it." Betsy repeated what Jill and Lars had told her: "No matter how friendly they appear, no matter how much you want to explain, sit tight and don't give them any information that's not on your driver's license, and say over and over that you want to talk to a lawyer."

Again Tommy nodded, this time more thoughtfully. "Okay, gotcha. Invoke my right to silence." He picked up his burger and took a bite before continuing. "But it's not gonna come to that, right? I mean, you're gonna do your magic thing and I'll be out of trouble."

Betsy gave him her most level look and said, "A very dear friend of mine was arrested for a murder he did not commit and spent weeks in jail before I could clear him. What I do is not magic, Mr. Shore, it's justice."

Tommy swallowed thickly. "Okay, okay, I see what you're getting at. But really, honestly, as strong as I can put it, I didn't murder Teddi."

Betsy took a bite of her salad, which was fresh and delicious.

"Okay, let's go in another direction, for now. What do you do for a living?"

"In the winter, I work in a drugstore." He named it, a national chain. "Just clerking, and just under thirty hours a week — the bastards, so they don't have to give me any benefits. And I'm also part-time for an office-cleaning company, working four thirty to nine six days a week — which, you will

169

also notice, is less than thirty hours, God bless bosses everywhere."

"And in the summer?"

"I manage a miniature golf course. I do everything — sell tickets, maintain the grounds, paint the office, everything. That's a full-time job, so in the summer I'm covered. I like my boss, too, he pretty much lets me run things my way." He smiled and ate three french fries together in two bites.

"You'll pardon my noticing, but you have the appearance of a farmhand." Betsy speared a cherry tomato with her fork.

"Oh, yes, I kind of have another job, very part-time, and I get paid with a cut in my bed and board. My landlord owns a hobby farm, he raises goats, sells milk, and, once in a while, meat. I help feed the animals, muck out the barn, rake the corral, mend the fences, do a little painting, like that. I don't milk them and I stay in the house on butchering day. Goats are okay; I mean, not like cows and horses, you can push them around and if they step on your foot it doesn't hurt." He smiled and sniffed twice. "They do have an odor, however."

Betsy smiled. "My grandmother's neighbor had a baby who was allergic to cows' milk and his parents kept a goat just for him. Grandmom said the creature smelled worse than the cows." She broke in half a cracker that came with the salad. "Now, tell me about Teddi Wahlberger."

Tommy strained to keep the casual air going. "What can I say? I wasn't really close to her, but anyone could tell she was beautiful in mind as well as body, and everyone said she was a really good person."

Betsy did not reply to this slab of boilerplate. She ate her cracker half, then got out her reporter's narrow notebook and took her time writing Tommy's name and the date on the top page. After a full minute of silence, he began to writhe subtly. He took a big bite of his burger, clearly hoping that she'd break the silence, but she waited through it.

"Okay, okay," he yielded. "Let's get real about Teddi. First, she was really pretty, that's the truth. But not stuck up about it. Not just her face, she had a great figure." His hands moved expressively. "She loved to party. She had parties at her house, cookouts mostly. Plus, I saw her around, I mean, it seemed like every time I was out, there she was. She never got sloppy drunk, but she liked to drink. She was a great dancer, knew every kind of dance, some I never heard of, I mean, like the cha-cha. She told funny jokes, she was sexy, really hot. She would flirt with anyone, even me, especially when she was drinking. I liked her. Everyone liked her."

"Apparently someone didn't," Betsy pointed out.

"Yeah, well, that wasn't me. I mean, it wasn't serious between us, the kind where I might get really mad if we had a fight, which we never did, not really. We were just — uh — friends."

She quirked an eyebrow. "With benefits?"

"Well, uh, yeah."

"So how did it come about that you got her pregnant?"

He boggled a little at this, and Betsy said, "I mean, didn't you take care that this wouldn't happen?"

"Oh, sure. She was on 'the pill.' " He put down his burger to waggle his fingers in quotation marks.

"And you didn't use some kind of backup?"

"I didn't think we had to." He picked up his burger. "I mean, she told me we were good to go." He put it back down with a little sad sigh. "Obviously, I was wrong."

"How long did you know Teddi?"

He stuffed a long french fry into his mouth and thought while he chewed. "Close to a year."

Betsy wrote that down with an air so skeptical that he amended his reply. "Well, maybe six or seven months. If you count up to right now."

"How did you meet?"

"At this club we go to, the Bar Abilene. It's in Uptown and it has a dance floor." Uptown was a section of Minneapolis featuring lots of bars, theaters, and ethnic restaurants.

" 'We'?"

"There's three, sometimes four or even five of us, we sort of hang out together, bring our dates or steady girlfriends. There was three of us this one night, and my girl, Dell, she couldn't be there, so I was flying solo, and Teddi danced with me a couple times and gave me her number. Next time I had a fight with Dell, I called her."

"How many times did you go out with her?"

He shrugged and again his blue eyes shifted just a little before he said, "Hardly any. Three at the most."

"And yet —"

"Yeah, well . . ." He sighed heavily and said, as if it were his own original thought, "All it takes is once."

Betsy put her pen down in a pointed way. "Mr. Shore," she began, then stopped.

"All right, all right," he said, raising both hands, one with the last of his burger in it, the other holding a french fry. "Maybe it was more than once." He put his food down on his plate. "Look, are you going to help me or not?"

"I can't help you if you're not going to answer my questions truthfully."

"But I am answering truthfully." His smile turned charmingly rueful. "Eventually."

"Mr. Shore, I don't have time to pry the truth out of you. You can go ahead with this game you're playing — with yourself or others, I'm not sure which — but personally, I am done."

"But Uncle Phil and Aunt Doris are good friends of yours! I mean, they said they could get you to help me!"

"I'm sure what they actually said was that they'd ask me to help you, which they did. But you're giving me false answers to questions. And I have better things to do than to chase after shadows."

"But —"

Betsy signaled for the check. Leona, the slim, dark-and-silver-haired owner of the Barleywine, brought it over, glanced at Tommy, and then, seeing something in his eyes, leaned over him and said with quiet conviction, "Whatever the problem is, you're not helping." Leona was uncanny at reading people, perhaps because she really was, as many people believed, a witch with psychic powers. Or perhaps because she'd been in the hospitality business all her life, dealing with every kind of person.

Tommy stared at her, openmouthed, as Betsy handed Leona her credit card.

When Leona walked away, Betsy said, "You think she's good? Wait until a really experienced police detective starts in on you." She stood.

"No, wait! Please, wait!" Now he looked seriously frightened.

Betsy sat back down. "What?"

"What do you want from me?"

"I want you to tell me how you came to impregnate a young woman you barely knew, and how you reacted when she told you."

He wiped his mouth with his hand, then grabbed his mug of beer and took a big swallow. "I thought she liked me, but later I guessed she just felt sorry for me," he muttered, shamefaced. "And when she told me she was pregnant, I didn't believe her." He wiped his mouth again, this time with the edge of his hand.

"I mean, okay, it wasn't once, but it wasn't like every other night for a month, it was only a couple of times." He was speaking to the top of the table, one trembling hand resting on his unfolded napkin. He spoke rapidly but with emotion. "So I asked her, I went, 'How do you know it's mine?' I mean, she wasn't a — you know — but she got around. I mean, I'd see her leave a place with a guy, and you know they're not going out for a smoke. You know? But she said the timing was right, and it was mine, for sure. I was scared, then I got mad. I mean, she said she was on the pill and there wasn't anything to worry about. Now she's saying maybe she forgot to take it a couple of times. I say, 'Well, maybe you shouldn't forget to get an abortion,' and she goes, 'Maybe I don't want one.' "

Tommy rubbed his forehead hard with the fingers of both hands. "I can't afford child support! Hell, I'm barely supporting myself! I mean, what was I supposed to do?" Suddenly realizing what a culpable statement that was, he swore in a low whisper and said, "I didn't kill her. I really, truly, honest-to-God didn't kill her."

"Where were you the night she was killed?"

Again his eyes shifted. "I was working. I did half a shift at the drugstore, then went with a gang to clean offices. You can ask both my bosses, like I'm sure the cops have. Then I went home."

"There's been a second murder, you know, this time of a woman who lived at Watered Silk."

Tommy looked seriously alarmed. "Whe— When did *that* happen?"

"There's a problem with this crime. It was a setup — someone interfered with a medication that a nurse administers — so while the time of death is known, the setup could have occurred any time between when Teddi was killed and the day this new victim died."

"Hey, that's not fair!" Tommy said. "How can I — how can anyone give an alibi for that?"

"He can't," said Betsy. "So what I'm looking at is opportunity — and access to what is needed for the setup. I have found out that both the medicine the victim was given — *and the poison introduced into that medicine* — are found at a pharmacy." She watched as his frightened mind stumbled over the implications.

"But — but wait! I'm not a pharmacist, for God's sake! I don't have access to all those pills and things! And, even if I did, I don't know what's poisonous and what's not! Oh my God, I *am* gonna get arrested! You've just got to help me, please! Please

177

help me!"

"I don't know if I can. Let me get some more information." Betsy wrote down the names of Tommy's supervisors at both jobs, and then the name and phone number of his landlord. For good measure, she asked for the name and contact information for his parents and his other girlfriend, Dell Wheatly.

"Tell me about going skinny-dipping at Watered Silk," she said, still writing.

"Who says I went skinny-dipping?" he asked sharply, trying to sound scandalized.

"Did you?"

"The cops asked me that and I told them I never did. I never even heard of the place."

"Was that a lie?"

"No." When Betsy didn't write that down, he waggled his head back and forth while grimacing as if in pain. "Damn," he muttered.

Betsy waited.

"Okay, I mean yes, I heard of Watered Silk. But I never went. This one guy says he knows a place to go skinny-dipping, which you can't do at the Y."

"Who was that?"

"I don't remember."

With a sideways pull of her mouth, Betsy stood and went to the bar to pay for the

178

meal. Tommy didn't try to call her back this time but sat crestfallen, not moving, while she put on her coat and walked out of the pub.

"I'm really sorry," she said to Phil and Doris that evening over wine and cheese in her apartment. Connor sat on a kitchen chair pulled into the living room, while Phil and Doris sat side by side on the deep-purple couch. Betsy was sitting in the comfortable champagne-colored chair she used when working on her stitching. A bright lamp stood behind the chair, its shade tilted so it was looking over her shoulder.

Betsy had redecorated her living room not long ago, replacing the love seat with a proper couch and reupholstering the chair. Crewel-worked pillows in complementary shades — with two in bright yellow for contrast — ornamented them. The carpet was new, a neutral buff, and she had painted the walls in a pale cream. The room was large, low-ceilinged, with a big pair of windows overlooking the street, guarded by buff sheers and heavy drapes that matched the carpet.

"I'm sure he's sorry, too," Phil said in a grim tone that boded ill for Tommy.

"I wonder if it could be true that he

doesn't know who told him about people using the pool at Watered Silk," said Doris.

Phil gave her a frowning look, clearly annoyed that she wasn't on his side, but she continued bravely, "Now, you know how it is among a group of people when they're drinking. They say all kinds of things, tell stories, make jokes, all of them talking at once."

"But he remembered that one thing," said Phil. "No details, just that one bit of information."

"It was more than a bit," Betsy said. "He remembered the name of the place as well as the fact that people went skinny-dipping in its pool."

"We used to skinny-dip at the Y," said Phil, going off on a tangent. "People don't do that anymore."

"Not at the Y, anyway," said Doris.

This time Phil was the one who looked surprised. Doris laughed at his expression. "Or so I've heard."

He laughed then, too, and nudged her with an elbow.

"I still don't think he's a murderer, but what are we going to do with the boy?" Doris asked, turning serious again.

"Maybe after he's been arrested, his memory will improve," growled Phil.

But Doris turned sad, concerned eyes on Betsy, who knew she wouldn't be giving up her investigation just yet.

# TWELVE

Later that night, Betsy checked her notes on her conversation with Tommy Shore, thought for a minute or two, then shrugged and dialed Dell Wheatly's phone number.

The woman who answered was Dell's roommate, and she called Dell to the phone.

"I don't think I know you," Dell said in a faintly angry tone, when Betsy identified herself.

"I'm a friend of Doris and Phil Galvin, Tommy Shore's aunt and uncle," said Betsy. "Tommy's in a little bit of trouble and they've asked me to see if I can help."

"Has he been arrested?" Now Dell's voice was alarmed.

"No. But he may be. Do you know anything about the trouble he's in?"

"I — don't want to say. Maybe you should talk to Tommy," suggested Dell.

"I have talked with him. He gave me your number."

"Why did he do that? What have I got to do with it?" Now she sounded truculent.

"I think he wants you possibly to be a character witness for him."

"Oh, he's a character, all right!"

"Did you know he was seeing Teddi Wahlberger?"

"Not until he told me he was the father of her baby." She gave a sad sigh. "But I knew he was seeing someone. You can always tell, y'know?" Another sigh. "So now you want me to say nice things about him, huh?"

"No, I want you to say true things about him. You know Ms. Wahlberger was murdered, and the police are looking hard at Tommy."

"Yes. You would not believe how scared he is about that. But I'm sure he's not the murderer. I don't think Tommy would kill anyone. You should've seen how sad he was when his favorite goat was butchered. He hates that part about farming, when the animals go for meat."

"How long have you known Tommy?"

"Oh, for years and years. Since middle school. He wasn't good at school. I wonder if he's not dyslexic or something. He just didn't get studying, he never learned his times tables, his handwriting was terrible, he still can't spell. And he's a bad liar. He's

183

been drinking too much lately, which doesn't help. People take advantage of him, they've done that for a long time. Once he got arrested because two people he thought were his friends asked him to keep some stuff for them that turned out to be stolen. He agreed because he's *nice.* He's sweet and kind to everyone and just *hopeless.* He'll never amount to anything, I know that. He needs someone to take care of him." After a pause, she said softly, "Maybe someday he'll realize that's me."

Betsy thanked Dell for talking to her. After they hung up, she made some notes, shook her head, and logged on to the Internet.

She checked her e-mail, replied to an inquiry on the shop's web site, then did a search for Teddi Wahlberger's Facebook page. She was pleased to find it had not yet been taken down.

The page was colorful and featured lots of pictures. Teddi made the common young person's statement that she was not religious *"at all!"* but was very spiritual, especially when in a forest or beside a lake. She believed cats had souls just like humans and dogs. She was touched by any show of compassion or act of kindness — "My friends are SO GOOD to me!" She believed that if more people thought hard about peace, it would happen. She believed that Girls Rule. She liked studly men who were sensitive. She liked dancing to loud music, swimming, long walks, skiing, bowling, and partying hearty (or sometimes "hardy"). New Year's Eve was her favorite holiday, "more fun than Christmas."

Looking through the pictures that Teddi had posted, Betsy realized with a start that she had already seen the house Teddi lived in. It was on Third Street, about four blocks from Betsy's building. A two-story white clapboard, it had a blue-gray roof and sky-blue shutters, and a new wooden deck out back. With her two roommates, Lia (Amelia Perrin) and Frey (Gwenfreya Kadesh), Teddi had held barbecue parties there all last summer, with guests ranging in number from four to over a dozen.

In one photo Betsy saw Tommy, looking younger than ever, wearing the foolish expression of a drunk. His jeans were too big and his Trampled by Turtles T-shirt was faded. He was raising his can of beer in a salute to the woman in the center of the frame. That was Teddi herself, wearing a yellow bikini too small for her lush figure under a short, lacy cover-up. Standing sideways to the camera, she was posing provocatively, one hand pushing up the back of her long blond hair, the cover-up pulled off her shoulders. Also in the photo was a tall, handsome man, well-muscled and deeply tanned, wearing white shorts but no shirt. He appeared to be laughing indulgently at Teddi's posturing. There were two other young women in the background. One was frankly plump with dark, curly hair surrounding a beautiful face. She was wielding a spatula beside a freestanding charcoal grill, and wearing denim clam diggers and a sleeveless T-shirt with a Las Vegas casino logo on it. The other woman, tall and very slender, had a noble nose and deep auburn hair. Her blue short shorts showed off long legs, her orange camisole a narrow waist. She was smiling at the camera — and presumably at the person taking the picture. There were no captions or tags to identify any of the people, but from other posted photos Betsy was able to identify the dark-haired woman as Lia and the redhead as Frey.

There were other photos of parties held in the house. Tommy was in one of those photos, too; and in the later ones, a skinny-tailed white kitten appeared, at first tiny, then bigger — darkening around the edges into a blue point Siamese. It was usually being smooched by Teddi.

By checking the friends list, Betsy found Lia and Frey, and by clicking on their pictures, she was directed to their respective Facebook pages. She left messages on both, offering condolences on the death of their friend, and asking them as gently as she could to contact her at Crewel World to talk about Teddi.

Betsy clicked away from Facebook and went on to her e-mail, then to some of the blogs she followed, and finally to her books: employee hours, bills paid and due, profit and loss, checking her running inventory, giving a second reading to an e-mail from her financial advisor.

A Kathryn Molineux trunk show was coming. Kathryn's animal-themed, Asian-styled canvases were hugely popular with Betsy's customers. She made a note to check how Godwin was registering his usual enthusiasm on the shop's web site and newsletter, so she could echo or supplement it on her own web site. The company backing the designer had sent an e-mail with pictures that she and Godwin could use in publicizing the event. She chose the wood duck canvas — maybe she could persuade Phil to try needlepoint — and the white heron, whose design of exotic, curving feathers was particularly lovely.

She wanted to talk with Godwin about the shop's standing offer of a five percent discount to any customer on his or her birthday, and sent him an e-mail about that. When the idea was presented some years back, she worried that most women would not wish to show their driver's license as proof of their birthdays because it would give away the year of their birth. But it turned out that many customers didn't mind a store clerk learning their true age, as long as they got their discount. And some customers felt tempted to spend more than usual because of the discount, and their extra purchases often made up for the shop's loss. Betsy was sure there was an algorithm to figure out who came out better on the deal, customers or Crewel World, but she hadn't any idea how to compose one, especially if she wanted to factor in the goodwill generated by such an offer. Maybe Godwin could figure it out.

She copied Teddi's Facebook address and sent it to Jill, asking in the accompanying e-mail if Jill might be able to read something into Teddi's Facebook pictures that Betsy had missed.

She was undressing for bed when her phone rang.

"Are — are you the owner of Crewel

World needlework shop?" asked a young-sounding woman.

"Yes," Betsy replied.

"Ms. Devonshire," the voice continued, pronouncing it "Devon-shyre" instead of, correctly, "Devonsheer," "I'm Frey Kadesh. I lived with Teddi Wahlberger for a little over three years. I don't think I ever heard her mention your name."

"That's not surprising," Betsy said. "I never met her. But I've been asked by a friend to supplement the police investigation into her death. It's something I do, to help clear a person who's been falsely or mistakenly accused of a crime. Teddi's murder was a deeply distressing event, and now there's been another suspicious death apparently connected to it."

"There has? Who?"

"A resident of Watered Silk, who may have had information about the person responsible for Teddi's murder. The police are redoubling their efforts, of course, but now so am I."

"Oh God, Lia and I are so upset about this! Teddi was such a good, good friend, such a great person! This has been really hard for us!" There was a sound like a sob.

"I'm sure it has. I'm sorry you two are having to suffer all this distress and sorrow."

"Thank you. The police are doing all they can, I'm sure. Do you think you really can help them?"

"I hope so. But I need to talk to you and, if possible, Lia."

"I wish I knew what to do," Frey said fretfully. There fell a thoughtful little silence. "Say, wait a minute," she said, "I think I've heard of you. Someone told me about this embroidery store woman who figured out how a man killed himself and made the gun disappear so everyone thought it was murder. Happened over in Navarre, right? Was that you?"

Well, word certainly did get around. "Yes," said Betsy.

"Wow. And you really think you can find out who killed Teddi and this other person?"

"I'm going to try."

"And it would help if you could talk to me about Teddi?"

"You and your other roommate, Lia. I want to get a clearer picture of who Teddi was, what she was like."

"I'll have to ask Lia, but I'm sure she'll say yes. Right now she and I are still roommates, so you could talk to us together. When do you want to do this?"

"When are you available?"

"I don't want to do it without Lia, so let

me ask her and I'll call you back."

"That will be fine. I hope to hear from you first thing tomorrow."

"All right, then, you will. Oh, this will be so great, to be able to help solve her murder. Whoever did this seriously needs to go to prison."

Lia was much less sure about talking to Betsy about Teddi. She called at around eleven the next morning to say she would sit in on the interview, but her reluctance was obvious in every syllable of their brief conversation. They agreed, however, that it would be best to get on with it as soon as possible. By the time Betsy got off the phone, they'd decided she would visit the women that evening.

"Now we'll see some progress," predicted Godwin. "I want to know everything they tell you, all right?" He was an avid follower of Betsy's cases. "Call me when you get home, especially if you learn something interesting."

"All right." Godwin was Betsy's most valuable employee (and the only one who worked full time), the most knowledgeable, and the one most willing to work long hours and on holidays; and in return, Betsy was willing to keep him up to date on her investigations.

She had a hasty supper with Connor, who gravely wished her success, and offered one of his favorite Americanisms: "I'll leave the light on for you."

Like most houses in the prosperous little town of Excelsior, the house Teddi Wahlberger had shared with Lia Perrin and Frey Kadesh was in good repair. A two-story clapboard in a neighborhood of similar houses, its small front yard featured a huge elm tree that was probably twice the age of the house. A winding brick walk led to the shallow front porch. Betsy stood for a few moments in front of the bright-blue door, painted to match the shutters, before pressing the doorbell.

The door was opened promptly by a young woman, tall and slim, her dark auburn hair pulled back in a casual ponytail. She was wearing a thick purple pullover, tight green jeans, and jeweled sandals. Her ears were studded with numerous earrings. She was easy to recognize from the photos on Teddi's Facebook page.

"Hello, Ms. Kadesh. I'm Betsy Devonshire."

"Hi. Call me Frey. Come on in." Frey stepped back, opening the door wide.

The living room was a recent remodel,

laid with diagonal hardwood flooring, or perhaps a good laminate, and open to the kitchen with a breakfast bar between the two rooms. Two brightly patterned carpets interrupted the lines of the boards, one of them in front of an oversize squashy sectional upholstered in dark gray and covered with many pillows in bright solids and prints. It looked opulent and comfortable. In front of the sofa stood a coffee table with chrome legs and a gray stone top. Beyond the sofa were French doors leading out to a big, dimly seen snow-covered deck.

The house smelled of hot cocoa and freshly baked sugar cookies. Betsy could see another young woman in the kitchen, stout but very attractive. "That's Lia," said Frey unnecessarily, gesturing toward her roommate.

"Hello," Lia said without enthusiasm. Well, Betsy thought, she really *was* nervous about this meeting. Or maybe she was merely shy.

"May I take your coat?" said Frey.

"Thank you," said Betsy, unbuttoning her black wool Jean Paul Gaultier coat — which she'd found, rejoicing, in an upscale consignment store — and letting it slide off her arms. She was wearing a thin brown sweater she'd knit herself and taupe slacks.

"Do you want me to take off my boots?" she asked. It was a common question in Minnesota.

"Please," called Lia from the kitchen.

"The sand they spread on the streets scratches our floors," said Frey apologetically.

Betsy pulled off her sensible low-heeled boots and set them on a rubber mat alongside two pairs of outrageously high-style boots, and Frey handed her a pair of thin, stretchy slip-ons, taken from a box of them behind the mat. She showed Betsy to the couch, which was as comfortable as it looked, if a little enveloping.

Betsy pulled on the slippers as Frey disappeared into another room with her coat, and Lia entered the living room carrying a bright red wooden tray on which rested three steaming mugs and a plate of cookies. "I hope you like these," she said in a neutral, low-key voice.

"I'm afraid I'm very fond of home-baked cookies," said Betsy with a smile.

"Me, too." And Lia smiled back.

When Frey returned, they all sat on the couch, well separated from one another. Everyone took a cookie and a mug. The cocoa was rich and not too sweet, the cookies crisp, almond-flavored, and still warm.

"These are delicious, thank you," said Betsy, taking a second bite.

"Lia is a fantastic cook," said Frey. "We were so pleased when she joined us."

"How long did you three live together?" asked Betsy.

Frey spoke first. "Teddi and I and another girl, Alison Reynolds, moved in here almost three years ago. But Alison's mother had a stroke — she lives in Fargo — so Alison went out there to help take care of her. She'd only lived here nine months. We advertised on craigslist and found Lia. Alison was great, but I think Lia is even better."

Lia said, "I think I was lucky to find Teddi and Frey."

"How did you and Teddi get together?" Betsy asked Frey.

"At a party. At two parties, actually. We met at one and kind of hit it off, then at the next party, there we were again. We liked the same things; we were both employed, with steady jobs; and we were both unhappy with our roommates at the time. Teddi knew about this house for rent, but we needed a third person to live with us in order to afford it. I knew Alison was looking to move out on her boyfriend, who was a controlling jerk, so I contacted her, and she said yes, please. We split everything three ways: rent, utilities, groceries. But then she had to leave and we got Lia to move in. After a couple of months, we made a deal with her: We'd buy the groceries if she'd cook, because she's like a chef, she took classes at Le Cordon Bleu College of Culinary Arts in Mendota Heights." Frey smiled at Lia. "She can make a delicious meal fast or slow, and she can even cook low-cal meals when we start putting on too much weight from her regular stuff."

Lia said, "Except I can gain weight even on low-cal meals. I could gain weight eating bread and water."

Betsy said, "Me, too. Not only that, I have a cat like the both of us. No metabolism at all. I feed her diet cat food, but she weighs twenty-one pounds." She pulled her shoulders up. "I'm sorry, I shouldn't have said that, you're not a cat, and you're not as overweight as my cat."

"That's all right," said Lia, though her tone made it clear that it wasn't all right at all.

"Speaking of cats," said Frey, as a half-grown cat came galloping into the room. He was the Siamese from Teddi's Facebook pages, his points now darkening toward chocolate. His tail had that hump in the middle that meant he was playing, though his back was also arched, and he danced sideways close to the stools at the breakfast bar, staring in mock-alarm at Betsy.

"Oh, Thai, how did you get out of the bedroom?" said Lia crossly.

Frey said, "I told you he knows how to turn a doorknob."

"It's all right, I like cats," said Betsy. "Here, kitty, kitty." She put down her mug of cocoa to snap her fingers at him. "Tie. Where did you get such a cute name for him?"

"It's Thai, like from Thailand, which used to be Siam," said Lia, "because he's Siamese."

"You won't like him," predicted Frey.

Thai trotted across the floor, leaped into Betsy's lap, put his forepaws on her chest, and licked her on the chin. His gleaming eyes were a clear blue, the color of a summer sky. Betsy stroked him, a little surprised to find his bones prominent under the fur. "What a sweet cat!"

"You want him?" said Lia and Frey in unison.

"Didn't I just say I already have a cat?" said Betsy lightly. "Besides, what's wrong with him?"

"Nothing!" said Lia, grimacing at Frey.

"Oh, don't lie to the nice lady," said Frey. "He gets into everything, he sheds, he licks you on the face, he wants to be part of whatever you're doing, and he barfs a lot."

"And he's a tomcat," said Lia. "You know what that means."

"What does it mean?" asked Betsy, imagining a number of possibilities.

*"Spraying,"* said Frey. "Tomcats spray." Her nose wrinkled. "And it *stinks.*"

"We're taking him to the Humane Society this weekend," said Lia.

"Oh, not *this* weekend!" objected Frey.

"Gwenfreya . . ." warned Lia.

Frey waved her hands to ward off the rebuke. "All right, I know, I promised. But what if he doesn't get adopted?"

"Why don't you get him neutered?" asked Betsy.

Lia said, "Teddi didn't want to do that to him. She said it's cruel. Anyway, it's too late now."

Betsy didn't think it was too late, but she didn't want to get into an argument over an issue that wasn't germane to the reason she was here.

Lia said quietly, "We have to get him out of here before he starts stinking up the house." They both looked at Betsy, as if hoping she might save the cat from a terrible fate. But Betsy put the cat on the floor. "I already have a cat," she repeated firmly.

Thai trotted away behind the couch.

"So it's too bad, he really is darling," said Frey.

"And funny," added Lia. "You should see him chase a ball. Sometimes he'll even bring it back to you."

Betsy felt something lightweight land on the back of the couch, and suddenly something was nuzzling her hair. Thai was back. His paws slipped around her neck, the nuzzling became more intense, and he started to purr.

"See what we mean?" demanded Lia. "I wish we'd never let him stay!"

"Then why did you?" asked Betsy reasonably.

"He's Teddi's," said Frey. "She loved him." Suddenly her eyes filled with tears. "She really loved him. And he loved her. That's why I hate, I *hate* throwing him away!"

"Yes, but we both *hate* that litter box, and his barf on the bed, and he won't use his scratching post, and —" Lia cut herself off, realizing again that she was spoiling any chance of persuading Betsy to take the animal off their hands.

"And he gets lonesome spending all day

and a lot of nights all alone in the house," said Frey, trying to put their dilemma in a better light.

"Teddi bought him all kinds of toys, so he's not bored," said Lia, shifting ground. "I suppose you did the same for your cat?"

"Oh, Sophie spends her days down in the shop with me and my customers," said Betsy. "She's lazy, she doesn't get into things. Her only fault down there — and it's as much my customers' fault as hers — is that she eats anything they'll give her. She's especially fond of potato chips.

"But I came here to talk about Teddi." She put the cat on the floor, giving him a little push on the rump to encourage him to go away. "Let's start with her job. Where did she work?"

"She was administrative assistant to the vice president of Goldman Fields, a CPA company in Minneapolis," said Frey. "She'd been there going on six years. She started out in their bookkeeping department while she was still getting her associate's degree in accounting. She was supposed to be working on her bachelor's in business management, and she was, but not very hard. She was comfortable where she was at Goldman, didn't want a promotion. Plus, she wasn't what you'd call a scholar."

"But she was a whiz at other things," offered Lia with a chuckle. "Things like dancing and parties — and beer pong, she'd win at beer pong almost all the time. Actually, we're all three party types — that's why we get — why we got along so well. We're not alcoholics, we don't let the parties interfere with our jobs, but we enjoy going out a lot. Or having people over."

"Like every weekend, one or the other," confessed Frey, smiling. "Here or somewhere out, doing something fun."

"Did Teddi have a lot of boyfriends?" asked Betsy. She had gotten out her reporter's notebook, which caused both girls' eyes to widen.

"No, not really," said Lia, toning it down a little. "I mean, she was beautiful, she attracted a lot of attention from a lot of men. And she liked that, a lot. But she wasn't like . . . promiscuous or anything."

"No, not at all," agreed Frey emphatically. "She was just popular, like she couldn't help it. And why should she? I wouldn't have, if I looked like her."

"You're both really attractive," said Betsy.

"Yeah, but not like Teddi," said Lia.

"Was there anyone special she was dating lately?"

"Well, there was that little boy-man

Tommy something," Lia said.

Frey added, "He's cute but looks about eighteen, though he's twenty-four. He showed us his driver's license to prove it. He's kind of shy, very sweet, but not the sharpest knife in the drawer." Frey chuckled. "Not that Teddi's IQ was off the charts. And they both liked corny jokes. They were well matched."

Lia said, "But then there's our favorite carpenter, Noah Levesque — it's spelled L-E-V-E-S-Q-U-E, but pronounced Le-VECK. He was hired by our landlord to build the deck out back, and he came over to get started on Teddi's day off, and caught her out back getting a suntan. He was hot for her from that minute; I think he took about a week longer finishing the job than he had to, just so he could hang out with her. Not that Teddi was fighting him off. I mean, she was so gorgeous, and he's so handsome, it was like they belonged together. Poor Tommy was feeling tossed aside — don't you think, Frey?"

"Definitely. He was more sad than jealous, but feeling cast off, for sure."

"Anyone else?"

"Well . . ." Frey looked at Lia, then at Betsy's notebook.

Lia said, "There was this other guy, older,

strange looking — no, that's not what I mean. That is, he looked like the guy in a movie who turns out to be a vampire." She touched her hairline. "What's it called when your hair comes to a point on your forehead?"

"A widow's peak," said Betsy, amused.

"Okay, widow's peak. Dark hair slicked back and cheekbones that kind of stick out and he likes to wear leather. Dark eyes, intense and just a little slanted. Teddi loved the way he looked. But I think he's married."

Frey said, surprised, "You do?"

"Yeah, I do. He never told her where he worked, for example, or what he did for a living, or where he lived. Teddi loved how he was so mysterious, but I think he had a wife and kids. And he's old, like thirty-seven or even older."

"No, he wasn't!" Frey was scandalized.

"Yes, he was. He had lines on his face. And he talked kind of creepy."

"I like the way he talked, so cool. And I never saw any lines."

"You hardly ever saw him. And you won't, either. Look on Teddi's Facebook page — you won't see a single picture of him."

Frey grew thoughtful. "Yeah, now that I think about it . . ."

"Yes, think about it," said Lia. "I was looking at Facebook today, getting ready for Ms. Devonshire's visit, and I couldn't find a single picture of him."

"What's his name?" asked Betsy.

"Preston something, or something Preston," said Frey.

Lia said, "I think it's Preston something — I can't remember if I ever knew his last name. Teddi called him Pres."

"What about the other two? Any sign they were married?"

Frey said, "Sweetie-face Tommy is definitely single. He couldn't afford to be married."

"And Noah was just getting over a divorce. No kids. It was one of those quick-to-get-married, quick-to-be-sorry-about-it things, but he and his ex are still friends."

"God, what a hottie he is!" said Frey. "I mean, fan my brow, as my grandmother used to say." She giggled, then sobered. "Sorry."

"Anyone else?"

"No, not really, but . . ." said Lia, and she exchanged a look with Frey.

Frey said, "Now don't get the wrong idea. Teddi was just friendly and . . . impulsive. She dated a lot of men just once or twice. No harm in that, not at all." Betsy thought

Frey was trying to explain away a lifestyle she thought Betsy might disapprove of.

Lia drew herself up tall and said boldly, "Okay, let's be honest. All three of us were up for a booty call once in a while."

Frey tilted her head to one side. "Well . . . once in a while."

Lia said, "The three we're telling you about were more like her regulars. Men she would invite over, to parties."

"Except the vampire," said Frey. "He'd come by to pick her up, take her someplace."

"Now," said Lia, "twice I came into the kitchen late at night and saw him sneaking down the stairs, dressed like he put his clothes on in the dark." She looked at Betsy. "I was up stirring the marinade for a roast I was preparing. I love to marinate. But you have to pay attention to what you're doing."

"You should get a job as a chef," said Frey.

Lia shrugged, smiling. "I've thought about it, but if I did, I wouldn't want to cook at home anymore."

Frey retorted in mock horror, "In that case, please forget I mentioned it!"

Betsy had a feeling this was an old, familiar exchange, a way of explaining their domestic arrangements to outsiders. She needed to steer them back to the subject at hand. "Lia," she said, "you're sure, then, that Preston had been in the house, upstairs."

Lia nodded. "Up in her bedroom, yes."

"How about Tommy? Or Noah?"

"Yes, both of them have been in her bedroom," said Lia, nodding.

"Yes," said Frey, also nodding.

"Do you each have your own bedroom?"

"Yes, I'm downstairs, with my own little bath; and Frey and Teddi each have — had — a bedroom upstairs with another bigger bath they shared."

Frey said, "There used to be just one bathroom, downstairs, but when our landlord remodeled this place, he turned the smallest bedroom upstairs into a really nice bathroom." She drew her shoulders up and rubbed her upper arms. "The police now think maybe Teddi was drowned in that tub. I've been using the downstairs bathroom ever since they told us that."

Lia said, "Do you want to see it? Scene of the crime, right?"

"Yes, thank you, if you're willing."

Frey led the way. Unlike downstairs, the upstairs was carpeted, or at least the hallway was — as was the one bedroom Betsy got a glimpse of as she walked past it.

The bathroom was really nice. It might

once have been a small bedroom, but for a bathroom it was quite large. The floor and walls had been tiled in a pinky lavender, and its window was set with imitation stained glass in a semiabstract pattern of purple irises. The fixtures were ivory and brushed nickel, with a two-sink travertine vanity, and an enormous bathtub standing alone on claw feet. Betsy stood beside it and found it easy to imagine a strong man pushing a small woman down into its depths.

A large armoire in antique green served as a linen closet.

Frey said sadly, "This used to be my favorite room. I've always wanted to live in a house with a bathroom like this. Our landlord wants to put the house on the market in a few years, that's why he redecorated, but at least he let us help design the upgrades."

"That's why our kitchen has a gas stove with a double oven and amazing counter space," said Lia. "I can really cook in there."

"Teddi's favorite space was the deck out back," said Frey. "She invited the carpenter to our first barbecue. She was still cooking out there after the first snowfall this winter. And Noah came to that last one, too."

Lia said, "And why not? She was so beautiful, and fun, why shouldn't they have

207

made a great couple?" She frowned. "The only problem was, Teddi wasn't ready to settle down, even a little bit, and he was, I think. She was a player, and she was playing him. I mean, she was still seeing Tommy, and there was Pres, too. I tried to warn her about Pres, but she wouldn't listen."

"I bet she heard you, loud and clear," said Frey. "She just didn't care. She wasn't really serious about any of them, so she would think it didn't matter that Pres might be married. And anyhow, maybe he wasn't."

Lia raised one finger and said thoughtfully, "Mrs. Pres might have taken it seriously, if there was a Mrs. Pres and she found out about Teddi."

Frey gaped at her, then looked at Betsy. "Wow," she said. "Is that like a clue?"

"Do you know if this possible wife of Pres's might have known about the therapy pool at Watered Silk?" Betsy asked Lia.

"There's too many ifs in that question," said Lia.

Betsy nodded. "You're right. But so long as the subject has come up, did either of you know about the pool?"

Big-eyed with alarm, the two were quick to declare ignorance.

"Did Teddi?"

Lia and Frey consulted each other silently;

the look between them showed uncertainty and raveling loyalty. "No," Lia decided, and Frey nodded agreement. But Betsy could tell they weren't sure.

Betsy sighed significantly to encourage them to rethink their reply, and went for a closer look at the armoire. It was a beautiful thing, possibly a real antique, though the paint job was obviously recent.

Betsy touched its shining surface and the door opened itself under her hand.

"The latch doesn't always catch," said Frey.

Curious, Betsy pulled the door the rest of the way open. It was shelved top to bottom and there were stacks of thick towels and washcloths, numerous perfumed soaps and shampoos, half scented in strawberry and half in lavender, and a shelf devoted to feminine products and cosmetics, carefully divided in half with a space between them. The bottom shelf held bed linens: a few sheets and pillowcases edged in lace.

"Those are Teddi's," said Frey. "Aren't they beautiful? They're antiques, they belonged to her great-great-grandmother. We don't use them, we keep the ones we use on our beds in our rooms. These are here to be ornamental. Like, *decor.*" She used the word self-consciously.

Two pillowcases sat on top of the stack. Betsy could see that their fabric was worn thin, and as she looked closely, she noticed that they were edged not with lace but with Hardanger embroidery. Frowning, she bent and reached in to pull one out.

"Um," began Lia, but Frey gestured at her to be silent.

Betsy unfolded the pillowcase. The patterns, skillfully done, looked familiar. The edging was Spider Web Flowers, and here was the lovely, complex pattern called Edelweiss.

A penny dropped. "Is there a sheet that goes with this pillowcase?" Betsy asked.

"Yes," said Frey, and she stooped to reach to the bottom shelf. "Now where — ?" She lifted the two other sets of bed linen. "Why, that's funny." She straightened and looked at Betsy with a puzzled expression. "It's gone."

# THIRTEEN

"Oh, that's impossible!" cried Lia, crowding Frey out of the way as she reached into the armoire. She lifted the other sheets, then pulled them all out, tumbling them onto the tiled floor.

"Careful, careful!" warned Frey.

"But of course it's here. Oh my God, Teddi will have a cow —" She cut herself off and, pressing both hands to her face, turned away. "Sorry, sorry!" she said in a strange, high voice. "Oh, Teddi!"

Frey immediately pulled her away from the wardrobe and embraced her. "It's all right, it's all right," she said.

"I can't believe she's gone!" wept Lia. "She was so *alive*!"

"I know, I know," said Frey, who was looking apologetically at Betsy over Lia's shoulder.

Betsy said, "I'm sorry this has upset you. Maybe this was a bad idea. Do you want me to leave?"

"Maybe that's best," moaned Lia.

"No!" said Frey, releasing Lia and holding her at arm's length. "Now you listen to me, Lia Perrin. You agreed with me that we should take every opportunity to help find out who did this terrible thing to Teddi. Ms. Devonshire just now found something that the police missed. It may be important. So pull yourself together and stop being messy. Okay? *Okay?*"

"Okay," said Lia, sniffing and nodding. "Yes, okay."

"Good girl." Frey turned to Betsy. "Is the missing bedsheet important?"

"I don't know how important it is, but it's definitely a clue. Someone brought the missing sheet to my shop, torn and dirty. She found it in her garbage bin, with no idea how it got there."

Lia whirled to face Betsy. "How did that happen? Who put it there?"

"I don't know. But it will be helpful to try to find out who took it away from here. Did either of you take it, perhaps to show it to someone, or even to wrap around something?"

"No, no, the only person who ever handled those bedclothes was Teddi," said Frey. "Even when we were cleaning in here, she insisted on being the only one to take them out and put them back, and we mostly just dusted around them. They were too fragile to survive much handling, she said."

"That's right," seconded Lia. "One thing that made us good roommates was that we never touched anything that wasn't ours. And it helped that we each had our own bedroom."

"May I see Teddi's?" asked Betsy.

"You show her," Lia said to Frey. "I can't go in there."

Teddi's bedroom wasn't large, but it was tastefully decorated in deep pink and silver with pale pink accents. The bed was thickly draped with a rose-pink duvet over a pale pink dust ruffle, and the border of the tufted headboard had been painted silver. The wall behind it had been hand-painted with a gnarled tree covered with pale pink flowers visited by silver butterflies. The carpet was silver-gray.

One pink wall was covered with pen-and-ink and watercolor portraits and landscapes, some framed and others held on by painter's tape. Betsy recognized Lia and Frey in two of the drawings. The paintings were well done, though not quite professional. A lowercase wooden initial *t*, painted silver, was centered over a deep pink Ikea desk and chair. A silver laptop computer sat on the desk, its lid closed, and beside it stood a plain glass vase holding a single branch of silk cherry blossoms.

"Teddi bought a capital *T* for this wall, but decided it looked too much like a cross and replaced it with the lowercase *t,*" said Frey.

"Was she anti-Christian?" asked Betsy.

"Oh, no, not at all! She went to church twice a year, even after her parents retired to Florida. She just didn't want a cross . . . in her bedroom." Frey shrugged and looked uncomfortable.

"I understand. Is all this artwork hers?" asked Betsy.

"Yes, all of it. She even painted the wall."

"That tree is amazing," said Betsy, turning to look at it again.

Frey said, "She loved to paint and draw. She did what-do-you-call-them, like cartoons — caricatures, that's it, and landscapes and people. There are whole albums of her work, not just the things on this wall."

"Would there by any chance be a drawing of this fellow Pres?"

Frey stared at her as if suddenly realizing she was sporting a halo. "My *God,* I never thought about that! Yes, yes, she did! You are incredible, even the police never thought of that!" Frey ran to the bedroom door and pulled it open. "Lia! Lia!" she called. "Get Teddi's albums out!"

"What for?" Lia called from downstairs.

"To look for a drawing of Pres!"

"Who?"

"Drawing! Sketch! Of Pres!"

"Holy cow, I never thought of that!"

Frey, pleased and excited, turned back to Betsy. "Is there anything else I can show you up here before we go back downstairs?"

Betsy shook her head, then thought of another question. "Was Teddi using birth control?"

"Yes, of course. She was on Enovid." She offered a sideways smile. "We're all on Enovid, actually."

"Apparently Teddi told someone she sometimes forgot to take her daily pill. Could that be true?"

"I don't know. She was kind of a space cadet, it's true, so it would be just like her, but I don't know if that's what happened. I mean, I never looked at her meds or in her jewelry box. We all kept our meds and anything pricey in our own bedrooms so we could lock them up during parties. Because you never know, right?"

"Right," Betsy agreed. "Do you know where in her bedroom she kept her birth control pills?"

"No — and anyway, why do you want to know that?"

"Because the autopsy showed she was pregnant. And I —"

"Oh my God! Oh my *God*! Are you sure?"

"The medical examiner's report said she was ten weeks along."

"But then — Could that be why . . . ?"

"Possibly."

"Oh my God!" Frey turned to lean against the door and gasped brokenly, trying not to weep. "I can't believe it, this is so awful!" She thumped on the door with her fist, twice, hard. "This is so *sad*!"

Betsy put her hands on Frey's shoulders. "I'm sorry. I thought you knew. Didn't the police say anything?"

"No, they never said anything about that!" Frey turned, shrugging off Betsy's hands. Her own hands pressed against her cheeks. Tears poured out of her eyes, wetting her fingers. "This is so wrong! I can't believe it!" she shouted angrily.

Suddenly the door pushed against her. "What's going on in there?" demanded a voice. Lia's.

Frey hastily stepped aside and opened the door. "Lia, did you know Teddi was pregnant?"

"Really?" She looked at Betsy, who nodded. "So *that's* what it was."

"What what was?" asked Frey.

Lia came into the room, walked to the window, and pulled aside a very pale pink sheer curtain to look out briefly before turning back. "I kind of wondered what was going on with her," she said to Betsy, her face full of grief. "She'd gotten odd, kind of moody. She wasn't eating junk food — which she loved — and wasn't partying so much."

Frey said, "Yes, I noticed it, too. But I never guessed *that*. I thought maybe it was something at work."

Lia nodded, "Me, too. So I finally asked her about a week before she" — Lia choked over the word — "died, if something was going on. She said everything was going to be fine. You see what I mean about odd? Not that everything was fine, but *was going to be fine.* I didn't remember that till later."

"So usually she was good about taking her daily Enovid?" asked Betsy. She was trying to get a straight answer from them.

Both girls shrugged. "I never asked her about it," said Frey.

"So that's how it happened," said Lia. "She *was* kind of a bubble-brain."

Frey said to Betsy, "Go ahead and look.

They shouldn't be hard to find. Only . . . will you look on your own? I don't think I could stand going through her things just yet." Frey went to stand by Lia at the window, folding her arms tightly, her eyes cast down. Lia put an arm around Frey's shoulders.

There was a pink chest of drawers next to the closet door. Above it a big poster featured just three words: DREAM SEEK ACHIEVE. Betsy opened the top right-hand drawer. It was packed full of thong panties in every color. As she rummaged through the drawer, she asked, "When are Teddi's parents going to arrive?"

Frey replied, "Tomorrow. Her body is going to be released any day, or so I've been told. They're going to take her back to Florida with them." She choked on a sob, a sound echoed by Lia.

The other little drawer was full of toiletries, mostly fingernail polish, but also a nearly empty prescription bottle of a medicine Betsy couldn't identify and a round plastic container of Enovid, the kind that displays a month's worth in individual spaces. The user punches one pill out of the foil bottom every day. They were about half finished — but there were pills not punched out here and there, just as Tommy had said

Teddi told him.

"Did you find them?" asked Frey.

"Yes." Betsy put the packet back in the drawer and closed it.

"Did she skip some days?"

"I'm afraid so."

"She should've gotten that kind the doctor slides under the skin of your arm!" said Lia fiercely. "Stupid girl! Stupid, stupid, stupid!" She ran out of the room.

"It may not have been being pregnant that got her killed," offered Frey tentatively.

"That's true. Maybe the man who got her pregnant was pleased — some are, you know."

"Yes, I know," Frey said, but her tone of voice indicated she didn't know any man like that.

"Let's go see if Lia found a drawing of Pres," said Betsy.

They found Lia downstairs, in the kitchen by the sink. The water was turned on full force in an attempt to drown out the sounds of her wailing.

"Lia, Lia darling!" called Frey, running to her, putting one arm around her, shutting off the water with the other. "Hey, now, pretty baby, what's the matter? Calm down, calm down, everything's gonna be all right!"

"Oh, Frey, oh, Frey, I can't stand this, I

don't know how to deal with this!" sobbed Lia. "This is all so *wrong!*"

"I know, sweetie, I know. And I agree. But we have someone here who can help put things back together, at least a little bit. So come on, dry those tears, stiffen your spine, and let's show Ms. Devonshire how helpful we can be, okay?"

"Yes, I guess that's right." Lia sniffed lengthily, wiped her eyes with the edges of her hands, and blew a gusty breath. "All right, I'm finished, at least for now."

"Good girl." Frey looked around the kitchen and saw a box of tissues. She pulled out several and handed them to Lia. "Dry your eyes and show us what you found in Teddi's art albums."

"Yes, of course." Lia looked shakily at Betsy, who was standing beside the big, squashy couch. "I'm sorry I lost it back there."

"I can't even imagine your pain," said Betsy. "I'm sorry to be inflicting this on you."

"Oh, I was an even bigger mess when the police were here," said Lia with a tremulous smile.

"Yes, she was, you should have seen her," said Frey, starting for the couch. "Come on."

Lia pouted. "You weren't such a big help, either," she said, following.

"I know, I know. But say, did you find anything?"

"As a matter of fact, I did. I can't believe the police didn't think to ask about it. They were in her bedroom for over an hour, so they saw her artwork, signed and everything."

"The two portraits she did of you were quite good," said Betsy.

"Yeah, well, we posed for those," said Lia. "She did the ones of Pres from memory because he refused to pose for her." By now she had just about recovered herself, and only let out an occasional sniff. She opened the first of two scrapbooks sitting on the coffee table. She had marked two pages with tablespoons. "It's what I had at hand," she said defensively.

"Never mind, let's see what you found," said Frey.

On the first marked page was a cocktail napkin with a smear of lipstick on a corner of it, which featured a thick-line caricature — probably drawn with a light brown eyebrow or eyeliner pencil. It was just the head of a handsome man, drawn in profile, with a straight nose; a high forehead marked by a widow's peak; a firm, manly chin; and a sensual curl to the wide mouth. The large, slanted eyes had long lashes. It was done with few lines, more a suggestion of a face than a detailed portrait, but the effect was striking and eloquent; Betsy felt she would know the man if ever she came across him.

"Now that's remarkable, really clever," she said.

"It kind of exaggerates him, I think," said Frey. "He's not that handsome."

"I agree," said Lia. "And yet, it *is* him."

"What's on the other page you have marked?" asked Betsy.

It was a trio of pen-and-ink portraits, done on a single page from an artist's sketch pad. The largest was of the head and shoulders of a handsome man, recognizably the subject of the caricature but more realistically drawn. Again, the widow's peak split the top of the high forehead, and the dark hair on either side was combed straight back. The eyes were dark and intense, almost glowering under slightly arched eyebrows, the wide mouth turned down at the corners. The expression was that of someone intensely interested in the viewer. Whether that interest was friendly or threatening was beyond the artist's ability to signify — or perhaps ambiguity was what the artist was trying to capture. The two smaller drawings were a three-quarter profile of Pres smiling, which put Betsy in mind of C. S. Lewis's devil Screwtape, and a full-length version of him, very slim in tight-fitting jeans, dress boots, and a leather jacket with the collar turned up.

"Very theatrical," said Betsy. Why young women were attracted to sinister young men was a conundrum that Betsy could not solve. She remembered her own youth, when she was that way, but could not now remember why.

"He probably isn't as dangerous as he looks," said Frey.

"Of course he isn't, it's a trick, a . . . a *pose* he uses to get gullible girls' attention!" asserted Lia.

"You're probably right," said Frey, and to Betsy, "She generally is."

"May I borrow these drawings?" asked Betsy.

"You know, I don't think so," said Lia. "I think we should give them to the police."

"You're right, of course, you're absolutely right."

"But I can scan them on my computer and send them to you," said Frey. "Maybe I should also post them on my Facebook page, too?"

"No, don't do that," Betsy said quickly.

"That could be a dangerous thing to do. But first thing tomorrow, do contact the investigator who talked with you and tell him what you've found."

---

## FOURTEEN

Betsy called Godwin, as promised, as soon as she got home. She was sitting in the upholstered chair in her living room. On her lap, purring, was a half grown Siamese tomcat.

"You brought home a *cat*? What's Sophie going to say about that?"

"So far, nothing. She's in her basket under the window thinking bad thoughts at me."

Connor, sitting on the couch, glanced over at Sophie and chuckled.

" 'You're a better man than I am, Gunga Din,' " quoted Godwin. "So what else happened?"

Betsy obediently launched into a description of her visit to Lia and Frey. When she'd finished, she asked, "Goddy, where do young people go clubbing nowadays?"

"Straight young people?"

Uh-oh, Betsy thought. "Yes."

"You're asking *moi*?" he returned, mock

surprised.

"I know, I know, but I have to start asking somewhere. I want to show those drawings around, and I haven't gone clubbing since I moved here from San Diego."

"And probably some while before?" he asked slyly.

"Goddy . . ."

"All right, all right, sorry. Let's see, how young are these people?"

"Mid-twenties, college-educated most of them, respectably employed — except one of them. Tommy Shore is playing above his pay grade. Bowling's probably more his style."

"You'd be surprised at how many young professionals will take a night to go bowling. It's inexpensive and fun."

"All right, and you make a good point — Teddi mentions bowling on her Facebook page. But I don't think this fellow Pres goes trolling for impressionable young women at bowling alleys."

"Point taken. The warehouse district on the edge of downtown Minneapolis is popular — and I would imagine someone who looks as sinister as the man those girls described would do well there. But it's maybe a little rough for people like Teddi and Lia and Frey. Suburban moderns like them prefer Uptown."

Uptown, Betsy knew, was a section of Minneapolis quite separate from downtown. Smaller, shaggier, without high-rises or business offices, it featured ethnic restaurants, boutique shopping, movie theaters, and nightclubs. Every summer an enormous art fair clogged its streets.

"Okay, thanks, Goddy."

She hung up. The young cat, tiring of Betsy, jumped down and climbed up on Connor. He stroked him and said, "He's rather skinny, isn't he?"

"The girls said he barfs a lot. He seems lively enough, it may just be they've been feeding him the wrong food." In the kitchen was a plastic grocery bag with seven small cans of cat food. "He also needs a trip to the vet for another little problem."

Connor crossed his legs, looking alarmed, and Betsy laughed.

"Hey, Sophie's fixed," said Betsy. She thought for a moment, then raised a forefinger. "Have you ever read John D. MacDonald?"

"Sure! Great writer back in the sixties and seventies. Tough guy. Why?"

"He wrote a biography called *The House Guests,* which focused on the two tomcats his family shared their home with. He said

227

something . . ." She thought some more, then quoted: " 'Owning an unneutered tomcat is curiously akin to working in some menial position for one of the more notorious lotharios of show business.' "

Connor burst into laughter. Startled, the kitten jumped down, looked around the room, and spied Sophie, whose eyes widened in alarm at his attention.

He walked slowly toward her, and she rose to her feet. Sophie's long fur made her seem even larger than her twenty-one pounds. Thai, on the other hand, was small, smooth-coated, and couldn't have weighed more than three or four pounds.

Sophie opened her mouth and gave her strangely thin, high-pitched cry, and when Thai continued his approach, she hissed.

Then he belted her in the chops with his paw.

Connor got there before Betsy could. Laughing, he scooped up Thai. "No, no, no!" he said. "Bad cat, bad cat!"

Betsy knelt beside Sophie to look for blood or other damage. Fortunately, there was none. But Sophie was speechless with shock and outrage. She kept trying to look past Betsy for her new enemy.

"There, there, Sophie," crooned Betsy. "Did that nasty little kitty hurt my darling big cat?"

Sophie let out a mew.

"I know, darling, I know. But it's just temporary. We'll find a home very quickly for that awful other cat."

"Achhhhh," hissed Sophie, catching sight of the Siamese, now standing on Connor's shoulder and looking at her.

"*Row!*" cried Thai. He jumped, but Connor caught him before he could get to the floor.

"Hold on, pal!" said Connor, struggling to contain the tiny animal. He finally succeeded by wrapping both arms around him. After a few moments Thai surrendered. He looked up at Connor with those sapphire eyes, patted him on the front of his sweater, and began to purr.

"Oh, lord," sighed Betsy.

"Yes," said Connor. "We'd better do something right away about Thai."

"Well, first, he goes to the vet. Nobody is going to want a sick, unneutered tomcat."

While Connor introduced Thai to the litter box in the bathroom, leaving him there behind a closed door afterward, Betsy logged on to the Internet to look up entertainment possibilities in Uptown. She found three that looked good: Chino Latino, Uptown Tavern, and Bar Abilene, which

Tommy had mentioned. The last had a Facebook page with lots of photos, an article entitled "Craft Beers," and a look-ahead at *Cinco de Mayo*. There was also a curious little sidebar put together by the manager, who was either an old man or a connoisseur of old-fashioned newspapers, because he called it "Remembering Walter," after Walter Winchell, the hugely famous former gossip columnist of radio and the *New York Daily Mirror.* A note under the title stated: "Our most widely read feature!"

The column consisted of snippets of gossip about regular customers. "Maggie D has a brand new recipe for happiness, and is he good lookin'!" read one. "Is Joe the Head ever goin' to master the salsa?" read another. "A little Byrd told us The Willowy One is infanticipating! Club soda from now on, sweetie!" Next, "Who's the clumsiest bar maid in the Twin Cities? Drop by and cast your ballot for Linnie!" And so forth.

Betsy was amused by the snippets, and could have read on, but she had things to do. She went to check her e-mail.

She was pleased to find a reply from Jill, who said she would be delighted to review the Morgan lap stand.

Another e-mail came from Thistle. "The chief of staff here isn't telling us anything about Wilma's death, which makes us think it's probably murder. So sad, and lots of us are angry about it. But really hope you are going to continue the class on punch needle."

Betsy replied in the affirmative.

Next was an e-mail from Emil Pedersen of Just Kidding, which was the name of the goat farm where Tommy lived.

"Thomas Shore is a fine young man, very honest, and he works hard. He doesn't drink too much. He has his own car and doesn't get tickets. He is kind to animals."

Braced by that good recommendation, Betsy logged off and went to bed.

The next morning Betsy found a downloadable file containing the drawings of the outré Pres. She printed them out and put them on the table next to Connor's plate of coddled eggs on toast.

"Would you like to go out hunting this weekend?" she asked when he picked up the printouts with a questioning air.

"Shall I bring along my little derringer loaded with a silver bullet?" he asked, lifting the printouts a little higher.

"He only thinks he's a vampire," she replied with a laugh. Then she added, more soberly, "But he may be a murderer."

231

Godwin looked at the printouts down in the shop later that morning. "This is going to sound weird, but I think I've seen him somewhere. Not out clubbing, not at a party, but doing something else. I think Teddi exaggerated his weirdness — because she liked it, maybe? I mean, I'm thinking he sold me something, like in a store." He frowned over the drawings for a minute, then shook his head. "Can't tell you where it was, sorry."

One piece of information Betsy had gotten from Frey and Lia was the name of the contractor their landlord had hired to build the deck behind their rented house. When Betsy phoned him to ask how to contact Noah Levesque, he gave an exasperated snort.

"Now look," he fumed, "I am not the owner of a dating service, nor am I a giver of advice to the lovelorn! If you want —"

"Wait a minute, wait a minute," Betsy interrupted — then had to take a calming swallow as her request brought a sudden memory of an old woman's voice making the same demand. "I am probably old enough to be Mr. Levesque's mother, and

I'm not in the least interested in having an affair with him. I want to speak to him about a project he worked on last summer."

"If you have a building project in mind, I'm the person to talk to about it."

"I don't want to talk to him about building a deck, either."

The penny dropped, but into the wrong slot. "Oh, Jeez, are you a cop?"

"No, I am privately investigating a case and I think he can give me some useful information."

"Oh, yeah?" His snort this time was less emphatic. Then he said, "What the hell. Tell you what, you give me your name and number and I'll ask him to call you."

After thanking him and hanging up, Betsy called the Excelsior Police Department and asked to speak to Sergeant Mike Malloy.

"All right, whatcha got?" Malloy growled at her a minute later.

"I went to talk to Lia Perrin and Frey Kadesh last night and found a pair of antique pillowcases in the armoire in their upstairs bathroom."

"And?"

"The pillowcases were edged in Hardanger embroidery. Shortly after Teddi Wahlberger's body was discovered, a woman came into my shop with an antique bedsheet she found in her garbage bin with the same pattern of Hardanger on its leading edge."

"And?"

"The bedsheet isn't hers. She found it when she went out at the last minute to put a bag of trash into the bin, which she'd put out to be picked up the night before. It was stuffed in with her garbage. Lia and Frey say the last time they looked, that same bedsheet was in the armoire, but it's gone missing."

"So how come this lady brings the bedsheet to you?"

"Because I wrote a little something about Hardanger on my web site, and she saw it and wanted to know if she could rescue and reuse the embroidery on the ruined bedsheet. I told her how to do it. Then I saw the pillowcases in the armoire and realized the pattern on the found bedsheet was the same. I'm wondering if perhaps the murderer didn't wrap Teddi's body in the sheet to carry it to Watered Silk. And if perhaps on his way home afterward, he tossed it in a handy bin sitting on the curb."

"You wouldn't by some chance have the name and address of the woman who found it in her garbage bin?"

"As a matter of fact, I do." Betsy gave him

the woman's name, Edith Ball, and her address.

Godwin was standing, agog, at the other end of the checkout desk, listening to her end of the conversation. "Wow," he breathed, "you've done it again, outsleuthed the police! Oh, Betsy, you're so *clever!*"

"No, it was just luck. A coincidence. I just touched the door of the armoire and it opened, and I saw the pillowcases on a shelf. Frey told me they were Teddi's great-great-grandmother's, too fragile to be used. I recognized the Hardanger pattern — a really gorgeous one, very elaborate — as the same one on Mrs. Ball's sheet."

"But suppose Mrs. Ball is mixed up in this somehow?"

"If she were," Betsy said, reasonably, "then under no circumstances would she be carrying it around asking how to save the embroidery."

"Good point," Goddy agreed. "Like I said: You're so clever!"

The phone rang after lunch, and Betsy answered it. "Crewel World, Betsy speaking, how may I help you?"

There was a brief pause. Then a man said, "I think I may have the wrong number."

"Are you Noah Levesque?"

"Uh, yeah? Who is this?"

"My name is Betsy Devonshire, and I'd like to talk to you about the murder of Teddi Wahlberger."

"Oh, shit! I beg your pardon, but dammit, I think I've done all I can with regard to that mess. I'm sorry as hell she's dead, but I'm not the father of her baby and I don't want to talk any more about it."

"Did you ever go skinny-dipping with her at Watered Silk?" asked Betsy.

The pause this time was longer. "Who are you again?"

"My name is Betsy Devonshire and I want to know if you ever went skinny-dipping in the therapy pool at the Watered Silk Senior Complex. Before you answer that, I will say we may have an eyewitness." Of course, Betsy thought to herself, if there had been an eyewitness, she was now dead. But she wasn't going to mention that to Mr. Levesque.

The pause this time was so long that Betsy began to think he had quietly hung up. But she bit her tongue and waited, and at last he spoke. "What do you want?" His voice was quiet.

"I want to talk to you."

"I'm pretty sure I don't want to talk to you."

"Why not? You know you're suspected by the police. If you didn't murder Teddi, you should want the real murderer to be caught."

"The real murderer is the person who got her pregnant."

"But you didn't know until just recently that you weren't the person who got her pregnant."

Another pause, this one not so long. "I can tell you right now, I don't know a damn thing that could help you."

"Neither of us knows that until we talk."

"Lady, you got an answer for everything, don't you?"

"Hardly. If I did, I wouldn't need to talk with you. Please, why don't you suggest a time and we'll find a public place to meet."

Noah Levesque was even handsomer than his picture on Teddi's Facebook page. He was perhaps thirty-five years old, about five eight or five nine, but so lanky he looked taller. His workman's tan had not entirely faded even this late into winter. He wore old skinny jeans and a fleece-lined denim jacket over a heavy flannel shirt, which did not disguise his broad shoulders and narrow waist. There were faint laugh lines around his eyes and on his forehead, and he had a dimple in one cheek that deepened dramatically when he smiled, which he did as he sat down.

Noah's brown hair was thick and just a little unruly, his dark brown eyes were densely lashed, and his teeth were white and even. His hands were large and blunt-fingered, without rings. And, though it was only noon, he had a beard shadow. "Hi," he said, in a rich voice with just a hint of sand in it.

Betsy, drinking in the delicious details, wished she were twenty years younger, thirty pounds lighter, and inclined to whisk handsome strangers off to Cancun for a winter week's romp in the sun.

They were at the Barleywine. Leona gave Betsy an approving smile when she saw the two of them in the same booth that Betsy had shared with Tommy. That Leona had picked up on Betsy's sudden fantasy — and approved! — recalled her to her mission, and made her get a grip.

Noah and Betsy greeted each other politely — he seemed a little wary. He ordered a turkey wrap and chips and, in a show of confidence, a big mug of Don't-Be-Afraid-of-the-Dark ale. Betsy had her favorite multilettuces salad — this time with a scatter of shrimp — and a Diet Coke. They chatted about the weather — cold and snowy — until their food arrived.

"So what do you want to talk to me about?" he asked after taking a bite of his wrap.

Betsy speared a shrimp and got right to the point. "Were you in love with Teddi?"

Her directness obviously surprised him. He hesitated, then replied with a little nod, "I think I was falling in love with her."

"Was she in love with you?"

"Not . . . yet."

She pressed. "Were you surprised to learn you weren't the father of her baby?"

He put his wrap down, his face troubled. "I don't think I like the way this conversation is going."

Betsy ate her shrimp, speared a tomato. She asked, "Where do you think it's going?"

"I think you're going to try to make me admit I was angry with her because she was playing around."

"Were you?"

"First of all, we were both free to date other people; second, I didn't know she was playing to that extent." He picked up his wrap.

"But you knew she was seeing other men."

He shrugged as he took a bite, then said around it, "Sure. She was young and beautiful and taking advantage of her youth and beauty, living life full on, right up to the hilt. She was enjoying herself. I couldn't blame her for that."

"Were you dating other people, too?"

He looked over the little heap of potato chips on his plate as if it held the answer to her question. "No," he said at last.

She made a swift mental note: *He doesn't know what I might know.*

"How did you meet?" she asked, changing tack.

He took another big bite of his wrap, chewed and swallowed. "Through my job. Dick Richards — he's the owner of the house she lived in with those two other girls — hired Maurice and Company to build a deck, and they hired me."

"Did they supply the crew, or did you?"

He offered a friendly smile at her ignorance. "What crew? It was just a ground-level deck, they only needed one person."

"So they hired you? You aren't an employee?"

"I'm a freelancer, I work for whichever contractor is looking to hire me for a job. I do demo — demolition — and drywall, roofing, framing —" Relieved to be wandering into familiar territory, he put down his wrap to count his skills off on his fingers.

"Flooring, plastering, painting, even a little plumbing. I work twelve, fourteen hours a day spring, summer, fall. In the winter I do hardly any work so I can collect unemployment." He lifted one eyebrow and smiled a charming, crooked smile, again deepening that dimple. "Anyway, one of them, Richards or Maurice, I'm not sure which, consulted with Teddi, Frey, and Lia to come up with a date for me to come by to start the build. Teddi happened to be the one at home the day I showed up. She'd taken the day off from work, I learned later. But nobody answered the door. I went around back to at least start measuring, and there she was, out in the yard, getting a tan." He smiled, remembering. "She was just about the prettiest woman I ever saw, just a little bit of a thing, but hot. And she was friendly and nice, we hit it off right from the start."

Betsy ignored the urge to question the intelligence of an adult woman who considered lying in the sun in her backyard the equivalent of being at home waiting for the doorbell to ring. "When was this?" she asked.

"Last year, second week in May." He ate a potato chip. "A real pretty day, warm and sunny, I remember that — that and Teddi's yellow bikini."

"And you asked her out to dinner that same evening," Betsy guessed.

"No, she made me wait about a week. One day while I was cleaning up, getting ready to go home, she invited me in to supper. Her roommate Lia cooked a great curry that just about melted my back teeth — they all three like spicy food, and fortunately, so do I. We dated pretty steady from then on."

"How did she let you know she was pregnant?"

He stiffened. Now they were coming to it. "She sent me a text saying we needed to talk. Urgent, she said it was. I called her as soon as I got home, but she had company and said she'd call me back later, which made me think maybe it wasn't so urgent. And she didn't call until the next morning. And she was kind of flip about it, she says, 'Hi, baby daddy,' and I said, 'Whoa, what does that mean?' and she says, 'What do you think it means?' and I said, 'Don't tell me you're pregnant?' and she says, 'Yes, and guess who the father is?' and I said, 'It's not me.' "

He leaned across the table toward Betsy, his triumphant, angry smile not reaching his eyes. "And I was right!"

"But you didn't know that when she told you."

He sat back, took a deep drink of his ale, and looked at her over the top of his mug. "No, I didn't, that's true. But I was pretty sure it wasn't."

"Why?"

"Because I am pretty damn careful about that sort of thing. Women like Teddi sometimes aren't, you know. She was having a wonderful life, dancing every dance, drinking every drink, going to every party. I wanted to laugh and have fun with her — and also take care of her, okay? But that isn't what she wanted — until this happened. Then she was scared, then she *did* want someone to take care of her, tell her what to do. But I don't think she knew for sure who the father was. I think she was trying it on with different men."

"Why did you think that?"

He shrugged and ate a potato chip. "I just did. I heard the cops took DNA samples from another guy plus me. And that they were looking for more candidates." He offered, umprompted, "I did ask her what she planned to do about it — you know, like get an abortion, keep the baby, give it away, plan an open adoption —"

"You seem to be familiar with the available choices," Betsy said. "Have you been through this scenario before?"

He looked surprised, then nodded. "Yes, a few years back. My sister got pregnant, and she wasn't married. She went round and round for weeks about what to do. Her boyfriend left town, the worthless piece of — Anyhow, she had all those choices. She finally chose open adoption. She had a girl, Jillian, a cute little kid who looks a lot like her daddy. When the boyfriend came back to town still not ready to step up to the plate, I went and had a talk with him, and this time he moved to Atlanta, which in my opinion is just barely far enough away."

"But your sister knew who the father was. Why did you think Teddi didn't?"

He ate another potato chip in two crisp bites before answering. "Because she didn't call back right away. Because when she did call back she didn't say, 'I'm pregnant and it's your fault.' She was, like, trying it on, to see what I'd say. When I said it wasn't mine, she didn't blow up at me. She said, 'Well, I think it is,' and I said, you ever hear of a DNA test, and she started to cry, so I hung up. I never heard from her again."

"Did you kill her, Mr. Levesque?"

"No, I did not."

"Is it true you're divorced?"

He blinked at the swerve in topic, then nodded. "Yes."

"How long were you married?"

"Not quite three years. It ended two years ago. No kids — her choice."

"Do you have any contact with your former wife?"

"Not lately. She's engaged to someone else now."

"Talk to me about skinny-dipping."

He raised his eyebrows in surprise, then took a long pull at his ale without looking at her. "Some people enjoy naked swimming." He put down the sweating mug and wiped his wet fingers on his napkin.

"I'm sure they do. Did you tell the police that you and Teddi used the therapy pool at Watered Silk to go nude bathing?"

"No, of course not." He picked up his wrap.

"Even though you did?"

He said cunningly, "Why do you have to ask? You said something about an eyewitness."

"That's right."

"Are you willing to produce her?"

"How do you know it's a woman?"

"You said it was. Didn't you?" When she merely looked slantwise at him, he tossed down his wrap. "Okay," he dared her, "what did this alleged witness tell you?"

Betsy said, "She showed me the way you

gained entrance: through a wooden door off the alley into the machine room, up the metal stairs, and through the men's locker room to the pool."

Noah was clearly rattled. He quickly said, "But she's crazy, right? A crazy old lady who's liable to say anything."

So he didn't know Wilma was dead. "Was she wrong?"

He looked away for a long while. Betsy bit her tongue and waited. "No," he said at last.

"Who rigged the door?"

"Dunno."

"It wasn't you?"

"Hell, no."

"But you're a carpenter."

"I'm the only carpenter in the county?"

"Who else used the pool?"

"I don't want to say."

"Even to save yourself from a charge of murder?"

"I didn't kill her, and they can't prove I did!"

"I have been involved in a number of cases in which an innocent party was nevertheless arrested for murder."

After another pause for thought, Noah said reluctantly, "That dorky guy, Tommy. He came once."

"Was he the one who showed you the way in?"

"No, he just turned up one night. Brought another guy I never saw before. I don't know who told him. Maybe the guy who came with him."

"Come on, who showed you this back way in?"

"Teddi did. I don't know how she found out — or maybe she told me who told *her*, and I don't remember the name. Seriously, I can't remember. It didn't seem important at the time, you know? It was like a prank, going to the pool. And it wasn't all that wonderful, anyway. The pool isn't very big, there's no diving board, and the water's too hot, like being in a bathtub." He shrugged.

"Who else was there when you and Teddi went?"

"There was a man and another girl."

"Lia? Or Frey?"

"I never saw either of them there. Look, it was only maybe three or four times, okay?

"When was the last time you were there?"

"Some weeks before Christmas, maybe the middle of December. It was snowing like a son of a gun, and we had a hard time getting out of that alley, and I could just see trouble all around if I got stuck, or damaged my truck sliding around back there.

It'd be embarrassing explaining how I came to be in that alley. Plus, I need my truck, can't afford to bang it up."

"But Teddi kept going back."

"I don't know that." He drank the last of his ale and pushed away his plate, with the remnant of his wrap still sitting on it. "Are we about done?" he asked.

"Where were you the night she was drowned?"

Noah tried for a dismissive tone. "As it happened, I was home alone. I caught some kind of bug and was sick for two and half days."

"Did you see a doctor about it?"

"No, it wasn't that serious. But I shut off my phone, just laid on my couch and watched some old movies. Slept a lot between visits to the bathroom." He shrugged. "Threw it off with no aftereffects." He wrinkled his brow. "But that's not much of an alibi, is it?"

"It's not an alibi at all. When did you last see Teddi?"

"About a week before she called to say she was pregnant. Maybe longer."

"Did she hint about it then?"

He frowned, then shook his head. "No, not really. We went out to dinner and were going to go dancing at our usual place, Bar

248

Abilene, but she was in some kind of bad mood, so I brought her home early." He frowned over that for a few moments. "I guess that was a sign, but it went right past me." He sighed. "I thought we were a couple, y'know? I knew she sometimes went out with other guys, but I was putting up with that, thinking fine, let her play, get it all out of her system, right? But when she got pregnant, that meant she wasn't just dating these other men. I was . . . disappointed."

"And maybe a little angry?" asked Betsy.

"No, that wasn't the way it was. I was upset, yes, but once I calmed down I was concerned about her. But she didn't call again — and then I heard she was dead."

"That must've upset you."

He sighed. "Yeah, it did. I was really depressed over it. I liked her, she was more fun than anyone I ever knew — in a nice way, and not . . . mean, I guess is the word, she didn't tease in a mean way, she didn't ever hurt anyone. When she got mad, she didn't yell or call anyone names, she'd just start bawling. Made you want to hug her. She was a good kid, she just wanted to have fun."

Betsy felt a twist of sympathy for Teddi. "Did she cry when she told you she was pregnant?"

"Only when I mentioned getting a DNA test. 'You don't believe me!' she said and started to cry, but I wasn't ready to hear that, so I hung up."

# FIFTEEN

On her return from lunch, Betsy found Godwin winding up a consultation with a customer who was jazzing up a relatively simple needlepoint canvas. He was just closing *The Needlepoint Book,* with its three hundred illustrated stitches. Beside it was a heap of wools, silks, metallics, beads, and charms. The total for the materials would add up to over two hundred dollars, including the needles, new scissors, and laying tool. The hand-painted canvas had been purchased at a sale price, further discounted because it was the customer's birthday, so she was paying more for the materials than the canvas — not an uncommon event.

The customer, a prosperous-looking matron in her middle forties, was wreathed in smiles as she left. Godwin turned to Betsy and said, "So?"

"He seems nice enough. He's unwilling to say he was in love with Teddi or that he was angry with her for being unfaithful to him. And he's got no alibi at all. He's really good-looking," she added irrelevantly.

"So what do you think? Is he a murderer?"

"I don't know. He had been skinny-dipping a couple of times with Teddi at Watered Silk." She thought for a moment. "Of course that doesn't necessarily make him a killer."

Godwin said, "But he's a carpenter, so he could be the one who rigged that back door."

"He denied it — and before I could conclude that he might have done it, I'd have to connect him to Watered Silk, either as an employee or as someone hired to work there. Or maybe as someone with a relative living there. I don't think he would just wander by accident down a narrow alley and on spec cut his way into a machine room. There would be no way he'd know that to be a back way to an indoor swimming pool. And something else: I told him I had a witness to the goings-on in the pool, and he said she was a crazy woman, liable to say anything. So he must have known I was talking about Wilma. On the other hand, I don't think he knows she's dead."

Upstairs that evening, Betsy found that

Connor had become very close to Thai. The cat, still a little tender in his hindquarters, was lying across the back of the couch, one dark paw just touching Connor's shoulder. Connor was knitting a tiny green cardigan that was meant to be a gift at Jill's baby shower in the summer.

He looked up and smiled at Betsy as she came into the living room — Sophie had detoured into the kitchen, where her dish lay hidden in a cabinet. In another minute she would start demanding her suppertime pittance of Science Diet cat food. That and an equal pittance in the morning gave vitamins at least a fighting chance against the junk food she cadged from customers all day.

"How's Thai doing?" asked Betsy.

"Much better." The cat had come home from the vet yesterday sore and still confused from the anesthetic. The "cone of shame" he'd been given was gone; his distress at wearing it was so obvious, Connor had taken it off and thereby made it his responsibility to keep the animal from pulling out his stitches.

The two sat and talked while Betsy decompressed from her day in the shop. Then she went into the bedroom and had a conference with her closet. What she thought of as her "good" clothes were appropriate for church or a sedate evening out at a fine restaurant or a meeting with her banker. But what to wear going out clubbing?

She did have a heavily sequined top, bought for a giddy New Year's Eve party years ago, but too out of fashion for an ordinary night on the town.

Finally she went with her old standby: the Little Black Dress. She fancied it up with a sparkly scarf and her most dazzling earrings. She emphasized her eyes and cheekbones with makeup, put on her strappiest sandals — then remembered the weather forecast: sleet turning to snow. She thought for a while of wearing boots and carrying her sandals, then remembered her tendency to leave a trail behind her wherever she went, of purses, shoes, toiletries, even pajamas, hose, and jewelry. She sighed and took off the sandals and put on her high-heeled boots. She stuffed her second-tiniest purse with her driver's license and medical insurance card, forty-five dollars in assorted bills, a lipstick, her smartphone, a tiny notebook and pen, and the folded-up copies of Teddi's drawings of Pres. Connor's admiring look when she came out of the bedroom told her she would do.

He wore a navy blue suit, an ice-blue shirt, and a pale pink tie. His black shoes were polished to a mirror finish.

They put on their winter coats and headed for Uptown. It was a little after 7 p.m.

There was a public, ground-level parking lot behind the Lagoon Theater. Connor, driving, pulled the ticket from the dispenser and found a space near the front end. They came out onto Lagoon Street and paused to take their bearings.

The many lights that ornamented the theater and flanked the nightclubs reflected merrily off the snow piled on curbs, and on the wet streets and sidewalks and the dark windows of passing cars. The air was also wet with a fine sleet. Or maybe it was tiny snowflakes; it was hard to discern. Betsy huddled deeper into her overcoat and was glad she'd decided to wear boots.

They crossed Hennepin and started up it. They passed the Uptown Theater, which was offering a midnight showing of *The Rocky Horror Picture Show* — and had been doing so since the movie was released. Beyond the theater was a hat store featuring fedoras for men and women, and then came Chino Latino, a restaurant and nightclub, where they had reservations for dinner. The entrance led into a long, narrow hallway with a wall made of tufted turquoise leather.

From a very high lectern at the end of the hallway, a black woman smiled down at them. "Reservations?" she asked.

"Sullivan for two at eight," said Connor. "May we wait at the bar?"

"Certainly."

They walked past a deeply sunken dining room to the bar, a long room backed by a ceiling-high, orange-lit mirror lined with glass shelves. On the shelves rested hundreds of bottles of liquor. The room was otherwise dimly lit and the orange color reflected flatteringly off the faces of the customers.

After a brief wait, they found two bar stools. A hasseled-looking bartender took their order for a scotch and water and a glass of pinot noir. "We picked a bad night to come," said Betsy, looking over the crowd. A row of small, tall tables bordered the other side of the narrow room. All were occupied by wildly assorted groups of people: young and middle-aged, black, white, Asian, brown, well dressed or in decidedly casual clothing. One couple even wore cowboy gear.

"Why is this so bad?" asked Connor, also looking around. "Lots of people to ask, don't you think?"

"I was hoping to have a couple of minutes to chat with the bartenders. They're the ones here night after night. But they're too busy right now. A busy man will glance at the drawings and say, 'Nope,' and move on to the next customer."

Which is what happened when the bartender came back to see if either Connor or Betsy wanted a refill. "Uh-uh," he said. "Don't recognize him."

But they got a different reaction from the second bartender. He paused to consider the drawings, rubbing the dark little fringe of whiskers on his chin. "Yeah, I seen him in here before. Nice enough fella, kind of quiet, but sharp eyes, know what I mean? And he drinks nothing but ginger ale with a twist, that's why I remember him."

"How often have you seen him?" asked Betsy.

"Oh, let's see. Five or six times? Maybe more — it takes a while for a face to stick."

"Over how long a period of time?"

"Huh, lemme think. Six months, a year? Probably longer. I been here almost two years, and it could be he's been in before I came, y'know?"

"You know his name?"

That amused him. "Hell, no." And he moved on.

When Betsy and Connor were summoned to their table on the other side of the big room, they were shown to the middle of a row of three dark-painted booths. A single light wanly lit an Asian-style wooden mask on the wall over each one. The mask hanging next to their booth looked authentic, though under it was a label reading "Miso Horney." The waitstaff wore chinos and black T-shirts that announced they were souvenirs of Thailand, some with naughty mottos on them.

The drinks menu came on newsprint and offered cocktails aimed at the youthful: Tootsy Roll, Honolulu Hummer, Raspberry Beret. Connor had another scotch and water, Betsy a Ganesha's Dance "mocktail," which was good if a little sweet.

The waiter told them the food menu featured dishes from "around the equator around the world." They selected the Senegalese peanut curry for two, which came on a single platter.

The waiter did not remember ever seeing Pres.

There is something intimate about sharing a platter. Betsy, after eating a particularly tasty tidbit, searched for another like it and fed it to Connor, and he returned the favor. The curry was spicy enough to heat their lips, and it tasted delicious. They polished off the whole thing in no time at all.

The busboy agreed to look at the copies of the drawings when he came to clear the table. "Somebody can draw really good," was his sage remark. "But I don't know who it is a picture of."

"Thanks for your help," said Connor and, making a comic bit out of looking for eavesdroppers, slipped the fellow a five dollar bill. The young man, who seemed a little slow, echoed the movement before slipping it into one of his pockets with a huge grin.

Then they donned their coats and went out to find that the snow had turned real, falling so thickly that distant objects were obscured as if in a fog. The flakes set sparkles in their hair. Connor took Betsy's gloved hand in his. "Sorry we aren't finding out much."

"We've only just begun. Besides, I really liked that curry."

They crossed Hennepin at Lagoon and walked up the street to the Uptown Tavern. Climbing steps, they found themselves in a long room divided by a lectern, with the restaurant on their right and the bar on their left. The bar was extensive with little, long-legged tables down its center and big-screen TVs near the ceiling, all showing a basketball game — but the sound was turned off and rock music was playing, although not loud enough to destroy conversation.

The DJ on duty was taking a break. Connor and Betsy found a pair of stools at the bar. Connor switched to Coke, Betsy ordered a ginger ale with a twist — "Just to see what it tastes like," she said.

When their drinks came, she showed her drawings to the bartender, a plump Hispanic man with a goatee.

"Ah, yes, I see him in here three, four, fi' time," he said. "He is ver' handsome, kind of quiet, but close, close with his lady."

"Always the same lady?" asked Betsy.

"Oh, not always."

"What else can you tell me about him?"

"He wear a beautiful coat, all dark leather, yes, and long, and he open it and it move" — he made a gesture with both hands. "Like a, a clock — no, a cloak." He smiled, amused. "An' then he order what you order, a ginger ale wit' a twist!"

"Do you know his name?

He had to think. "Ah, yes: Press. Like Elvis Presley, only jus' Press. He act like a movie star, but he drink pop!" And laughing, the bartender went to serve another customer.

The other bartender said he didn't recognize the man in the drawing.

They finished their drinks and went out and just up the street to Bar Abilene.

The snow had already slowed, although about half an inch had already fallen. The sidewalk's fresh white surface was seriously marred by dozens of footprints.

Bar Abilene had a covered patio out front lit by a multitude of old-fashioned incandescent lightbulbs in red, yellow, green, and orange. Loud music could be heard through the wooden doors.

As Connor opened them to enter, he and Betsy were assaulted by a blast of salsa music with its chik-chika rhythms. The room was big and packed with tables. Straight ahead was the bar, with a longhorn steer's skull attached to the back wall. There was a dance floor off to the right, crowded with people doing the salsa, with its fancy footwork and hip-and-shoulder waggle.

Connor asked for a booth and they were led to one near the back corner. The music was deafening and the dancers lively, and the room smelled of spiced hamburger, beer, and mixed drinks.

They sat for a while, studying the menu and watching the dancers.

One couple's movements were beautiful, complex, and coordinated. The woman wore a mid-calf skirt that fell in a straight line when she was barely moving, then flared widely when her partner twirled her.

Another couple danced so closely that they were right up against each other, their hips moving in perfect synchronicity, their eyes locked on each other. Connor nodded toward them, then blinked empathetically and wiped imaginary sweat from his forehead. Betsy laughed.

There were two women who danced so well together it was obvious they were a couple, not two girls merely showing off their moves to attract men.

A short, stocky Latino man wearing a black pinch-brim cap danced with such skill and ease that it was clear he'd grown up hearing this music.

In honor of the music, Betsy and Connor ordered Cuba libres and guacamole — the latter to be prepared at their table. While they waited for it to arrive, Connor swept Betsy onto the dance floor, where he proved to be light of foot and inventive of movement. The dances had no pause between them, and at last, Betsy, out of breath, signaled with a fanning motion of her hand that she had had enough.

They came back to their table to find their drinks waiting and the guacamole ready to be mixed. The waiter, a good-looking man in his forties, wore a tan western shirt and fancy cowboy boots. He expertly mashed the peeled avocado halves in a stone bowl, dashed on the Worcestershire and hot sauces, stirred in the onion and chopped tomato, all very quickly.

"Anything else?" he asked, already looking around to see what else needed his attention.

"Yes," said Betsy, presenting the drawings. "Do you know this man?"

"Say," he said, "I remember watching a young woman do that drawing!" He touched the caricature with a forefinger that had a dab of avocado on it. "Oops," he said, and wiped his finger on a napkin. "I'll get you a fresh napkin, okay?"

"Oh, never mind that," Betsy said. "When was it you saw this being drawn?"

"Oh, I don't remember, maybe a couple months ago. I do remember the drawing, though, because it was so clever. He'd gone away from the table and she got out her eyeliner and did it very fast on a napkin."

"Do you remember anything about the man she drew?" asked Betsy.

He pulled back a little, eyeing her suspiciously. "What's your interest in this?"

"I'm doing a private investigation. The

young woman you remember is dead, and I'm trying to trace her last movements. The man was just a friend of hers, but naturally I'd like to talk to him." This was sort of the truth, Betsy told herself.

"All right, I guess I buy that." He thought briefly. "She seemed like a nice person, but he was, like, totally focused on her, in an almost theatrical way, kind of like Dracula with his next victim." He frowned. "Maybe I'm exaggerating, but there was his exotic look, that long leather coat he wore . . . But it could have been a pose. I mean, maybe he was one of the good guys. But he was just so —"

"Intense?"

"Yes, exactly."

"You didn't by any chance learn the name of the man?"

"Hell, no. Or hers, either."

"May I ask your name?"

"Will McNally. I'm the manager here. But we're busy tonight — and shorthanded. Will you excuse me?"

# Sixteen

Betsy was feeling a little droopy when she came in to work on Monday — not because she was hung over; she'd been careful with her liquor consumption. But the outing had been a failure. Okay, yes, she'd found a new restaurant she'd like to return to, and it was fun to discover that Connor was great at salsa dancing, but the big goal of the outing, to find out who this Pres person was, hadn't been met.

Then a regular customer came in with a problem that took her mind off her failure. Mrs. Cunningham — Betsy had never learned her first name — was in love with a counted cross-stitch pattern by Maxine Gold of an ethereal woods fairy called Chrysella, and wanted to stitch it as a birthday gift for a dear friend. But the friend's living room was done in not quite the same shades of green, and it would seriously clash with the green family of Maxine

Gold's pattern. Mrs. Cunningham was familiar with the custom of changing the colors of a pattern to fit a decor, but this piece had a lot of subtle color changes in it and she was unsure how to make the changes so the new pattern would be coherent.

Betsy called Godwin over for a consultation.

"What colors are you thinking of?" asked Godwin.

"Well, first, I want the fairy to have white hair instead of blonde," said Mrs. Cunningham, "and her dress and wings in shades of brown or russet, buff, and gold instead of green, gray, and ivory."

"Ooooh," said Betsy.

"The front of her dress is ornamented in ivy," Godwin pointed out. "And there are more green leaves in that flowered headdress."

"Yes, well, DMC 320 and 368 would match Glory's living room."

But those weren't the greens the pattern called for.

"Also," said Betsy, having had a minute to think about it, "if you're doing an autumn-themed piece, the ivy leaves could have turned red."

"Well, I hadn't thought to make it

autumn-themed — but, on the other hand, maybe I should," said Mrs. Cunningham.

"It depends on what you're thinking to bring in along with the browns," said Godwin. "Bright, glowing oranges and reds, like DMC 742 and 946, say autumn, but brown-reds like 355 and greeny-tans like 680 don't."

"Hmm . . ." said Mrs. Cunningham.

Half an hour later, she was seated at the library table surrounded by dozens of DMC flosses. Godwin had separated them into families of colors, so she could make the gradations of color come out right.

She was finding a lot to like in the gray-into-brown family, specifically the cool shades of 3782, 3032, 3790, and 3781. And she liked the equally cool gray-violets of 341, 156, 340, and 155. On the other hand, she liked Godwin's suggestion of going for warm tones for the skin, mouth, and eye colors of the fairy. "But don't forget, tow-heads have fairer skin than usual, so you might want to change the pattern's tones there, too," he pointed out.

"This is why I love your shop!" she declared. "You are *so* helpful, and you're willing to let me spread myself out like this — I can't imagine sitting on the floor at Michael's with floss all around me. Not that I would even have thought to do this on my own."

Betsy came to look at the choices she was making, and noticed how she was leaning toward the cool rather than warm shades. Then Betsy glanced again at a picture of the original pattern. "See the veining in the wings?" she asked. "What if you did that in Kreinik silver braid?"

There was a little silence as Mrs. Cunningham visualized the result. "Oh," she said softly, then, "Oh, my, that would be lovely."

After she left, Godwin said smugly, "There goes another satisfied customer." Then he mused, "I wonder if that fairy is a gift for Leona."

"Why would you think that?" asked Betsy.

"Well, they're both Wiccans, you know."

"Yes, I know. But both are solitaries — not members of a coven. And I don't think fairies are Leona's style. She's more into the pragmatic uses of magic. Like brewing."

"Is brewing magic?"

"Well, you take a powder that contains invisible living creatures and mix it with roasted barley sprouts and well water while you recite a spell. Then you boil it in a cauldron, and it will make beer."

Godwin laughed. "All right, magic. But don't you think Leona and Mrs. Cunningham know each other?"

"Sure — the same way you know every gay man in the area."

"Oh. Well, yeah, I see what you mean." A little embarrassed, Godwin went to the checkout desk to file the receipt for Mrs. Cunningham's purchase.

When the phone rang, he picked it up. "Crewel World, Godwin speaking, how may I help you?" he said. He held the phone a little away from his ear. Betsy could hear a frantic voice shouting incomprehensibly. "Hold on, hold on!" said Godwin. "Slow down. Who is this, please?" He listened briefly, then said to Betsy. "It's Frey Kadesh. Something about Teddi's parents." He held out the phone.

"Hello, Frey?" Betsy said. "Is there a problem?"

"Oh, yes indeed! Mr. and Mrs. Wahlberger are here to begin sorting out Teddi's things. They brought the clothes that were left at the Watered Silk pool — the ones Teddi was supposed to have worn? Well, they're *mine*! I don't know what to do, I was going to call Sergeant Malloy, but they don't want me to. They say the police are rude and incompetent, but I say this might be important. So what should I do?"

"The clothes are yours? Are you sure —

I'm sorry, of course you're sure! That's very strange, isn't it? And anything strange could be important."

"Could you come over and tell Mr. and Mrs. Wahlberger that?"

"How about I tell them over the phone?"

"No, come over, could you?" Frey's voice suddenly dropped to nearly a whisper. "They're being very difficult. I tried to tell them who you are, and I don't think they believed me."

Betsy thought briefly. "All right, I'll be right over."

"I have to go over to Frey and Lia's house for a little while," she told Godwin. "Teddi's parents are there, and Frey says they're being difficult." She thrust her fingers into her hair, a sure sign of frustration. "I'm not sure what she expects me to do with them."

"You'll calm them down. You look perfect for a meeting with people who are being difficult," said Godwin.

Betsy looked down at herself. She was dressed in a sedate navy blue suit with white piping on its cuffs and collar, the jacket over a white camisole. She refreshed her lipstick, put on her Jean Paul Gaultier confidence-building coat, and hurried out the back door. There was a tiny parking lot behind the building. It ended in a steep, tree-dotted rise currently covered in snow. Betsy's Buick was crouched beside a Dumpster kept there for her tenants. A thin layer of salt and sand crunched under her feet, and her breath smoked as she hurried to her car.

The car's heater had barely stirred to life before she pulled up in front of the blue-shuttered house where Teddi had lived — and died. Betsy was already regretting her decision to come over. What could she possibly say to these people, who were angry and grief-stricken?

Still, she'd agreed to come, and she was already here. *Suck it up,* she told herself, and got out of the car.

Frey answered the door, lifting her eyebrows and rolling her eyes in a swift signal of distress, as she said with false cheer, "Why, Ms. Devonshire, how good of you to visit! Come in, come in!" She was wearing jeweled sandals, tight blue jeans, and a loose-fitting dark green shirt. Her ears twinkled with lots of earrings, and she was wearing too much mascara in an attempt to disguise the redness and puffiness of her eyes.

Betsy came in and remembered to take off her shoes. She selected a pair of stretchy slippers and went to the squashy couch to put them on. The house smelled of freshly brewed coffee.

"How's Thai?" asked Frey.

"He's fine," said Betsy, not wishing to burden the young woman with complaints about the war between Thai and Sophie, as each battled for a place in the household. She stood and took off her coat, which Frey took away with her out of the living room. Only then did Betsy notice the handsome senior couple behind the breakfast bar in the kitchen. "Hello," she said.

"Hello," said the woman, who was short and stocky, with silver hair and a deep tan. She was wearing a black dress, and a silver crucifix hung around her neck.

She looked at her husband, who obediently said, "How do you do?" He was medium-short, even more darkly tanned than his wife, with thick silver hair and a deeply creased face dominated by a lot of nose and small, sad eyes. He was wearing a purple turtleneck sweater.

"My name is Betsy Devonshire," said Betsy. "I own a needlework shop here in Excelsior."

"I'm Stan Wahlberger," said the man, "and this is my wife, Louise. We're from Marathon, Florida."

Betsy smiled. "Isn't that out on the Keys? I've always wanted to visit the Keys."

"Yes," said Louise. She sipped from a mug.

"Good fishing," contributed Stan, earning a quashing look from his wife.

"I understand you are here to begin the sad business of picking up your daughter's possessions," said Betsy.

"Are you three getting acquainted?" asked Frey brightly as she came back into the room.

"Not really," said Louise. "Why did you ask her over?"

"Because she's a detective, a private eye," said Frey. "And I wanted her to tell you to tell the police about some of my clothing ending up over at Watered Silk."

"I thought she owned a needlework shop," said Stan.

"I do," said Betsy. "But I also sometimes try to solve crimes when people ask me for help. I don't have a license, but the police are aware of my work."

"Ms. Kadesh, did you ask Ms. Devonshire to investigate?" asked Louise, her eyebrows raised in surprise.

"No. It was someone else." Frey looked at Betsy to explain.

"Your daughter was murdered, which is absolutely horrible," said Betsy. "I was shocked to hear about that; you must be

273

devastated. The police are investigating, of course, and have shortened the list of possible suspects to three people. One of them is Thomas Shore, who is the grandnephew of two very good friends of mine. Those two friends have asked me to look into the case, with an eye toward clearing Tommy."

"And have you, er, 'cleared' him?" asked Louise, her voice hard.

"No, not yet."

"Of course you haven't — and you won't, he is the father of Teddi's unborn child . . ." She sobbed once, a heavy, choking sound, and her husband gathered her into his arms and looked angrily at Betsy.

"But don't you see," Frey broke in, "this case can't get solved if the police — and Betsy — don't have the information they need to solve it."

"What information?" demanded Stan, still angry. "So the filthy beast who murdered our daughter grabbed some clothes from the wrong closet to take along with her body —" He stopped to take a high-pitched breath. "Her body," he continued, struggling to get the words out, "to that indoor pool. I don't see how that's relevant. And I don't want to subject my wife to more of that . . . that rude cop's questions!"

"But Sergeant Malloy —" started Betsy.

"I don't know any Sergeant Malloy. We've had to deal with a cop — what's his name — Burgoyne!"

"Oh, *him,*" said Betsy. "He does have some kind of attitude problem. But we're in Excelsior, not Hopkins. The policeman you want to talk to is named Mike Malloy. He's a good man."

"I don't care if he's Michael the Archangel," asserted Stan. "No more cops."

And they could not be moved from that position.

Betsy asked to see the clothing that had been returned, and Frey took Betsy upstairs, away from the couple — which was what Betsy wanted.

"I'm not sure this is a real problem," she said, once they were inside Frey's room with the door closed. The room was a little larger than Teddi's, painted, curtained, and carpeted in a neutral buff color, but with brilliant splashes of red and orange in the duvet, the peacock blue cushion on the little upholstered chair, and a single abstract painting on one wall that might have been the climax of a ballet performance as seen by someone needing glasses. On the duvet lay a sad little heap of clothing: gray wool slacks, a butter yellow sweater, a black bra and panties, a cropped fur jacket that looked like pale mink. On the floor were a pair of high-heeled boots with silver metal trim on the toes and heels.

"These are from your closet?" asked Betsy.

"Yes," said Frey. "Though I would never put these together as an outfit. I mean, those slacks and that sweater? Really! Especially with those boots!"

"And Teddi never borrowed your clothes?"

"How could she? I'm four inches taller and ten pounds lighter than she was! None of my stuff fit her, not even my shoes!"

"So obviously someone came into Frey's room and pulled this stuff out to take along with Teddi's body to Watered Silk," Betsy said to Godwin a little while later.

"I don't see why Frey wanted you to come over," said Godwin. "I agree with you, Teddi's parents couldn't control whether or not Frey called the police to tell them about the clothes. They weren't Teddi's clothes, after all."

"I think they made her nervous, and she wanted an ally to stand with her on her decision. Plus, she feels guilty about Teddi's murder."

"Why should she feel guilty?"

"Well, suppose something awful were to happen to Rafael — God forbid, of course

— but it happens in your condo. Now it's not your fault, perhaps you were not even there. Wouldn't you beat yourself up over it, anyway? 'Why wasn't I at home? Why didn't I see this coming?' Those kind of questions."

Godwin nodded. "Oh, wow, yes, you're right. I think anyone would think those things. Poor Frey. Poor Lia."

"And poor Stan and Louise Wahlberger. I have heard repeatedly that the death of a child is the hardest kind of loss there is. Even an adult child — she was still their baby, no matter how old she was."

"How *awful* this all is!" exclaimed Godwin. "I wish it were over!"

He looked at the drawings of Pres, picked up the one with the three images on one page.

"I keep thinking I've seen him somewhere," he murmured, attempting to distract himself.

"I wish you could remember where," Betsy said, a bit more sharply than she probably meant to. She walked into the back.

Godwin sat down behind the desk and thought for a minute, then took out a pencil from the soft foam fish head that was a souvenir of a trip to Florida. It was meant to hold a soft drink or beer can, but Betsy used it to hold pens and pencils, a pair of scissors, a crochet hook, a plastic ruler, and a pair of ebony knitting needles, size ten.

He opened a couple of drawers and found a thin box of tracing tissue paper, took one out, and placed it over the drawing. He traced just the face of the man, and drew a cowboy hat on him. He shook his head no, then traced it again on the same piece of paper, this time giving him lipstick, mascara, and a woman's bouffant hairdo. Again no. He sighed.

In the back, Betsy was restoring order to a slanted holder of counted cross-stitch patterns. A customer looking for something had pulled them out in handfuls and left them scattered on the floor. She grew so irritated when that happened.

"Hey!" shouted Godwin, "here he is!"

Betsy came rushing out to the desk and halted, surprised. No one was in the shop but Godwin. Nor was anyone walking by outside.

"Where?" she asked.

"Here! Here! Look at this!"

Betsy came for a look at the sheet of tracing paper Godwin was holding out. There were two faces on the sheet. On one of them Godwin had drawn a baseball cap with the Twins logo on it; on the other he had drawn hair parted on the side, hiding the widow's peak, and redrawn the eyebrows so they were less satanic. He'd lowered the eyelids, and adjusted the mouth from a firm line to an ordinary smile.

"Okay," said Betsy, confused. She still didn't know who he was.

"He's the manager at an auto parts store," Godwin said. "Remember when I needed a new pair of windshield wipers and a new brake pedal pad? I had worn my old one right down to the metal. And you would not believe what the Miata dealership was going to charge me for it. So I went to Halloway's Auto Parts, and this man" — he took the paper back from Betsy — "got out a huge catalog and looked it up and ordered it for me. Cost me less than half what the dealership would have, so it was worth putting up with his attitude."

"Attitude?"

"Rude. Partly because I'm gay, partly because he's so important and I'm a time-wasting, ignorant member of the public who just happens to keep his store in business."

Betsy smiled.

Godwin continued, "I had to ask another person to show me how to put the wipers on because he couldn't be bothered. I was mad at him for three whole minutes, and I broke a nail doing it myself, but it was worth it for the money I saved." He held out a slim-fingered hand complacently.

"So what's his name?" asked Betsy.

"I don't have the slightest idea. But hey," he added, "at least I've told you where you can find him."

Betsy took her Buick to Halloway's Auto Parts in Saint Louis Park. She noted the pale blue pickup trucks with the fiberglass tires on their roofs, a memorable advertising gimmick. The building was large, white, and single story. TONY HALLOWAY AUTO PARTS, read a long blue and yellow sign across the front, the o's shaped like tires.

Betsy pulled into a parking slot near the main entrance and went in to find stacks of tires — their smell was overpowering — and row upon row of automobile parts and supplies, from many kinds of engine oil to air filters to headlights to brake pads, and so on. After a brief search, she found in one aisle a bewildering number of windshield wipers in myriad sizes.

She went to the long counter in back to ask for help. There were three men standing behind it, none of whom looked like Pres. One of them was helping a burly man in work clothes. Cut into the middle of the wall behind him was a broad door into the back. There must be a big warehouse behind it, Betsy thought, remembering the sheer size of the building from when she first entered the parking area. She wondered if Pres was back there and how to summon him if he was.

But first, she might as well attend to the errand that brought her to Halloway's Auto Parts. The counterman she chose to talk to was young, of medium height and average build with dusty-brown hair, amiable blue eyes, and very large hands. He wore dark blue coveralls with a HALLOWAY logo over the pocket and above it his first name, James.

"My windshield wipers are streaking," she said, "so I want to replace them. Normally I go to my dealer, but I've decided to save some money by buying new ones here and putting them on myself."

"What are you driving?" asked James with a smile.

"A three-year-old Buick Regal," she replied, and added, in case it mattered, "four door."

James's amused smile told her it didn't. He consulted a thick catalog to find the right kind of wipers for her car. She went back to the wiper aisle to choose a heavy-duty variety that promised to sweep away sandy salt-water as well as snow.

She paid for the wipers, then went out to install them, a task she'd seen done many times in her driving lifetime but had never tried before. To her surprise, she couldn't even get the old wipers off.

Embarrassed, she went back inside, to the same young man, and asked him if he could show her how it was done.

He turned and went to the warehouse door and shouted, "Pres, you back there?"

And to Betsy's gratification, out came a medium-tall, slender man with dark hair and eyes, looking a whole lot like Goddy's reinterpretation of Teddi's sketch. He was not dressed in coveralls but was instead wearing a nice black sport coat and gray trousers. He followed James to where Betsy stood.

"This young woman," said James, "can't put the wipers we just sold her on her car. Okay if I help her?"

Pres looked at Betsy with an impatient grimace, looked around to see no customers waiting, then lifted a what-the-hell hand. "All right, go ahead."

James made his own grimace of apology at Betsy for the man's attitude, shrugged himself into a winter-weight jacket, lifted

282

the wipers off the counter, and said, "Follow me." He went down to the end of the counter and led Betsy out to the parking lot.

"Where — oh, there." He strode quickly to Betsy's car and in a few seconds had her old wipers off.

"Will you show me how to do that?" she asked.

"Sure." He put one of the old wipers back on and showed her the little lever on its underside that could be lifted so it slid off. "Easy peasy," he said with a smile.

She watched as he opened the package holding her new wipers. But before he could put them on, she asked, "Is your boss always so rude to customers?"

He almost dropped the empty package. "What did you say?"

"He gave me such a look when you asked if you could help me put those on. Is he always like that? Who is he, anyway?"

James looked over his shoulder at the big front windows as if afraid he'd find Pres watching. "He's the store manager, Preston Munro. And he's all right." But that last was said in a tone of resigned disbelief.

"Is he married?"

James looked shocked. "Why? You interested in him?"

"No, but he was dating someone I sort of know who thought he was single."

He raised his eyebrows, glanced again at the store windows, then shrugged. "Yes, he's married. He's married to the boss's daughter.

"He's Tony Halloway's son-in-law?"

"That's right." He turned away from her to begin putting one of the wipers on. "Now, first you lift up —"

"So that's how he gets away with that attitude."

He put the wiper down and turned back to her. "What's this about, anyhow?"

"The woman he was dating has been murdered."

"Sufferin' cats!" he said. "Hold on, are you a cop?"

"No, I'm conducting a private investigation. Have the police been here yet to talk to Mr. Munro?"

"No." He was staring at her, alarmed. "Will they?"

"I'm sure they will." Especially since Betsy was going to phone Mike Malloy as soon as she got back to Excelsior.

"Because he was dating a woman who's been murdered?"

"Don't you think they should?"

He thought about that. "Now, don't get

me wrong, I am not the president of Pres's fan club, but murder is serious business. Do you actually think he might have killed that woman?"

"I don't know. I'm just collecting information."

"Maybe I should warn Pres about this." He nodded toward the store. "Or Mr. Halloway . . ."

His expression was significantly enigmatic, so Betsy asked, "What do you think Mr. Halloway's reaction would be?"

James suddenly showed Betsy a malicious grin. "Whatever it is, Pres won't like it."

Back at the shop, Betsy searched the Internet phone directories for a Preston Munro in Minnesota and was surprised to find only one listing, right down the road in Minnetonka. It even offered his wife's name, Sonja.

She picked up the phone and dialed the Excelsior Police Department. "May I speak with Sergeant Malloy?" she asked.

"I'll see if he's here. Who's calling, please?"

"Betsy Devonshire. Mike knows me. It's important."

"One minute."

In slightly less than a minute Malloy's

voice came impatiently over the line. "I can't tell you anything about an ongoing investigation," he announced.

"Maybe not, but I can tell you something."

The tone mollified. "Is that so?"

"Did Lia or Frey get in touch with you about that drawing of Pres?"

"Yes, and I have the drawings here on my desk. That was good work, thank you."

"Well, I know who he is, and where he works, and where he lives. With his wife."

"Have you talked to him?" Malloy asked sharply.

"No."

"Good, that's good."

"But I talked to someone he supervises, and I'm afraid that man will purely enjoy telling Pres the police may come by."

"Dammit —"

"There's no way I could know that would happen, Mike."

"All right, all right, I can see that. How did you find him?"

"Goddy remembered buying a brake pedal pad at the Halloway Auto Parts store in Saint Louis Park from a man who resembled the one in the drawing. So I went there to buy a pair of windshield wipers and saw him in the flesh. But I bought the wipers from another employee, who gave me additional information about him. Pres is the son-in-law of the owner of that store." Betsy gave Mike all the information she'd gathered, including Pres's home address. "His wife's name is Sonja," she added.

"Nice piece of detective work," Malloy said, not too grudgingly. "Maybe you should think about getting a license."

"And give up needlework? Not gonna happen. But may I ask a favor?"

"What kind of favor?"

"Let me know what he says when you talk to him."

"I'll think about it."

# SEVENTEEN

"So, you're thinking it's one of those three," said Connor. He, Godwin, and Betsy were seated at the shop's library table enjoying a lunch of soup and half a sandwich — in Connor's case, a whole sandwich — that Godwin had fetched from Antiquity Rose. It was about half past one, and there were no customers present.

Betsy nodded. "I think that very likely."

"So which one are you leaning toward?" asked Godwin.

"I'm trying not to lean toward any of them." She took a bite of her sandwich, chicken salad flavored with dill on cracked wheat.

"But?" said Connor. He enjoyed watching the way Betsy's mind worked.

"Okay — Tommy. I hate saying as much, because he's Phil's grandnephew, but he lies like a frightened person." She dipped up two spoonfuls of soup, then added, reluctantly, "And if you trace the route between Watered Silk and the drugstore where Tommy was working that night, it passes right by Mrs. Ball's house." Mrs. Ball was the woman who had found the Hardanger-edged sheet in her trash.

"Strewth!" breathed Godwin. "Have you told Phil and Doris?"

"No."

"Maybe you should, just to give them a heads-up before Tommy gets arrested."

"I know, I know."

Connor crumbled a cracker into his soup while looking speculatively at Betsy. "Do I hear some other kind of 'but' in there, machree?"

"Well . . . yes. Tommy is scared, but he's also weak. I can see him getting angry enough to dunk a woman under water — but to hold her under while she struggles? Halfway through he'd change his mind and let go. On the other hand, I think he was hurt and angry by what he interpreted as Teddi's pity. He thought he was winning her heart, but it appears she was allowing him to hang around because she felt sorry for him. That kind of pity can make some people really angry."

Connor said, "I think it would depend on whether Teddi told other people she was feeling sorry for him. Especially on Twitter or Facebook, where everyone could see."

"Hmm." Betsy hadn't gone far down the line of entries on Teddi's Facebook page. No doubt she should do that.

"And one other thing," Betsy said. "Wilma was poisoned by something applied to a medicated pad that was put on her back by a nurse every night. Tommy works at a drugstore."

"Whoa!" said Godwin. "That looks bad, really bad!"

Connor, listening to all of this, felt a need to be contradictory. "Well, okay," he said, "but what about the other two?"

"Noah has no alibi at all for Teddi's murder. He says he was home alone, sick, with his phone shut off. He's scared of being accused, and a little conflicted about his feelings when he found out someone else was the father of her baby. But his motive is weak. And, looking as far as Wilma's murder, although he knew the unguarded way into Watered Silk, he has no knowledge of or access to the poison used on her. Even more telling, he didn't seem to know she's dead."

"And Pres?" asked Connor.

"Yes, now there's Pres. He has a serious motive — he's married, and he works for his father-in-law, who, it seems, would be pleased to discover something seriously bad about him. The employee I talked to — his name is James — was very sure about that. James doesn't like Pres either."

"What kind of alibi does Pres have?"

"I don't know, I haven't talked to him yet, just to that employee at the auto parts store. Mike has warned me off until he has a crack at him. On the other hand, Pres lives in a house that's on a slightly wavy line between Watered Silk and the place where the torn sheet was found."

"Godfrey Daniels!" exclaimed Godwin. "You need to talk to him!"

"I'm sure Mike Malloy will be talking to him shortly. I wonder if James warned Pres to expect a visit from the police."

Connor said, "If Pres is as unpopular as James described him, I would think James took delight in telling everyone."

Betsy said, "But it's almost equally likely he'd take a secret delight in watching a police investigator come in and surprise him."

There was a thoughtful silence as they finished their lunch. Then Connor said, "Are there any other suspects?"

"Like who?" said Godwin, surprised.

"Oh, I don't know. Those two roommates,

Lia and Frey. A boyfriend of Teddi's we don't know about yet. Pres's wife. Or Noah's ex-wife — were they divorced because he has a violent streak? Or Tommy's girlfriend — What's her name? Dell?" he asked Betsy. "You talked to Dell, what did she say?"

"She said that Tommy's hopeless, and that she dreams some day he'll realize she's the one he needs to take care of him. Meanwhile, I'd like to talk to Pres's wife — only I don't know how to approach her. And you're right, I really should talk some more to Lia and Frey."

"You've been busy with Crewel World, machree, trying to do two big jobs at the same time. I think maybe you need to focus on one or the other."

"I can organize a crew to take care of the shop," Godwin said at once. "I think Connor's right, you need to spread your net wider if you're going to prove Tommy didn't do this."

Connor looked at Betsy's frustrated face and felt compassion for her. "Goddy, you can ask me to help in the shop," he said. He knew Betsy didn't want to involve him too deeply in the business. But why not? She was too damn independent, in his opinion, too determined to keep him at arm's length.

But Godwin was store manager, he was the one who made the hiring decisions. He smiled winningly at Godwin. "I work very cheaply," he said. He failed to see a swift look of alarm and anger cross Betsy's face — and so did Godwin.

But the next lead came from inside the shop. Ramona Tinsmith, who had once made a quilt that included stitched chicken patterns bought at Crewel World, came in looking for cat patterns.

"I have been instructed by my niece that the chicken quilt is to be hers after I die, so now my daughter wants me to leave her a cat quilt."

Godwin laughed. "You look kind of young to be thinking about leaving heirlooms to people," he said.

"It came up when my niece Lily, who is twelve, read an old mystery novel about a mean old rich uncle who draws up a will disinheriting some of his relatives. She started asking questions. Like, "Why don't you have a will? Why don't you write one leaving that chicken quilt to me?" Follow-up from my daughter, Hunter: "Make mine a quilt featuring cats." So I've been buying fabric that has cat-themed prints, and now I'm here."

Ramona picked first a simple pattern from Dimensions of a black, tan, and white kitten behind a big blue ball of yarn, then a larger and much more difficult Bucilla kit of the front half of a gray tiger cat asleep against a jug of yellow flowers. "That will go in the center, like the dancing Mexican cock was the center of the chicken quilt," said Ramona. Then she selected two Anchor kits, each featuring a head-and-shoulders cat portrait, one of a black and gray tabby, the other a brown tabby. She paused at the famous Frederick the Literate pattern, but decided it was too large and elaborate to be a quilt block, and instead chose Janlynn's Glamour Puss cartoon of a cat in sunglasses relaxing on a recliner.

She found a booklet full of cat patterns but made a face and put it back. "I need some little ones," she said.

Godwin said, "Hold on a second," and went over to the shop's computer. "Yes, I thought so!" he said a few moments later. "Look at this." It was a downloadable online pattern from Trina Clark called Cat Sampler, consisting of eight black silhouettes of cats in various poses. The whole thing was about ten inches by nine and a half inches, but it would be easy to make small squares from each individual silhouette, and piece them together to use as a border for the quilt. Ramona was delighted. It cost five dollars for the download, and Ramona gave Godwin the cash to print it out for her on the spot.

And because she'd put a fox in a bottom corner of the chicken quilt, she wanted a dog for the cat quilt. She wanted a barking dog, but they couldn't find one, so she looked for something else and finally picked a bookmark that included a silhouette of a Scottie dog at the bottom. "It'll mix in with the sampler cats to make it hard to find," said Ramona, happily.

She selected some floss in colors she didn't already have and a square of low-count aida fabric to go with the patterns.

Then while Godwin was adding up her bill, she went to the big board covered with tiny charms. It was near the checkout desk, where he could keep an eye on it — charms were a temptation to thieves, being so easily slipped into a purse or pocket.

Betsy had been in the back thinking of ways to reconfigure the displays — a cost-free way to stir interest in patterns was to stir regular customers from their accustomed paths so they'd find something new. She came out to see Ramona looking over a dozen or more charms lined up on the checkout desk. As she approached, Betsy saw Ramona select three, four, six, eight of them with a forefinger; then, hesitating, a ninth. Each was different from the others: some were Christian themed; some portrayed puppies or palm trees; there was even a jack-o-lantern.

"You must be planning a marathon of stitching patterns that call for charms," Betsy remarked.

Ramona turned and smiled at Betsy. "No, these are for my scrapbook."

"You scrapbook, *too*?" asked Godwin. "Where do you find the time?" Ramona had a full-time job as a nurse in a medical clinic, plus she was raising her daughter. And of course, she kept busy with her needlework.

"Oh, I'm a pretty good organizer," said Ramona. "How much for these nine, plus the floss, patterns, and kits?"

Godwin used his calculator to total everything up. It came to a little over a hundred and fifty dollars. Ramona opened her purse and took out a checkbook. "Bet you don't see many of these nowadays," she said.

"That's true," agreed Godwin. Most of Crewel World's customers used credit or debit cards. He took the check from her, confirmed that the amount was right, then turned to Betsy. "Can you approve this?" he asked, a little too casually. One of his eyebrows was raised significantly.

"Certainly," said Betsy.

She looked again at the check — and saw what he'd been hinting at: Ramona's home address was on a street just a few numbers down from Preston Munro's.

"Is something wrong?" Ramona's tone had turned frosty.

"No, not at all. I was just noticing your address. Do you by any chance know Preston Munro?"

"Not really — but I know his sister, Julie, and his wife, Sony." She pronounced it like the electronics manufacturer. "Sony's a scrapbooker. In fact, she's the one who got me interested in the craft. Her work is amazing. She does beautiful calligraphy on her pages, and she has a real eye for design." She paused for a moment, frowning. "Why do you ask? Sony's not a stitcher."

"Actually," Betsy said, "it's her husband I'm interested in. What can you tell me about him?"

"I told you, I hardly know him at all." Ramona persisted, "Why do you want to know?" Then her eyes brightened. "Hey, are you doing another investigation?"

"Yes," said Betsy. "The grandnephew of a friend is a suspect in two murders, and I'm trying to find out if he really did it."

"*Two* murders? Wouldn't they know by the second one if he did it or not?"

"You'd think so. And in all candor, things do look bad for him. But I think his personality makes him an unlikely suspect. I've now got two alternative theories to look at, and some people may have some answers for me."

"Including Pres? Oh my God, you can't seriously suspect him! Sony thinks the sun rises and sets just for him! I don't like him, he thinks he knows everything and he treats her like a dumb kid, even though she's really smart. She went to school to became a surgical nurse, you know."

"Where does she work?" asked Betsy.

"Nowhere, now. She's a stay-at-home mom. They have an adorable little boy named Tony, after his grandfather. He's just turned three." Ramona leaned in toward them to confide, "She wants another baby, but so far no luck, which is kind of sad, because she's a wonderful mother."

"Maybe Pres doesn't want another child," said Betsy.

"He wants whatever she wants — that's one of his good points. And it's not like they can't afford it, he makes good money."

"I want to talk to him — and maybe her,

too," said Betsy. "Do you think they'd be open to answering some questions?"

"I don't know about him, but Sony loves to meet new people, especially if they're crafty. Tell you what, I'll talk to her and let you know."

"Thanks, Ramona."

Betsy called in two part-timers so she could take the afternoon off. "You know what this is doing to my bottom line," said Betsy, who could be of two minds about anything. She was complaining to Connor in the apartment upstairs, where she went to change out of her work clothes.

"You want to take back the arrangement, maybe drop this case?" asked Connor.

"Well . . . no."

"So hush, and get on with it."

So Betsy got on with it. The first thing she got on was the Internet. She went to Lia's and Frey's Facebook accounts and found, as she suspected she would, an almost daily diary of their activities. Both spoke of an agreement they'd made with each other and with Teddi before she died: that if one of them wanted to entertain a guest, the other two would make themselves scarce for the evening. In this case they had gone out clubbing together with dates — making solid alibis for the night Teddi's body was taken to Watered Silk. Their alibis were weaker, though, for the period during which Betsy estimated someone got into Wilma's room and doctored her Exelon patches with atropine.

Tommy, on the other hand, didn't have a Facebook page at all.

Noah had one set up to describe his professional skills, with little about his personal life — though he did have two photos taken at a barbecue party at Teddi's house, designed apparently to show off his deck-building skills. In one of the photos, he and Teddi stood smiling in the backyard with the deck behind them. They did make a handsome couple, Betsy had to admit.

Preston didn't have a Facebook page, either; but Sony did, full of photos of their happy-looking and adorable dark-haired son, Tony, and some pages from her scrapbooks. Ramona was right, the pages were beautiful, cleverly and skillfully designed. Of the photos that included Pres, none featured him in "vampire" mode. The closest he came to it was a photo from last Halloween, when he and Sony went to a costume party where he was a 1930s gangster in an outsize fedora and she was his tall and sturdy moll in a deeply fringed dress. He was laughing but she was looking serious, a pose underlined by the fact that she was holding a plastic tommy gun.

"I love to keep souvenirs of my life," Sony wrote above a series of photos of documents ranging from her baptismal certificate to a report card from fourth grade to her high school diploma and a college examination paper she had aced; even to her big plastic name tag from St. Luke's Hospital.

Here and there Sony mentioned that she didn't want baby Tony to grow up as an only child, and that she hoped for a baby sister for him some day "soon." There was even a photo of an empty nursery waiting for an occupant, as Tony had been moved to another bedroom with a "big boy bed" shaped like a sports car. The word "VROOOM!" — ornamented with streaks indicating movement and clouds of exhaust — was spelled out on the wall over the bed, painted there by Sony.

Wow, thought Betsy, what a lucky little boy. She could just imagine the pleasure his mother would take in decorating her prospective daughter's room. Ponies, perhaps? Or, more likely, a princess's boudoir.

She got out her notebook and looked for the pages of notes she'd taken while interviewing Tommy Shore. She found the contact information for his bosses for both of his jobs, and also the web site url for his landlord. On that web site, Betsy found adorable photos of kids and adult goats, which were unfortunately close to photos of cuts of goat meat. But there was a "Contact Me" link, too, and she left a note there asking the landlord to e-mail her about Tommy Shore. She was careful to word it as if she were seeking a reference rather than an alibi.

Then she called the pharmacy. The manager told Betsy that Tommy was pleasant with customers and fellow employees, rarely late to work, but obviously not interested in getting promoted. "He prefers outdoor work. He quits every summer to work at a golf course," she said.

Tommy's supervisor at the office-cleaning company said the same thing. "I offered to make him a crew chief if he'd quit taking the summer off, but he wouldn't accept my offer."

His work schedule had enough holes in it to make his alibis worthless.

Betsy was composing a little article about Thai — its central question was, Does anyone want a fine, healthy, neutered Siamese tomcat? — when her cell phone rang. It was Godwin.

"Ramona called. She talked with Sony

without giving her any details, and told me that Sony would like to talk to you. She gave me her cell phone number — or you can contact her via e-mail or Facebook."

But Betsy did not want to advertise to stray readers that she was talking with Sony, so she called her cell.

Sony's voice was pleasantly deep and resonant. She spoke slowly, as if she wanted to make sure she was not misunderstood. "Little Tony," she said, with an emphasis on "little" to make clear to Betsy that she was not speaking of her father, "has a playdate this afternoon, so we can talk on the phone without interruption. Is that okay?"

"Well . . ." said Betsy, "actually, I'd prefer to see you face-to-face. I'm much better at in-person interviews than conversations over the phone. Would you like to come here? Or should I come to you? Or shall we meet somewhere in between?"

"Why don't you come over here? That way I can show you my work, and anyway, I want to be nearby in case Little Tony's play-date gets interrupted and I need to pick him up early."

"All right, thank you. In, say, twenty minutes?"

"Fine."

A little while later, Betsy was driving up a winding street in a Minnetonka development of large, attractive houses, not quite McMansions but multistoried stone-and-clapboard homes on large lots in a newer development not far off Highway 3.

The Munro house was on a corner lot, a pale blue wood-and-stone structure marked by a tall picket fence. The two-car garage had its door either up or missing, and sawhorses and ladders showed some kind of work was going on inside, though no workmen were present. Betsy pulled into the driveway and got out. A flagged walkway led in a curving line from the driveway to the house.

Sony was a dark-honey blonde, tall and solidly built, with a calm strength in her face that Betsy found very attractive. Betsy had called Sony on her cell to let her know she was arriving, and Sony stood in her doorway waiting for her. She was wearing a deep yellow velour jumpsuit with honeybees embroidered all over it, and brown leather slippers.

"Hello, Ms. Devonshire," she called in her warm voice. "Please, come in out of the cold." The sun was shining, but the temperature was in the midtwenties. "Excuse the mess, we're putting in a new door and insulating the garage so Pres can work on his car in there."

"I suppose since he works in a car parts store, he gets good advice as well as a price break," said Betsy with a smile, coming up three steps and into the foyer.

The entrance area was tall with a pale oak staircase at the end of it. Sony led the way into a big living room, deeply carpeted, furnished comfortably in earth tones. A triple bookcase stood against one wall, full of books that looked well read; and a huge, deep green plush chair sat in a bay window, where the sun pouring through could provide good reading light. A children's book was on the seat, and Betsy could easily imagine Sony reading to her son there. There was no television in sight — probably in the family room, thought Betsy. A good-size palm shrub was growing in a large green pot standing on a wheeled platform next to the chair. It looked healthy. Everything looked new or well kept.

"What a pleasant house you have," said Betsy, shedding her coat.

"Thank you," said Sony. "Won't you sit over there?" she added, gesturing toward the couch. It was long and modern, a color somewhere between tan and gray-brown with subtle stripes of darker gray-brown. Two pillows were standing stiffly upright on it, printed in thick wobbly stripes of gray-brown, green, and white. Betsy was glad to tuck one of them behind her back — the couch was deep. On a coffee table she saw three fat scrapbooks, closed.

Sony curled into the plush chair and regarded Betsy with friendly brown eyes. "Tell me, what can I do for you?"

This direct question surprised Betsy, but amused her just a little, too; it was a technique she'd used herself not long ago.

"I've been asked to find chinks in the armor of a homicide case the police are building against the grandnephew of a good friend." Seeing Sony's surprise, she added, "It's something I've done before."

"What do you mean?" Sony was sitting up, her manner no longer friendly. "I thought you were here about my scrapbooking, to ask me to give a program or teach a class in your store!"

"No, not at all. My shop doesn't sell any scrapbooking products. Oh, I see what's wrong here. Ramona said she didn't tell you what I was after. I do have a needlework shop, but I sometimes supplement the efforts of the police in their criminal investigations. I'm looking into the drowning death of Teddi Wahlberger. The poor young lady was murdered, possibly by someone she accused of being the father of her unborn child."

"How . . . interesting. But why do you want to talk to me?"

"Well, it seems Teddi and your husband knew each other."

"Now hold on," Sony said heatedly. "I don't see how that's possible. I never heard of this Teddi person."

"I'm sorry about that, but there's no doubt Pres knew her. He took her out on several occasions, even came to her house for parties."

"I don't believe you!"

Betsy spoke gently. "I'm really sorry, but people had seen them together, and Teddi drew a really clever sketch of Pres one night while they were out, and another more formal portrait of him. He was careful not to allow his photograph to be taken, but Teddi was a talented amateur artist, and apparently she couldn't resist capturing the face of a man she found fascinating."

"I don't know why you are telling me these lies," Sony growled quietly, but her eyes were blazing.

Betsy, oblivious to the warning in Sony's voice, said, "Perhaps you'll believe a police investigator when he comes to talk to you. I believe he's talking right now to Pres."

"You're trying to scare me! I won't listen to any more of this!" Sony jumped to her feet. "You leave this house immediately! Right now, do you hear? Out, *out,* or I'll hurt you!" Sony was standing tall, her teeth actually bared, her arms reaching out as she started to move toward Betsy, her fingers curled like claws.

Betsy grabbed her coat but didn't wait to put it on. She ran for the door, with Sony at her heels. She managed to wrench the door open and jump through it before Sony could get her hands on her.

She hurried down the walk without even slowing to pull the door shur behind her, and didn't pause to look around until she was pressing hard on the button that unlocked her car door. Safe inside, she clicked the doors locked, then peered out the side window.

Sony was standing in the open doorway, her face red with fury, mouth open as she shouted threats.

Betsy backed hastily out of the driveway and sped away.

"Whew!" she whispered, as she went too

fast around a curve. The car swerved as she made her way to a side road that would take her back to the highway.

Then the adrenaline rush subsided and, with trembling hands, she sighed in relief. That had been a close call. She even managed a shaky laugh. "And I never got to ask her about an alibi!" she said to herself.

# EIGHTEEN

Detective Sergeant Mike Malloy checked in with the Saint Louis Park Police Department before he went to find Tony Halloway's Auto Parts store. One of the detectives, Investigator Alex Webster, elected to come along. Webster was a taciturn man, a little above medium height, overweight, with decidedly Asian features. He listened closely to Malloy's account of the case on the drive over to the store, but didn't ask any questions.

They entered the premises and headed to the counter at the back of the store. "May I help you, gentlemen?" said the tall young man standing there.

Malloy produced identification, as did Webster. "We'd like to speak to Preston Munro," said Malloy. The counterman, who had the name James embroidered on his jumpsuit, managed, barely, not to smile. But his eyes sparkled with glee. He cleared his throat twice and said, "Just a second." He went to a broad door in the back of the store and called, "Pres! Some people here to see you!"

"All right," came the reply, and a man Malloy recognized from Teddi Wahlberger's drawings came out and up to the counter. "Help you?" he said in a surly tone of voice.

Malloy displayed his badge a second time, and the color drained from Munro's face.

"We'd like to talk to you for a few minutes, if that's all right," said Malloy.

Munro suddenly grew much more polite. "Certainly," he said. "There's a break room back here where we can talk. Okay with you?"

"Sure," said Malloy.

James looked disappointed. Evidently, he'd been hoping for a takedown ending in handcuffs.

Munro went to the end of the long counter, where he lifted a hinged section to allow Malloy and Webster through. The two followed him through another door that led to a very clean break room furnished with soft drink machines, two white formica tables littered with car magazines, and eight orange plastic chairs.

"This okay?" asked Munro.

"Sure," said Malloy. He went to the nearest table but waited for Munro to choose a chair. They all sat down.

"Do you know why we're here to talk to you?"

"Um . . . no, not really."

Malloy got right to the point. "Did you know a woman named Teddi Wahlberger?" he asked.

"Wahlberger?" Munro appeared to think briefly. "No, I don't think so."

"You didn't take her out, to dinner or dancing or to parties?"

Munro frowned in disapproval. "Of course not, I'm a married man."

Malloy reached into an inside pocket, a movement which clearly alarmed Munro. Malloy paused to make sure of the reaction, and glanced at Webster to ensure that he saw it, too. When Munro saw there was just a piece of folded paper in Malloy's hand, he relaxed.

But when Malloy unfolded the paper — which turned out to be two sheets, photocopies of Teddi's drawings — and smoothed them both out on the table, Munro stared at them wordlessly for nearly a minute. Then, too late, he looked up at Malloy. "Am I supposed to know who this person is?"

"I think it's pretty obvious who this is."

Another long pause. "Where did you get

these?" Munro asked. He started to touch them, then withdrew his hands and placed them in his lap.

Malloy said, "Teddi Wahlberger drew them. See her initials on the corner of the second sheet?"

Munro didn't look at the second sheet, but nodded. "Okay, she saw me out somewhere, was taken by my appearance, and drew some pictures. So what?"

"That little cartoon drawing was done by Ms. Wahlberger at the Bar Abilene, where the two of you were sitting together. You left the table briefly, and she drew this on a napkin while you were gone. I have an eyewitness who saw you two together and watched her make that sketch." As Malloy watched Munro trying to think up a response, he thought to himself, *Thank God for that Devonshire woman. Although she continues to foolishly involve herself in murder investigations, at least she keeps me abreast of her findings, which are frequently sound.* Though of course he would never, ever say that to her.

"All right," said Munro in a low, defeated voice. "I took her out a few times." More strongly, he asked, "So what?"

"Did she later contact you with an accusation that you were the father of her baby?"

He twisted his face into a grimace, upset that they knew that, too. "Shit. Yes, she did." His chin came up. "But she was lying. I knew it wasn't possible."

"Why is that? You were seen coming out of her bedroom." That was close enough to the truth that it didn't matter.

Munro said in a low, shamed voice, "Because I had a vasectomy over a year ago."

Why was he ashamed? Having had a vasectomy was a terrific defense against an accusation of having impregnated a woman.

"Did you tell her that?" he asked.

"Absolutely. She sent me an IM, I sent her one right back. 'So sorry, honey,' I said. 'No way it's mine. Vasectomy.' " His tone shaded into impudence. "I might've misspelled 'vasectomy.' "

Aware he'd missed some point, Malloy shifted ground. "Where were you the night of Monday, January twenty-eighth?"

"Is that when Teddi drowned?" asked Munro. When Malloy didn't answer, Munro's eyes moved to Webster, who sat as impassively as the Buddha he resembled.

Munro appeared to cast his mind back. "Let's see. Yeah, I remember that day. I had left work early to pick up a salesman named Marvin Beasley at the airport. He represents McGowan Import Auto Parts of Atlanta. I

314

brought him to the Doubletree Hotel here in Saint Louis Park, where we had a couple of drinks at the bar and talked for an hour. Then we went out to dinner at Benihana, that Japanese place in Golden Valley where they juggle the cleavers while they grill your food right in front of you. Had a couple more drinks there, then I drove him back to Doubletree and went home. Sony — that's my wife — and I watched the late news and shared a bottle of wine, and we went to bed, where I slept like a liquor-soaked log, with her beside me, till seven-forty the next morning. She can tell you I was there all night — she wakes up if a leaf falls from a tree in the yard. Took a shower and downed half a bottle of aspirin and went to work. Okay?"

As Malloy drove Webster back to the Saint Louis Park police building behind city hall, he asked, "What do you think?"

"I think once you confirm his story with that Beasley fellow, and his wife in Minnetonka, you'll be able to eliminate him as a suspect." He smiled. "Okay?"

Malloy sighed. "Okay."

"Honestly, I thought she was going to knock me down," said Betsy to an open-mouthed Godwin. "She came at me like a mama griz-

315

zly bear defending her cub."

"But her cub is Little Tony," said Godwin, puzzled. "And you weren't threatening her cub."

"That's true," said Betsy, and frowned. "Still, she was protecting her husband, that seems obvious to me. No matter what she said, I think she at least suspects that he dated Teddi. Maybe she even suspects — correctly — that he's been dating a lot of other women. Remember that bartender who said he came in with different women?"

"If someone came to me with proof that Rafael was tomcatting all over town, the person I'd be mad at would be Rafael," said Godwin, with an air of stating the obvious.

"Yes, but wouldn't you also be mad at the person who told you the bad news?"

"No, of course not . . . well, maybe . . . okay, yes. But I'd definitely be mad at Rafael, too. I bet if you could be a fly on the wall of their bedroom tonight, you'd hear them go at it something fierce."

Betsy brooded about the episode, and finally called Ramona.

"Oh, hi, Betsy, did you get to talk to Sony?"

"Yes, but she blew up at me before I could ask her any questions, and ran me off her property."

"Seriously?"

"Very seriously."

"Golly, how did that come about?"

"Probably my own fault. Instead of feeling my way into the subject of her husband's infidelity, I came right out with it, said I had proof."

"Uh-oh."

"What do you mean, 'uh-oh'?"

"Well, um, Sony knows way far back in her head that Pres is not exactly faithful. I mean, he came on to me at a party at their house one time, and I made kind of a joke about it to Sony — you know, feeling her out about it — and she cut me out of her life for three months. I had to apologize to her, say I must have been mistaken, before we were friends again. But she's like that about him. She tries hard to pretend she doesn't know the truth about him. No, she tries hard to pretend he is as devoted to her as she is to him. You know those comedy scenes where someone puts his hands over his ears and goes 'la-la-la-la' when he doesn't want to hear what's being said? She's like that. She absolutely ignores any hint he's not the perfect husband, because — well, I'm not sure why. Maybe because she's crazy in love with him."

"Uh-oh," echoed Betsy.

"Exactly."

"So why didn't you warn her that I wanted to talk to her about a murder investigation that might involve her husband?"

"Because then she wouldn't have let you come over. Or, she might've contacted Pres and together they would've concocted a story for you. I kind of let her think that you wanted to talk to her about scrapbooking."

Betsy recalled the set of scrapbooks on the coffee table in Sony's living room. "Yes," she told Ramona, "she thought I wanted her to give a talk about the craft, or maybe teach a class. I'm sure she felt blindsided. How long have they been married, do you know?"

Ramona's voice was laced with amusement as she said, "About four and a half months shorter than they would be if Little Tony had been conceived on their honeymoon."

"I see."

"Not entirely you don't, not yet. The reason Pres married her is that Sony's father had a little talk with him. Sony wanted him, and Big Tony likes giving her what she wants. And he can be, um, extremely convincing. Big Tony had that nickname even before Little Tony came along, you know."

"I see. At least Pres didn't flee to Atlanta."

"What? Well, no. Mr. Halloway is well off, and he was willing to bring Pres into his car parts business, so Pres decided not to leave town."

"This is wonderful information — but how did you come by it?"

"Pres has a sister who is a stitcher and a quilter. We met in college. She adores her nephew and likes her sister-in-law, but doesn't like her brother."

"In your opinion, is Pres capable of murder?"

"I don't know. I believe Paige would tell you he is. But like I said, she doesn't like him — I mean, she *really* doesn't like him."

Betsy went upstairs to find that Connor had gone grocery shopping — he'd left her a note — so she went into the kitchen to prepare a sandwich for her lunch. She gave Thai a snack — he was doing splendidly on grain-free canned cat food, but needed to be fed at least three times a day. She had purchased a rimmed plastic pet food place mat and kept it on the kitchen counter. Aging, fat Sophie could no longer jump high enough to get up onto the counter — another point of contention between the two cats. But right now there were no complaints, Sophie was down in the shop. Godwin would put her out at closing time.

Betsy had barely sat down with her sandwich when her phone rang.

It was Sergeant Mike Malloy, wanting to talk to her about her interview with Sony Munro. He knew she'd talked to her because Sony had given him an earful about Betsy's visit.

"She wanted to know what right you had to talk to her like you did, telling lies, she said, about her husband," said Malloy. "What the hell did you say to her?"

"That I had a drawing of her husband made by a woman he was dating, and that there was a witness to his presence at a tavern in Uptown with a number of women."

"She said you approached her under false pretenses, claiming that you wanted to talk about scrapbooking."

"No, I never said that to her," Betsy said. "The woman who put me in touch with her may have given her that impression."

"Which you instructed her to do."

"No, it was her own idea. The woman is a friend of Pres's sister, who doesn't like him."

"Oh, I give up," said Malloy, exasperated.

"What did she tell you?" asked Betsy. "No, wait, first tell me what Pres told you. Does he have an alibi?"

"He said he went out to dinner with a representative of a wholesaler in foreign auto parts, then came home around eight-thirty or a little after, played with his son, talked to his wife, and went to bed early. Sonja Munro says he didn't come home to dinner because he had an appointment with a salesman, that he got home close to nine o'clock, watched a video with his son, shared a bottle of wine with her, and they were in bed by ten thirty."

"What time did you talk to Pres?"

"First thing this afternoon, why?"

"Because that gave Sony Munro time to call him after my visit and work up an alibi with him."

"You're right, it would have given her time to do that. But Mr. Halloway says that Preston left work early to meet a car parts salesman flying in from Atlanta who wanted to meet with Halloway the next day. I don't think Pres or Sony persuaded Halloway to help with their alibi. By the way, did you know that Halloway Auto Parts has three stores? One in Saint Louis Park, one in Fridley, one in South Saint Paul."

"No, I didn't know that."

"Preston manages the Saint Louis Park store — but the old man keeps his office there, probably to keep an eye on Pres. You were right about one thing, he doesn't think much of his son-in-law."

"Does he think he is a murderer?"

"No, he thinks he doesn't have the guts to kill a woman — or the brains to think up a scheme like taking her to an indoor pool so we'd think she drowned there. But he does think he's an adulterer. He's got no proof, but he's convinced of it nonetheless."

"Here's an odd question," Betsy said. "Would Tony Halloway kill a woman his son-in-law was seeing in order to protect his daughter?"

"From what? Disappointment in her husband? Such a degree of disappointment that her eyes would open to what he really is and she'd divorce him? Not a chance."

"I see what you mean."

"Anyway, Halloway says the salesman told him that Pres took him out to a Japanese restaurant, then dropped him off at his hotel around eight thirty."

"So, I guess that lets Pres out of the running as a suspect." Betsy sighed. "The only question I have left is, did Teddi Wahlberger call Pres to accuse him of being the father of her baby?"

"No, she didn't call him."

Betsy was surprised, but before she could

say so, Malloy continued, "She did text him, however. Munro says he wasn't worried. He knew he couldn't be the father, he had a vasectomy fourteen months ago."

"Oh, no! Really?"

"Why so shocked?"

"Mike, visit Sony's Facebook page and you'll see why."

*Whew!* thought Betsy after hanging up. *A vasectomy! And poor Sony has dreams of a sibling for Little Tony.*

She was suddenly hot with anger against Pres, not just for his infidelities but for the vasectomy he never told his wife about. "Wicked, wicked, he's a wicked man!" she muttered, "even if he isn't a murderer!"

She went back to her sandwich, but her appetite was spoiled. In a little while Connor came in with two bags of groceries. He was whistling a plaintive little melody that took Betsy a few seconds to identify:

If I should plant a tiny seed of love
In the garden of your heart,
Would it grow to be a great big love one
    day,
Or would it die and fade away?

Connor had a liking for old English music-hall songs, both comic and sentimental.

Betsy shared his interest, as her father used to sing these songs to her and her sister when they were children.

She smiled at Connor and sang with him the next verse of "If I Should Plant a Tiny Seed of Love":

Would you cherish it and tend it every day,
Till the time when we must part,
If I should plant a tiny seed of love
In the garden of your heart?

"Machree," he sighed tenderly. He put the groceries on a kitchen counter, then came to kiss her. "I'm so glad you know these songs, too."

"Connor, you are the dearest man in the world to me." Betsy was near tears.

"What is it, machree?"

"I've found out something about Preston Munro that makes me sick. I wish he didn't have an alibi supplied by his loving wife, whom he is deceiving and doesn't deserve!" She told him what Malloy had told her.

He made an ugly sound in the back of his throat and went to put the groceries away. In a few minutes he was back with a sandwich and a fistful of potato chips.

"So how did it go with Sonja?" he asked.

She told him. "She was enraged on his

behalf, poor thing."

"So what do you think? He's out as a suspect?"

"I think so. I mean, if he really wasn't worried about being the father of Teddi's baby, why would he murder her?"

"Maybe because she could raise such a stink about it that his wife would find out — and then Sony would find out about the vasectomy. If he had to tell Teddi why he wasn't the father of her baby, what would she do? Was she above a little blackmail? What might he do to keep her from contacting Sony?"

But after a minute's thought, Betsy responded to his theory. "Now wait, that would depend on whether or not Teddi knew about Sony. And I don't think she did."

"Why not?"

"Because according to everyone who knew her, she was a beautiful, sweet, funny, joyous, harebrained ninny. It never occurred to her that Tommy might be insulted by her pity. It never occurred to her that Noah might be hurt by her refusal to be exclusive with him. And it never occurred to her that Pres might be married."

"So now what?" Connor asked, eating the last of his chips.

"I wonder if Mike would agree to a lengthy sit-down, where we could both try to sum up what we know and who the evidence points to."

Connor looked at his watch. "Likely he's home by now." He stood and picked up his plate and hers. "I'll do the dishes while you call."

# NINETEEN

To Betsy's amazement, Malloy was open to
the idea of a meeting. In fact, he said, "Why
not get together this evening? My wife and
kids are going out to a movie I don't want
to see, so I'll have an excuse to miss it. Bring
your POSSLQ with you, if you like."

"Possel-cue?"

Malloy was surprised she didn't know the
acronym. "Person of the Opposite Sex Sharing Living Quarters," he said.

"Oh, you mean Connor."

"You mean there's more than one of
them?"

Betsy was fairly sure Malloy was kidding.
"See you in half an hour?"

"Fine."

The Malloy house was a good-size orange-
brick two-story about three blocks from the
commons, toward the beach end. Connor
and Betsy found handsome Mrs. Malloy
and their two good-looking redheaded

children putting on their coats and boots in the living room.

Quick introductions were made, and the movie-going party went out the door.

Malloy showed Connor and Betsy into the living room, neat and modestly furnished in blue and green. Old-fashioned slat window blinds covered the windows under ivory drapes. There was a gas fireplace lit by a brisk little dance of flames. A big flat-screen TV was mounted over the fireplace.

Malloy offered them a choice of LaCroix sparkling water or coffee, and a platter of cheese and crackers. So this was to be a friendly visit.

Still, as Betsy sat, she drew out her notebook, and Malloy chose the bow-backed occasional chair rather than the cushioned one. Connor sat next to Betsy, leaned back, and crossed his legs, prepared to listen.

"May I ask something right away?" said Betsy.

"What is it?"

"Would you and Mrs. Malloy be open to acquiring a cat?"

"No. But thank you for asking."

Betsy sighed. "Okay. Next question: Did you get that antique sheet back from Mrs. Ball?"

"No. She'd cut the lace off it and thrown

the rest away. Said it was torn and dirty and smelly."

"Oh, that's too bad!" She wrote in her notebook that the sheet was gone.

"Still, the existence of it in that trash can is significant, don't you think?" Malloy said.

"Oh, yes, especially when you look at where that trash can was located. But what I'm thinking now is that I've neglected the murder of Wilma. I don't understand how it was done and my one contact at Watered Silk isn't able to tell me."

Mike settled back a little and said, "Let me tell you what I know. Wilma Carter had been diagnosed with Alzheimer's and it had reached a stage where she could not live on her own."

Betsy nodded. She knew this already, and Mike knew that she knew.

He went on. "Her nearest living relative was a nephew, Tony Halloway."

Mike acknowledged her start of surprise. "Yes, the owner of the auto parts chain who has a son-in-law managing one of them. Which son-in-law has a good alibi for the murder of Teddi Wahlberger and an even better one for the murder of Mrs. Carter."

"I know Mrs. Munro says he was home with her when Teddi was killed, but where was he when Wilma was poisoned?"

"Down in Madison, Wisconsin. He flew down there for a motor parts manufacturer's convention and was gone four days." One of Mike's pale eyebrows raised on his freckled face. "Besides which, he hasn't got the connections or the knowledge to have done what was done to Wilma."

"What was done to Wilma?" asked Betsy.

"As I said, she had Alzheimer's. She wasn't bad enough off to be kept in a locked ward, but neither was she in a regular apartment with a kitchen. She was on various medications, including one called Exelon, which is administered by a patch. Every evening a nurse would come to her room and pull off the previous evening's patch and stick a new one on between her shoulder blades, where she couldn't get at it."

Malloy leaned forward and picked up a small notebook on the coffee table. He began a search through it, and finally stopped to read briefly.

"When she was found dead, an autopsy was ordered," he said. "There were no marks of trauma on the body. The usual screening test for drugs was negative — but those are generally done on drug addicts, looking for opiates and suchlike. So they did another, more detailed screening. And they came up with a positive for atropine.

"Now, atropine is used during surgery to regulate the heartbeat, and quiet muscles. In eye surgery, it relaxes the muscles and dilates the eye. Mrs. Carter hadn't had any surgical procedures recently to account for a medicinal dose of atropine, and anyway, the amount found in her system was more than would normally be used in such procedures.

"The conclusion is that she was poisoned with atropine."

"And somehow the Exelon patch is involved?" said Connor.

"Right. As soon as the body was taken away, her room was searched. The foil packet that held the patch was found in a wastepaper basket." He put the notebook down on a knee and made a pulling-apart gesture with his fingers. "You peel it apart," he said. "The patch is inside. And on the back of the foil cover was a tiny hole, such as you'd get by sticking a hypodermic needle into it."

Betsy sucked air through her teeth. "Oh, dear," she said.

"Damn clever," muttered Connor, with a movement of his mouth as if tasting something spoiled.

"Yeah," sighed Malloy. "The thing is, it could have been done at any time. The box of patches was about half gone, and it holds a dozen of them, so up to six days in advance someone could have come in there and interfered with that patch."

"Well, no," said Betsy, "not if it was done after Teddi was put in the pool, to keep Wilma from telling who she had shown that door to. There were a number of people sneaking into Watered Silk through that back door. Which one of our three suspects knew about it first?"

"Someone Wilma showed it to, I'll wager," said Connor.

Malloy nodded sharply. "That's my conclusion, too. But which one of them? Tommy Shore, Noah Levesque, or Preston Munro?"

"Did any of them have access to a hypodermic and atropine?" asked Betsy.

"Tommy Shore might have, since he works in a drugstore — but." Malloy raised a warning finger. "The atropine stocked in a drugstore pharmacy is low dose. It's used to treat eye problems. It would take a large quantity of drugstore atropine to kill someone. Putting a few drops of drugstore atropine on a skin patch might have made Wilma sick, but it wouldn't have killed her."

"So where would a concentrated dosage come from?" asked Betsy.

"A hospital. None of these men had access to a hospital pharmacy. In fact, nobody within spitting distance of this case has access to a hospital pharmacy."

Betsy frowned. "Sony was a surgical nurse," she said thoughtfully. "But that was before Little Tony came along, about three years ago."

"Is there atropine in lethal doses at Watered Silk?" asked Connor.

"No."

Betsy thrust her fingers into her hair and thought hard. Malloy leaned forward just a little bit, watching her expectantly. But she yanked her hand away with a sound like, "Bssshhhhh!" and added, "I can't see how it was done."

Connor said, "Maybe Tommy figured out how to concentrate the atropine."

Betsy scoffed. "Tommy couldn't figure out how to make a ham sandwich without watching an instructional video."

"Maybe he fell across an article while surfing the net," argued Malloy, but not as if he believed it.

"You really like him for this, don't you?" said Betsy.

"He's what I'd call my least objectionable suspect. I'll tell you something else: He had scratches on his forearms when I first talked to him. He said a goat did it, but I'm thinking of a struggling woman being shoved under soapy water. Neither one of the other two suspects had any marks like that."

"Oh, wow. Oh, wow," breathed Betsy.

"I'm this close" — Malloy held up his right hand, finger and thumb a half inch apart — "to arresting him. Don't you think I should?"

"I don't know. Knowing Tommy works at a drugstore, I do think he looks more likely than the others. But how can we link him to Wilma Carter? He doesn't know anyone at Watered Silk, so what was he doing visiting the place? Whereas Preston has a — what? A great-aunt? A great-aunt who *is* Wilma, for cripes' sake!"

"But his wife says he was at home, with her."

"She loves him, she may be lying for him."

"Humph, I suppose so. But I'm damned if I'd lie for a spouse who's been lying to me for years about infidelities."

"Not to mention that little old vasectomy," added Connor.

"Did you tell her about it?" Betsy asked Malloy.

He shook his head. "Not relevant."

"He is not a nice man," said Betsy. "And if I had to judge by likability, he'd be my murderer. But where would he get atropine?

And a hypodermic needle? And the knowledge to put it in that little patch?" She frowned. "Where are those patches kept? Surely not in Wilma's room."

"Actually, they were. Residents' medicines are kept in wooden cabinets about sixteen inches wide by twenty inches tall, fastened fairly high up on the wall. They're locked, of course. The nurse on duty has the key."

"And the keys are kept — ?"

"Key. One key unlocks any of the cabinets. A second copy is kept in the little pharmacy at Watered Silk — which is itself under lock and key. But the locks on the cabinets are fairly flimsy. They're meant to keep the residents out, not to foil a determined burglar."

"Did any of our trio know anything about this?"

"No. I checked the records, and Preston visited his great-aunt-by-marriage only once, eighteen months ago, in the company of his wife and father-in-law. Thereafter, his wife did the visiting, about once a month, sometimes along with her father."

"Typical," remarked Betsy.

"Now, machree," Connor said gently.

Malloy continued, "Tommy never visited the complex, except to swim in the pool, which he now says he did twice. He says

335

Teddi brought him both times, and he claims he doesn't know how she found out about it."

"And Noah?"

"Now here's one big black mark against Noah Levesque: He's an insulin-dependent diabetic, so he has access to hypodermic needles and knows how to use them. And here's another black mark against him: He worked at Watered Silk, helping to build a bistro in the complex. But that was before they installed the therapy pool, which he did not work on. And, he says he never went skinny-dipping over there. He knew about it — he says Teddi told him — but he also says he told her he outgrew skinny-dipping when he turned twenty-five."

"He's lying," said Betsy.

"What? About what?"

"I got him to agree to talk to me by telling him I had an eyewitness to his using the pool. He identified Wilma as 'that crazy old lady' whose testimony was not to be believed. But I described the route she showed me through the alley door, up the stairs into the maintenance closet and through the men's locker room. Then he admitted he'd used the pool several times."

"Son of a *bitch*!" said Malloy, making a note. "I better have another talk with that fellow. I wonder why he changed his story when talking to me."

"Because somehow he found out that Wilma is dead. And he assumed that the eyewitness I scared him with — who, by the way, never mentioned him by name or identified him by description — is gone. And he knows I'm not connected officially with the police, so he concludes that you and I never talk."

Malloy said, "Poor ignorant bastard," and wrote something else in his notebook.

Betsy said, "Have you talked to the former head of maintenance at Watered Silk?"

"Why should I talk to him?"

"Because he's a smoker, and his office down in that basement was far away from the official exit where smokers can stand outside and puff away."

"So?"

"So there's this great big door a few steps away from his desk that leads out into an obscure alley where a man can indulge his nicotine addiction quickly and safely, once he makes a few adjustments to the blockade on it. If you go look some more, you'll find a few stray cigarette butts in the alley near that door."

Malloy looked at Betsy for a few seconds while he thought about it. Then he turned to a blank space in his book and wrote something else down. Finally he looked up at Betsy, waiting.

"His name is Paul Juggins, and he lives in Hopkins," she said.

Connor looked fit to burst with amused pride.

In the car on the drive home, Connor burst into song: "She's a lassie from Devonshire, just a lassie from Devonshire, she's a lassie I love so dear, oh, so dear!"

"I believe the original lassie was from Lancashire," said Betsy, laughing. After a moment's thought, she launched into a new version of another old song: "Has anybody here seen Connor? S-U-L-L-I-V-A-N, has anybody here seen Connor? Find him if you can! For he came to me from 'cross the sea, tender as a man can be. Has anybody here seen Connor? Connor from Ireland!"

"Oh, my dear, that's good!" said Connor.

By the time they got home, their joyous mood was all spent, and they came up the stairs to the apartment quiet and thoughtful.

"I *liked* Noah," said Betsy, rinsing and filling Sophie's water dish before putting it on the floor for her. Thai beat her to it, though, and straddled it with his forepaws so Sophie couldn't get at it. Connor gently lifted the Siamese and tickled him under his chin. The animal reached up to lightly touch Connor's face, purring. Sophie meanwhile came to drink. "He was charming and seemed like a grown-up," Betsy continued. "I'm disappointed that he's proved a liar."

"He's scared. They're all scared, I suspect. One of them is going to be tried for murder, and each is hoping it's one of the others."

"And they're all lying."

"You don't know Pres is lying; you haven't talked to him."

"He's been false to his wedding vows, and he lied to his wife about his vasectomy. I cannot believe he wouldn't lie to me."

Connor put Thai down. "Do you think he really lied about his vasectomy? Maybe the person lying is Sony. Maybe she's insisting online that she wants another child, knowing she's not going to get one from him, turning wishful thinking into some kind of weird game."

Betsy frowned at him, then went into the living room to think. She sat down in the chair she used when knitting. Knitting was her way of clearing away the distractions in her mind so she could work things out. "I don't know," she said to herself, turning over his comments in her head. Sony's fury at Betsy during that one encounter certainly gave rise to a theory of an unbalanced personality.

Hmm . . .

Connor, knowing what she was about to do, joined her and got out his own project. It was a counted cross-stitch sampler pattern, done all in blue on linen, of old-fashioned sailing ships, mermaids, anchors, rays, starfish, dolphins, and more maritime-themed items scattered down the cloth, with a quote from *A Midsummer Night's Dream:* "And heard a mermaid, on a dolphin's back, uttering such dulcet and harmonious breath, that the rude sea grew civil at her song; and certain stars shot madly from their spheres to hear the sea-maid's music." The pattern was by Stickideen von der Wiehenburg; Betsy had found it at a needlework market last year.

They had purchased a second good lamp to match the one Betsy had placed behind her chair. This new one stood beside the couch, where it cast a good strong light over Connor's shoulder when he sat there. They both snapped on their lights and fell into a companionable silence.

Betsy reached into the carpetbag hanging suspended in its little wooden frame beside her and pulled out the knit scarf she was

340

working on. It was an experimental piece, using roving instead of yarn. Betsy sold roving down in her shop — a length of wool that has been cleaned and carded so the fibers all face in one direction. People who like to spin their own yarn but not go through the lengthy preparation process buy roving, as do people who do needle felting. But a woman who sold wool at craft fairs told Betsy it is also possible to knit or even crochet with it. So Betsy had bought a single ball of roving that came from a black sheep and was trying to knit a skinny scarf from it.

The roving was somewhat flat, but about an inch wide, far wider than any yarn she had ever used. It was not as solid as a strand of yarn — with little effort it would pull apart — so she had to handle it gently. The scarf she was creating from it was thicker than usual, but so narrow it was nearly round. As she gained experience of its properties, she was surprised to find it wasn't all that difficult to work with. As a bonus, there were subtle shifts in the natural black color, even here and there a fine strand of brown. She had a dark brown sweater that would go nicely with this scarf.

As she settled into the knitting, she felt the usual calming and clearing of her mind.

However, because roving was new to her, she had to keep some of her attention on the soft, fragile material in her fingers.

And, because this was a learning experience, she wasn't doing anything but straight knit stitches, using size thirteen needles, and easing the roving onto and off them. Her scarf was just ten stitches wide and so far just a little over four inches long.

Push through the last loop, lay the roving over the end of the needle, gently twist to catch it with the needle and pull it through, then slip the loop off.

Which of the three suspects knew Wilma's name? Noah thought he knew that she'd seen him in the pool, but that was a fact not in evidence. All Betsy knew was that Wilma knew how people were sneaking into the complex without going through one of the camera-guarded entrances. When she told Noah how it was done, he'd been convinced that Wilma had seen him there.

No, wait a second. Noah had described Wilma as a crazy old lady — how did he know that unless he had encountered her? Had she walked into the pool via that back entrance and accosted him? Who was there with him? Skinny-dipping is not usually a solitary activity.

What else did Noah know about her? Her

name? The number of her apartment? That she had a fresh Exelon patch applied to her back every evening? That he might know that last bit of information was impossible to believe — but her murderer knew.

Pres might know. Wilma was a relative by marriage. And his wife visited her at Watered Silk. Sony could easily have kept him aware of Wilma's status at the senior center.

And what about Sony? She had a temper and was not afraid to display it. Betsy could see her attacking Teddi . . . maybe. It seemed more likely she would go after Pres. And would she be willing to murder her own great-aunt, whom she knew well? And why? Did Wilma see her — or one of the men, or some other person — sneaking Teddi's body into Watered Silk to float it in the pool?

Hold on, that would mean Sony knew about Teddi — knew where she lived, in fact. And she could have gone over there to surprise her in her bath and drown her.

Betsy smiled. That seemed awfully unlikely. Pres was extremely careful about keeping his women from his wife.

So let's look at Tommy.

Poor ineffectual Tommy. Who was living hand to mouth, working two low-paying jobs, and couldn't even afford child support if he'd fathered a child. "What was I supposed to do?" he had whined to Betsy over a burger and fries. If Teddi had not wanted to abort her baby, Tommy was going to be stuck taking care of it for the next eighteen years. Probably he could see himself in court in a few years, convicted of being tens of thousands of dollars behind in support. He knew where she lived, he'd been in her house.

So had Noah, the lying liar. No, Tommy was a lying liar, Noah was a calculating liar, thinking Betsy and Malloy would never talk to each other. He'd assumed it was safe, once Wilma was dead, to deny to Malloy ever going swimming at Watered Silk. It was not impossible that he'd encountered the perpetually peripatetic Wilma while working on the bistro. And Noah knew how to wield a hypodermic needle, too. But did he know which room Wilma was in? Or that she used Exelon? And where would he get the atropine?

Where would any of them get the atropine?

Atropine. Wasn't it derived from belladonna, a plant? And called belladonna because it dilates the eyes, which makes a person look more beautiful? So how can it be a poison?

She put her knitting away.

"Time for bed?" Connor asked.

"In a little while," she replied. "I need to look something up."

She went into the second bedroom that was her office and booted up her computer.

A keyword search gave her lots of information. Atropine, in small or diluted doses, was perfectly safe. It had many medical uses: It could treat diverticulitis, spastic colon, certain heart problems, even infant colic. A doctor could easily write a prescription for a patient and it could be had from a drugstore.

It was also used in surgery, because in bigger doses it paralyzed the muscles and allowed a surgeon to cut or move through them. But by paralyzing the muscles, it required that a patient be given artificial aid to breathe, and there was danger the heart would stop.

None of her suspects had ever worked as a surgeon or even a surgical nurse or hospital pharmacist.

Except Sony, who was in bed asleep next to her husband, the lying fink, the night Teddi was drowned.

Rats. As Godwin said, quoting Mark Twain, it was "too many" for her.

She shut down the computer and went into their bedroom.

# TWENTY

Betsy found Connor reading in bed — he liked spy novels and was deep into a worn paperback copy of *The Miernik Dossier.* "I've seen you reading that one before," she said, starting to undress. "Why do you like it?"

"It's a collection of documents," he replied, closing the book on his thumb to mark his place. "You have to figure out the story yourself, rather than having the author tell it to you. Kind of like the detecting you do: You gather the stories and information, and from it you come to a conclusion that fits all the facts. It's fascinating watching you at work."

She sat on the bed to take off her shoes. "It's not quite so much fun from inside my own head. I frankly don't know where to look next. I have different reasons for liking each of the suspects — and different reasons for thinking they're innocent, too." She rubbed her forehead. "I don't like any of them for this, actually."

"So who is most likely?" he asked.

She sighed. "Tommy. Well, that is, Tommy for Wilma, and Pres for Teddi. Or maybe Noah for Wilma."

"Could it be there are two murderers?"

She considered that. "Oh, now you've complicated it even more!" She went to brush her teeth.

Later, asleep, she had a dream. A dolphin — colored an improbable pink — was leaping out of a dark, stormy sea, making a series of leaps, each exactly like the previous one, while whitecaps flung themselves high, breaking into a lace-like pattern at their tops, over and over and over. In her dream, she was at first fascinated by the precision of the leaps and the beauty of the whitecaps, then bored by the endless parade until a piece of classical music started to play. By then the dolphin wasn't leaping in time to the music, and then it was the clock radio playing something by Mozart and it was time to wake up.

Whew!

Connor began to stir, so she quickly shut off the radio and slipped out of bed. It was her morning for water aerobics at the Courage Center in Golden Valley. She made a quick trip to the bathroom to brush her teeth again, step into her dark blue swimsuit — the one resistant to chlorine — and dress in jeans and a sweater. She grabbed her zippered bag containing underwear, deodorant, a comb, socks, and a washcloth; rolled a towel on top; and went down the stairs to the back hallway that led to the small parking lot in back of her building. It was still dark out, the temperature well below freezing but not bitter cold. The sky was overcast, but it didn't feel like snow, and the roads leading eastward toward the Courage Center were clear.

Getting a bit of exercise three mornings a week had become a longtime habit, and one not difficult to maintain, as it happened so early in the morning that it didn't put a hole in her day.

She found her friends in the women's locker room chatting about travel, past and planned, but she had nothing to contribute. The women took quick showers and went into the brightly lit great room, where an Olympic-size pool waited, its surface smooth. Music set to a disco beat started, and their instructor came out of a side office, as the six women and three men stepped down into the delicious warmth.

Toward the end of the one-hour class, a new move was introduced. Everyone went to the side of the pool to do leg flutters and to step with alternating feet onto the vertical edge of the pool, and then were asked to pull themselves up by their hands out of the water, drop back down, and repeat. Whoosh, drop down, whoosh, drop down.

Betsy was thinking about Noah, Tommy, and Pres, and forgot to coordinate her movements and her breathing. She tried to take a breath while dropping back down so far that half her face was underwater.

One instant she felt water rushing up her nose and seemingly the next she was lying on her side on the pool's apron, trying to cough up a lung.

"That's it, that's it, breathe, Betsy, breathe!" Emily was saying, patting her on the back.

"What happened?" asked someone whose voice she couldn't identify.

Betsy was unable to reply.

"She was doing pull-ups with the rest of us and suddenly she was unconscious," said Jim, who was kneeling beside her. "Did you bump your head?" he asked her.

Betsy shook her head, then raised her shoulders. *Had* she bumped her head? There was no sore spot she could detect. She pulled herself into a sitting position, trying to slow her cough, which was turning into a retch.

" 'M all right," she managed. "B'okay. In minute. Two."

Somebody draped a big towel around her shoulders. "Try to relax," said the unfamiliar voice. Betsy felt her shoulders and back being massaged. "We've called an ambulance."

"No, no. 'M okay. Really." But she could not stop coughing.

The doctor at the emergency room of Methodist Hospital could not find any sign of trauma to her head, and so concluded that Betsy had simply inhaled when she should not have and, except for a sore throat and aching lungs, was fine.

Someone had gathered her clothes and swim bag and given them to the med techs in the ambulance, and miraculously, they were not mislaid, so she was able to change into dry clothing while Connor waited, his face a mask of concern.

"I'm okay, really I am," Betsy said in a husky voice. "I admit, it was scary. One second I was thinking about atropine and the next I was stretched on the pool apron unable to catch my breath. I don't remember inhaling water, I don't remember passing out. I just was gone, instantly."

"Nobody grabbed you by the ankles, as a prank, and yanked you under?"

"No, of course not, we're not that kind of a group!"

"I'm glad to hear that."

"What made you ask such a thing?"

"While I was waiting for them to release you, I had a few minutes to think. And what I was thinking about was a certain George Joseph Smith, an English serial killer."

"Why would you think about him?" Betsy asked. "You think someone from my group is a murderer?" She gave a rusty laugh, amused.

"Mr. Smith was a bigamist who killed several of his wives by drowning them in their bathtubs. He did it in a clever way, without leaving a mark on them — or himself. The way you almost drowned in the pool today made me think of it."

"Go on, tell me how he did it."

"He would go to the end of the tub where their feet were, grab them suddenly by the ankles, and pull back sharply to make their heads go under the water. It forces water into their nose and mouth, and somehow the shock brings about instant unconsciousness. A very clever forensic investigator back then tried some experiments on female volunteers using one of the actual bathtubs, and discovered how it was done. It's so fast and effective, he nearly killed one of the volunteers in the process."

"When did all this happen?"

"Smith was hanged in 1915." After another thoughtful silence, Connor asked, "Do you suppose any of your suspects ever read about brides-in-the-bath Smith? It's a famous case. Or do I mean infamous?"

" 'Brides in the bath.' I have heard about that case. I didn't know they'd found out how he killed his wives. I thought there were more than three."

"He married at least seven times, without getting a divorce between them. He'd marry them, then persuade them to give him all their money, and move on."

"He must have been charming," said Betsy, thinking of Noah. "I think we'd better contact Malloy and tell him about Mr. Smith's methods."

But Malloy was out of his office. Betsy insisted that Connor take her back to the Courage Center to retrieve her car. He did, and then followed her closely all the way home.

There, she changed into work clothes and went downstairs. Godwin came rushing up to throw his arms around her. "Oh my God, we were *so worried!*" he exclaimed, squeezing until she began to struggle against his hold.

"I'm all right, really I am. I got a bad scare, but I'm fine, truly."

He let go and stepped back. "Your voice sounds funny."

"That's because I coughed up about a quart and a half of highly chlorinated water a little bit at a time."

"Maybe you shouldn't be at work, then. What about heading back upstairs to lie down?"

"No, no, honestly, I'm fine." She looked around the shop. The sun, still in the north, poured light through the front windows, making all the fibers glow. The Bose was playing something spritely. A heady aroma of coffee permeated the air. Godwin and Betsy's part-timer, Vicki Sue, were doing some dusting and rearranging of displays. Sophie the cat was curled on her chair, the one with the blue cushion and needle-pointed sign reading NO THANK YOU I'M ON A DIET, meant to discourage customers from sneaking her treats. But there were no customers to discourage.

Betsy walked through the shop, looking for anything awry, but found nothing. She could have sent Vicki Sue away, but the young woman needed the money for college, so instead Betsy said, "I think I will go back upstairs. I'll check back in after lunch."

She went up to her apartment to find Connor mopping the kitchen floor. He was wearing an apron and rubber gloves, which meant he was going to scrub down the counters and appliances as well. He was whistling "Where Did You Get That Hat?"

Betsy blew him a kiss and went into the bedroom, where she changed into jeans and a chambray shirt and lay down on the bed to take a nap.

An hour later she was back in the living room, knitting the black roving. And thinking. After a while, Connor came in to lie down on the couch.

"Penny?" he asked, meaning a penny for your thoughts. Thai jumped up onto his chest and began to knead dough.

"I'm so discouraged about this case," she grumbled. "I want to go out and shake something loose — but I don't know what to shake. Or who." Her knitting took on a brisk movement until she realized she was in danger of damaging the roving. She slowed down.

Thai, still on Connor's chest, turned around three times and lay down. Silence reigned for perhaps half an hour.

"Connor," she said at last.

"Huh — what? What's the matter?" He had fallen into a doze.

"What do you think a good forensic technician could have gotten from that torn sheet if it was, in fact, used to carry Teddi to the pool?"

He sat up, dumping the cat onto the floor, running a hand over his face and yawning. "What would they find? Well, proof it was used to carry Teddi, probably. Her DNA would be all over it. Along with residue from the lavender-scented bath salts."

"But would there be any DNA from the person who carried her?" Betsy asked.

He thought about that. "I don't know. Maybe. But I'm thinking not."

"Yes, I think not, too." She frowned. "But maybe there would be traces from the vehicle he used. Fluff from the carpet in the trunk of the car, or God knows what from the backseat, or the bed of a pickup truck. And that sheet was splitting, so there would likely be fibers from it coming loose and remaining behind. The police could compare the sheet and whatever it had picked up to the material it rested on."

"I don't think Noah would be foolish enough to carry a fresh corpse in the back of his pickup truck. Someone he passed, or who passed him, in a semitruck or a bus might look down and see it. If that sheet was as thin as you describe it, and poor Teddi was still a little damp, her outline would be clear under it. Or the jostling might uncover her body."

"Oh, ugh! Stop, stop!" Betsy cringed in her chair, raising her knitting as if to ward off Connor's words. Then she lowered her hands. "But you're right. She would have to ride in the passenger seat if our culprit is Noah." Her expression grew pained at the picture she was creating in her mind, of a cooling, sagging corpse, its wet, lolling blond head poking out the top of the sheet. She looked over and saw an echo of her expression on Connor's face.

"What all this in aid of?" he asked. "Mike told you he doesn't have the sheet. You have some idea of playing a trick to winkle out an admission somehow from one of the suspects?"

"Suppose the word got out that Mike did recover that bedsheet, and has found proof that it was used to carry Teddi. Suppose word also got out that he intends to get search warrants for the vehicles that might have been used to transport her."

"Can he do that? Legally, I mean? Get away, Thai!" scolded Connor. The cat was sniffing at the ball of roving.

"It doesn't matter. If I had carried Teddi in my trunk, say, and thought the police were coming by to vacuum up stray fibers to compare them to fibers from the sheet, I'd be off like a shot to clean my trunk."

"So what does that mean?"

"A stakeout, so we can catch the guilty party at it."

Connor rubbed his face some more. "You may have a good idea there, machree. But why not pass it along to Malloy?"

"Because none of these people are within his jurisdiction."

"Okay, you're right. And anyway, how would he get the word out? If these men were living in Excelsior, he could tell a few people and inside three hours it would be all over town. But Preston lives in Minnetonka, Noah lives in Navarre, and Tommy lives way the hell and gone out in the country. So," he added, having just thought of it, "who is going to do these stakeouts?"

"You and I can do one."

"Hey!" protested Connor, alarmed.

"We're not going to arrest anyone, just let Malloy know what we saw. He can contact the proper authorities."

"Why don't *you* contact the proper authorities?"

"Because I don't know any of them, they

don't know me, and they'll just tell me to stay home and mind my knitting store."

"Which isn't bad advice, machree," said Connor.

Betsy set her mouth in a firm line. "I'm going to do it, and I'd really like your help. You and I can take one of them, and Jill can take another — and, well, maybe we don't really need to do Pres, because he's pretty solidly out of it." Her expression softened. "We'll do it as soon as I can think of a way to tell the suspects — even Pres, because Madison isn't all that far away, he could have driven up here and back again — that the police are coming with a search warrant and a handheld vacuum cleaner."

# TWENTY-ONE

After lunch, Betsy went into her carpetbag, dug past the roving in it, and took out a scarf she was knitting from yarn made of recycled silk saris. She sold the yarn in her shop, but had no sample of it on display. Its bright colors and incredibly smooth texture made it a treat for both eyes and fingers. She was doing her usual knit two, purl two stitch with an odd one at either end to keep it from curling over. It was forty-two stitches wide, enough so she wasn't turning too often.

As usual, she soon found herself lost in contemplation, first of the knitting, then of the case. She began ruminating about the information she had gathered from the start, from the first time she'd gone into the Watered Silk complex. She remembered meeting Wilma Carter, and hearing her call out, "Wait a minute, wait a minute, start over!" in the pool room of Watered Silk.

She remembered her shock at learning of a mysterious body afloat in that pool. She remembered Bershada's indignation that her nephew, Ethan Smart, was under suspicion. She remembered her sorrow when it was revealed that Teddi Wahlberger was ten weeks pregnant when she was drowned.

She remembered the torn and dirty sheet with the magnificent Hardanger embroidery across its top. She remembered Phil and Doris's concern when they discovered that Phil's grandnephew, Tommy Shore, was the father of the unborn child. She remembered Tommy's persistent, incompetent lying.

She remembered Frey's and Lia's anguish over Teddi's death, and their persistent and finally successful efforts to make Betsy take Thai home with her. She remembered the surprise discovery of a pair of pillowcases whose Hardanger trim matched that on the dirty, discarded sheet. She remembered the shock of Noah's good looks and the second shock of hearing that he'd lied to Mike Malloy about visiting the Watered Silk pool.

She remembered the fun but fruitless night out clubbing with Connor. She remembered Goddy's clever trick of tracing Teddi's sketch of exotic Preston Munro and taming it into a face he could recognize. She remembered Sony Munro's rage when

Betsy told her that Pres was dating Teddi.

She remembered the evening at Mike Malloy's home, where he told her that Pres was out of the running as a suspect, but Tommy, with his pharmacy access, and Noah, with his knowledge of the building complex and his insulin dependency, were not.

She remembered . . . Hold on, there was an idea in there somewhere. Her hands slowed, stopped, dropped into her lap.

Connor, reading his spy novel, noticed her stillness. "Have you got an idea, machree?"

"I believe I have, my dear, I believe I have."

She went into her office and booted up, found the web site for Bar Abilene, and called them on her phone. She raised her voice over the noisy background when the call was picked up, and asked for the manager.

After a pause, she heard a man's voice. "Bar Abilene, Morty speaking, who's this?" And the other phone was hung up. It had gotten a lot quieter; he must have an office in back.

"Hello, I'm Betsy Devonshire and I would like to talk to the person who writes the Winchell column."

"We don't take complaints about its

content," the man said at once.

"I don't have a complaint. I'd like to plant an item in it."

" 'Plant an item'?"

"I'm trying to spook a serious lawbreaker into doing something to give himself away."

"Who is this?"

"My name is Betsy Devonshire, I live in Excelsior, and I do criminal investigations. But I'm not a cop."

"Are you asking me to break the law?"

"No, of course not. I just want you to put an item in your clever gossip column that may cause my suspect to incriminate himself. It won't be an accusation or anything like that, just a piece of information that may cause him to jump to a certain conclusion."

"Is this person one of our regulars?"

"Yes."

"May I ask who he is?"

"I can't tell you that. Because if he doesn't jump — or if he's innocent — I don't want him treated any differently."

It wasn't hard to convince Morty to plant the item, but it took awhile to convince him that the message would mean something to her suspect.

After they hung up, Betsy sent an e-mail to Lia and Frey. "Please go to the Winchell column at the web site of Bar Abilene tomorrow after eight in the evening and read the item, 'Overheard: Mrs. Sherlock and her Irish BFF are talking about bed sheets, trunks, and fibers. Could they be planning a march up the aisle?' Please call Tommy and Noah, ask if they've seen it, and do they think it's about Betsy Devonshire? (My boyfriend is named Connor Sullivan, btw.) Thanks!" She sent another e-mail to Ramona, asking her to contact Pres about a strange message she'd seen on the Bar Abilene site.

And having set the trap, Betsy got on the phone with Jill.

"I don't know, Betsy, this could be dangerous."

"How? I don't plan on confronting anyone, I just think that if we witness one of them scrambling to clean out his trunk or the passenger cab of his vehicle, we can let Mike know about it. You know how good forensics people are nowadays, there's no way an amateur could clean up every single trace of evidence, and with one of us as an eyewitness, Mike will have probable cause for a search warrant. Right?"

"You're going to do this whether or not I come on board, I assume."

"You assume right. I'll watch Tommy, and

Connor will watch Noah."

"It would be better if there are two witnesses to the act."

"Okay, Connor and me, and you and — who?"

"Lars, of course. Though I'd like it better if it were me and Connor, and you and Lars. I want Lars to be with you watching Noah; Connor and I will take Tommy."

"Welcome aboard."

When Betsy told Godwin of their plans the next morning, he was indignant that he hadn't been offered a piece of the action. "A *stakeout*? For *real*? Just like *Dragnet*?"

"Don't you mean *CSI*?"

"*Dragnet*'s more fun. Dum-da-dum-dum!" replied the fan of old-time radio. "Let me and Rafael come along, please? *Please?*"

"Settle down, Goddy, for heaven's sake! From all I've read, stakeouts are boring! And we aren't going to be part of any action, we're just going to be sitting there watching. For hours and hours, probably. Even if something happens, we're not going to do anything, we're just going to report it to the police."

"Please? Please-please-please?"

"Oh, all right, I'll tell you what: You and

Rafael — if you can persuade him to come with you — can stake out Pres Munro."

"Awww, I thought he was cleared!"

"I have thought Tommy was cleared. I have thought Noah was cleared. Right now I think Pres is cleared. But I can't prove any one of them is guilty. For all I know it's Pres. Actually, it's probably a good idea to cover all our bases."

"All right, count me in. When do we start this stakeout?"

"Tonight. We should all be in place by eight o'clock. We'll take turns this afternoon scouting out the sites. Look for a place to park that isn't obviously overlooking their driveway. Then we'll close the shop early enough to give each of us time to get there. Make sure your cell phone is charged and your gas tank is filled."

"I will make it so," Godwin said, echoing Captain Picard from Star Trek. He went in back to call Rafael and soon Betsy heard him arguing and pleading with his partner. But he came back a little later all smiles. "Rafael thinks it's a wonderful idea, he's *so* excited! We're going to pack a picnic!"

Betsy had always thought of her Buick as a big car, but with Lars in the passenger seat, it seemed to have shrunk to the size of a sports car. While not in the least obese, he was a very big man, and he came dressed for the outdoors in snow pants and a heavy jacket. He overflowed the passenger side of the front seat; she could feel his jacket brushing her arm. She wondered if he had a gun under it. Of course he did, he was a cop, they were always carrying. She was sure it was a big gun. Probably an AR-15 — a man his size could carry one as a sidearm. Betsy had never felt so safe in her life.

Looking down at the huge boots he wore, she wondered what size they could possibly be. Seventeen? Twenty? Extra-extra wide? He must have to special order them. In the summer he could rent them out as cabins to tourists.

He also had the biggest thermos Betsy had ever seen. "Coffee," he'd said when she'd noticed it in his gloved hands.

Now his gloves were off, draped across one massive knee. His wedding band winked in the faint light cast by a light high up on a pole in the barnyard of Tommy's landlord's hobby farm.

They were parked alongside the road, hidden from the house by a short row of overgrown lilac bushes. Tommy's old car sagged in the driveway that crossed between the barnyard and the snow-covered front lawn. There was a garage, not attached to the house. Betsy was sure the landlord's car was tucked safely away in there.

An hour later she was getting cold. She wanted to start the car and run the heater, but there were lights on in the house, and out here in the country sounds carried. The sound of a car starting and then not moving away might draw a look out the window — and if Betsy could see the upstairs window, then someone looking out could see her car. She sighed and wiggled her bottom, hoping to stir up her blood.

"Coffee?" suggested Lars.

But Betsy thought about the lack of bathroom facilities and said, "Not right now, thank you."

A silence fell.

Betsy asked, "Have you done many stakeouts?"

"A few."

"How do you pass the time?"

"Talk about fishing. Or cars. Or sports." He sighed and looked out the window. "What do you and Connor talk about?"

"Needlework. English music-hall songs. Being a tourist in Europe. We're planning a trip to East Glacier Park this summer."

"Not much crossover there, huh?"

Betsy smiled in the near-darkness. "Not

much. I'm kind of sorry now I agreed with Jill to swap you for Connor — and I bet she's feeling the same."

"Are those pecans in the chicken salad?" asked Rafael.

"Yes. And cranberries instead of golden raisins. Isn't this exciting?"

"Not really, *mi gorrion.* But it is fun, more fun than I thought it was going to be. Do you think we will actually see something happening?"

"Probably not. I'm getting cold. Start the car for a little while. Is it time to check in yet?"

Rafael checked his watch. "Not yet."

Connor and Jill were discussing needlework. "I'm not a big fan of counted," Connor was saying. "I mean, the results are spectacular, but . . . well, all those damn *x*'s."

Jill nodded. "Of course you can use other stitches. Samplers are a great way to explore the possibilities."

"I saw a great quote on a sampler: 'You love someone because they sing a song only you can hear.' "

"Why don't you ask Betsy to marry you?"

"I have. I ask her about once a month. So far she says no." Uncomfortable with her question, he changed the subject. "What do you think Lars and Betsy are talking about?"

"Fishing," said Jill. "Children. Problems with owning a Stanley Steamer. What do you think?"

"Owning your own small business," he said, with a chuckle. "Knitting. Ireland. Cats. Speaking of which, would you like a cat? He's very lively, we've got his health problems straightened out, and he's been fixed."

"No, thank you. We have an absolutely enormous dog who would come to give him a big, wet kiss and accidentally swallow him whole."

"What time is it?" asked Lars.

Betsy pressed the button on her Indiglo watch. "Half past midnight. How much longer should we sit here?"

"Hey, you're the one in charge of this shindig. You tell me."

"Give me a cup of coffee. Then I'll be good for another hour, anyway."

"Disappointed yet?" asked Connor.

"I never was appointed," said Jill. "I don't think anything is going to happen."

"So why did you agree to go on this stakeout?"

"Because I've been wrong before. More often than Betsy, really. Is she this good about other things? I mean, she's some kind of phenom at sleuthing. Is she making you happy? Wait a minute, that's a rude question. I must be getting tired. You don't have to answer that."

"Thank you, I won't. But she does. How did you and Lars meet?"

Rafael yawned prodigiously. "How much longer do we sit here?"

"I'm not sure. Let's ask Betsy. What did I do with my cell?"

"Hush, look!"

"Where? Oh my God, someone's coming out of the house!"

"No, wait, it's not Pres, it's Sony."

Rafael leaned toward the window. "What in the world is she doing up and out? It's half past two! And what is she carrying? It looks like some kind of weird purse! Is she going somewhere?"

"Oh my God, she's opening the trunk! It's not a purse, it's one of those little vacuum cleaners! Call Betsy! Call Betsy!"

Godwin, hero of the hour, was sitting proudly at the head of the library table in Crewel World. Phil and Doris were there, and Bershada, Tommy, Noah, Rafael, Betsy, and Connor.

But not Sony or Pres, of course. Sony was in jail, and Pres was trying to convince his father-in-law that none of this was his fault.

"What did you do when you saw her open that trunk?" asked Bershada.

"Honked my horn," said Godwin. "Flashed my lights."

"What did she do?"

"Came across the street yelling at us. 'Who are you? What do you want?' I rolled the window down the least little bit and said, as nicely as I could, 'Oh, my dear, you are so busted.' "

He laughed delightedly. "And Rafael is on the phone, shouting at Betsy, 'Eet ees *not* Mister Preston, eet is *Sonja*!' " Godwin was exaggerating Rafael's Spanish accent — though it was true that Rafael, under great stress, lost some of his fluency in English.

Rafael, smiling broadly, nodded. "Just so," he said, "Just so."

"Then what did she do?" asked Doris in her husky voice.

"She ran back in the house, leaving the little vacuum cleaner on the ground and the trunk open. I found my cell phone on the floor and dialed 911, but they weren't interested, there wasn't a crime taking place. So I called Connor and while Rafael talked to Betsy, I talked to Connor. And then a squad car came up behind us!" Godwin laughed some more.

"Betsy called 911," guessed Bershada.

"No, *Sony* did! She reported us as *prowlers*! Too, too, too delicious! They actually made us get out of the car and searched us and *everything*! I finally persuaded one of them to take Rafael's cell — Betsy was still on the line! *She* explained what was going on, and meanwhile *Connor* had called *Mike,* and he called Minnetonka PD."

Godwin's great good humor diminished abruptly. "Well, Mike was *not happy* with these goings-on, but what could he do? We had caught her with her hand in the jelly bean jar, almost literally. So he got a search warrant and summoned a tow truck, and I imagine that a forensic search of that trunk is happening *right this minute*!"

He sat back and raked in the plaudits for a couple of minutes, then waxed serious. "But I still don't understand what she was thinking, Betsy. Why did she commit murder?"

"She was desperately in love with Pres, had been from the start. When she got pregnant, her father applied a *lot* of pressure on Pres to marry her. Mr. Halloway then tried to make an honest businessman of his son-in-law. But Pres was of the opinion that he had done the right thing by Sony and it was up to Tony to make it worth his while.

"He was pleased that his offspring was male, because he was the kind of man who thought having a son was better than having a daughter. Plus, his father-in-law was proud and pleased to have a grandson, and Big Tony had probably made it clear to Pres that keeping the father-in-law happy was a *good thing.* But Pres didn't want any more children. One reason, perhaps, was that he was a serial adulterer, and life was much less complicated without any 'accidents' to mark his passage. So he had a vasectomy — but he didn't tell Sony, because she wanted another child.

"Sony suspected that Pres was unfaithful, but she used all her considerable willpower to suppress that knowledge. Pres was good to their son, he was an ardent lover, he had a fine job with a future, they had a nice home. She gave up a promising nursing career to stay home and keep everything running smoothly.

"So see?" Betsy said, "there *was* someone who knew about drugs. And who kept her hospital ID in a scrapbook, so if she liked, she could pull it out and gain access to areas not open to the public. Such as the pharmacy."

"But why kill Teddi?" asked Phil. "She didn't know the girl, did she?"

"Sony intercepted a message from Teddi meant for Pres. Here was a reality she could not deny. Pres, who somehow was unable to give Sony another child, was giving one to another woman. It made a sham of her marriage, of her whole life. But she still loved Pres, and still wanted him as her husband — as her respectable, faithful, *employed* husband. What would her father do when he found out? Sony knew he already didn't think much of Pres. No, no, this would not do, this would not do at all!"

"So she killed her in cold blood," said Godwin in a shocked voice.

"Or perhaps in a hot, passionate rage!" Rafael pointed out.

"I wonder if it might have been an accident," said Betsy.

"How can you 'accidentally' hold someone under water until they die?" demanded Tommy.

"Let me tell you about a wicked Englishman named Smith," said Betsy, and she did.

Then she continued, "Now, here's what I think might have happened. Sony continued to monitor Pres's iPad or cell phone or whatever and found out that he'd made an appointment to meet Teddi late one evening. She goes over to Teddi's house and finds Teddi taking a luxurious bath in a tub full of lavender-scented salts. There is a confrontation. Sony, intending just to duck Teddi, grabs her by the ankles and pulls. Teddi is instantly motionless, and Sony stands horrified at what she has done. She has killed someone. She can't just leave her there; Pres is coming over, and if he finds the body, he will likely call 911 and may well end up charged with murder.

"There is no open water anywhere, she can't take Teddi's body to a lake or river and dump it in so people will think she fell through the ice and drowned. The snow is deep, the ground is frozen, she can't dig a grave. Then she remembers a place with a pool, a place with a secret entrance — a place her great-aunt showed her: Watered Silk's therapy pool.

"She takes the body out of the tub, and while the tub is emptying, she goes into Frey's bedroom to get some clothing — and that shows you how blind I was!"

"Blind how?" asked Bershada.

"The clothes were wrong! Sony went into the wrong bedroom. She didn't know which one was Teddi's. Tommy did, Pres did, Noah did. They wouldn't have made that simple mistake. But Sony had never been in Teddi's house before. Anyway, Sony gets the clothing. She doesn't bother to put it on Teddi's body; after all, she'd only have to take it off again. And she's in a hurry. She finds a handy sheet in the armoire and wraps Teddi's body in it. She is a strong woman, she can carry the body and clothing down the stairs and out to the car. She hides them in the trunk and gets home ahead of her husband. She plies him with wine and, when he is deep, deep asleep, she slips out of the house and takes the body to Watered Silk. She thinks people will conclude that Teddi came to Watered Silk to go skinny-dipping and drowned.

"But the autopsy made it clear that Teddi did not drown in the pool but in a bathtub full of lavender-scented bath salts. The police are called in and they are asking questions, like how did Teddi get into the pool?

"And delightful Wilma Carter, her great-aunt, is a chatterbox, and starts to hint that she has told many people about the secret entrance. What if she admits that she told Sony?

"So perhaps reluctantly, but with her

usual efficiency, she pulls out her old hospital identification, which, I'll wager, has a magnetic key that still opens a number of doors at St. Luke's, where she used to work. Penney's sells scrubs; she buys a set and slips into the pharmacy and takes a bottle of a powerful solution of atropine, the surgical kind that paralyzes the muscles and can suffocate a patient if their breathing is not mechanically supported. And she also takes a small-bore hypodermic.

"Then she jiggles the cheap lock on the cabinet in Wilma's room until it opens, takes out the box of Exelon, and uses the hypodermic to spill a lethal dose of atropine onto the patch inside its foil packet. She is nowhere around when the nurse comes in the next evening to put the patch between Wilma's shoulder blades. Wilma suffocates very quietly that night, because she is unable to move or call for help."

"Oh, *stop*!" cried Godwin. "That's *too* awful!"

"Okay, I'll stop. That's the end of the story anyway, really."

"It's Pres's fault," pronounced Bershada. "He drove her to it."

"No, it's her fault," said Noah. "She refused to face the facts about her husband."

"I'm just glad it's over," said Tommy.

Betsy stood. "My throat's gone all dry. Excuse me, I'm going to get a bottle of water from the back."

But Connor was faster.

"Sit back down, machree, I'll get it." He walked swiftly away from the table, toward the far back of the shop.

No one said anything for a minute.

Then Jill spoke up. "I wonder what will become of their little boy," she wondered.

Connor came back to the table, twisting the top off a bottle. "What a sad question! Of course his father, who loves him, will take good care of him."

"Will he?" said Betsy. "I should think Little Tony would put a big crimp in his lifestyle."

"He is going to be so fired from his job," said Tommy. "He won't be able to afford a lifestyle, much less a kid."

"Maybe the grandfather would want him," suggested Godwin.

"Of course!" said Jill. "Big Tony would gladly step in — won't he?"

"I don't know that," said Betsy. "He hates Little Tony's father. And his daughter has proved herself a half-crazy murderer. If he takes Little Tony in, I should think at least some of the time he'd be looking for signs of trouble in that child."

A sad silence fell.

"All that selfishness," murmured Connor. "What a pity, what a pity." He put the opened bottle of water down in front of Betsy with a flourish. "But you, machree, carry no blame in this matter. You have dealt a blow for justice and saved several innocent men from the loss of their reputations and, in one case, the possible loss of his freedom. To quote Proverbs, 'Give her credit for what her hands have made, and let her works praise her.' "

A murmur of agreement went around the table, and Betsy quickly took up the bottle to drink from it in order to hide her pleasure at the praise.

# DOLPHIN PATTERN

Photocopy the pattern. (Any copy shop can make your photocopy larger or smaller to fit the size you want.) Tape it to a window at eye level, and tape a piece of white weaver's cloth (or any thin, tightly woven fabric) over it at least three inches larger in all directions. Trace the pattern onto the cloth with a soft pencil. Punch needle work is a mirror image of the pattern — if you want the result to be the same as the pattern, turn the photocopy over before tracing.

This pattern can repeat to give a continuous band of dolphins and waves. Move the weaver's cloth left or right until the pattern on the photocopy butts up against the pattern on the cloth, and trace again. Stretch the cloth into a really good hoop that will hold the fabric tight.

You will want a skein of white and two skeins of blue floss — DMC 825 and DMC

813, for example. (Any two similarly related colors of gray, green, or aqua will work. The number of skeins needed depends on the size you make the pattern.) Use the lighter color on the belly of the dolphin. Fill the space around the wave and dolphin in white.

**Optional instructions — if crafters have a punch needle, they already know this:**

Cut about a yard's length from one of the skeins, and pull three threads from it.

Turn the needle so the beveled edge faces up. Push the threader through the needle toward the handle until it extends beyond the end of the handle. Pull a couple of inches of the three threads through the looped portion of the threader, then draw the threader back down the punch needle and out the beveled end. Pass the threader, with the thread still attached, through the eye of the punch needle. Slip the threader from the thread. Pull the thread back until only about a quarter inch is coming out the end.

Hold the punch needle's handle like a pen and keep the beveled portion of the needle turned toward the direction you are going. Work on the outline of your pattern first. Punch through the fabric and pull it back up so it barely clears the surface. Make your stitches small and make the lines close together.

The nap of the pattern forms on the underside of your fabric. Check it now and again to see how you are doing. When you near the end of your floss, lift the needle so that the end is on your working side. Refill the needle and continue. When you release the fabric from the hoop, it will close around the stitches, keeping them in place.

Ellen Kuhfeld

The employees of Thorndike Press hope you have enjoyed this Large Print book. All our Thorndike, Wheeler, and Kennebec Large Print titles are designed for easy reading, and all our books are made to last. Other Thorndike Press Large Print books are available at your library, through selected bookstores, or directly from us.

For information about titles, please call:
    (800) 223-1244

or visit our Web site at:
    http://gale.cengage.com/thorndike

To share your comments, please write:
    Publisher
    Thorndike Press
    10 Water St., Suite 310
    Waterville, ME 04901